Rigby's Romance

Rigby's Romance
Joseph Furphy

MINT EDITIONS

Rigby's Romance was first published in 1905.

This edition published by Mint Editions 2021.

ISBN 9781513134338

Published by Mint Editions®

MINT
EDITIONS

minteditionbooks.com

Publishing Director: Jennifer Newens
Design & Production: Rachel Lopez Metzger
Project Manager: Micaela Clark
Typesetting: Westchester Publishing Services

Contents

Prologue	9
I	14
II	17
III	21
IV	27
V	31
VI	35
VII	37
VIII	42
IX	48
X	54
XI	58
XII	63
XIII	66
XIV	72
XV	78
XVI	82
XVII	87

XVIII	92
XIX	96
XX	102
XXI	105
XXII	107
XXIII	111
XXIV	115
XXV	119
XXVI	124
XXVII	130
XXVIII	134
XXIX	139
XXX	144
XXXI	150
XXXII	153
XXXIII	158
XXXIV	162
XXXV	168
XXXVI	171

XXXVII   174

XXXVIII   178

XXXIX   187

PROLOGUE

W hilst conveying my own unobtrusive individuality into Echuca on a pleasant evening in the April of '84, I had little thought of the delicate web of heart history which would be unfolded for my edification on the morrow. My mind was running rather upon the desirableness of a whole bag of chaff for my two horses; a satisfying feed for my kangaroo dog (which is implying more than most people wot of); and a good sleep for myself. I would have been prepared to aver that I was merely bound for Yarrawonga, via Echuca, on business of my own; whereas the smoothly—running Order of Things had already told me off as eye-witness and chronicler of a touching interlude—a love passage such as can befall only once in that one life which is each person's scanty dividend at the hand of Time.

Making straight for my customary place of sojourn—namely, Mrs. Ferguson's Coffee Palace—I helped the landlady's husband to unsaddle and feed my horses; after which, I caused that unassuming bondman to bring about twenty lbs. of scraps for Pup, whilst I chained him (Pup, of course) in an empty stall. Then, with six or eight words of explanation and apology to Mrs. Ferguson, I sought my usual bedroom, and, shedding all my garments but one, threw myself into collision with that article of furniture which has proved fatal to some better men, and to a great many worse.

Here an opportune intermission of about ten hours in the march of events affords convenience for explaining the purpose of my journey to Yarrawonga. The fact is that I object to being regarded as a mere romancist, even as a dead-head speculator, or dilettante reporter, of the drama of life. You must take me as a hard-working and ordinary actor on this great stage of fools; but one who, nevertheless, finds a wholesome recreation in observing the parts played by his fellow-hypocrites. (The Greek "hupokrisis," I find, signifies, indifferently, "actor" and "hypocrite.")

I was booked for one of those soft things that sometimes light on us as gratefully and as unaccountably as the wholesale rain from heaven upon the mallee beneath. John C. Spooner, Rory O'Halloran and I had just bought the Goolumbulla brand. Or rather, the manager, Mr. Spanker, had given us the clearing of the run under certain conditions, one of which was the payment of £100.

Goolumbulla—centrally-situated in that wilderness between the Willandra and the Darling—had been settled for about five years. Six hundred head of cattle had originally been placed on the run, to the disgust and exasperation of Mr. Spanker, whose bigoted faith in the evil-smelling merino admitted no toleration for any other kind of stock. His antipathy was reasonable enough in this instance, for these were warrigals, even as scrub-bred cattle go. You know the class—long-bodied, clean-flanked, hard-muscled, ardent-eyed, and always in the same advanced-store condition. They had been wild enough when first brought from the ranges of the Upper Lachlan, and Goolumbulla was just the sort of country to accelerate their reversion to the pre-domesticated type. At the time I speak of, they could barely endure the sight of a man on horseback. As for a man on foot, they would face anything else on earth to get away from him; and if they couldn't get away, that man might either betake himself to his faith, or stand on guard. Which latter alternative sounds so dishonestly vague and non-committal that literary self-respect demands a slight digression.

To deal with fear-maddened cattle in confined spaces—as in drafting or trucking—the infantry man requires an alert eye, a cool head, and a suitable stem of scrub, terminating in a nasty spray of leafless twigs; also his flank and rear must be covered, in order to confine the enemy to a frontal assault. These conditions being fulfilled, the operator can reserve his mortal preparation for some future emergency, though it would, perhaps, be as well to abstain from anything in the nature of language until the draft is put through. A handy piece of brush, judicially presented, will check the charge of any steer. The animal will try to get round the obstruction, but he won't attempt to break through.

Here, by the way, I may seize an opportunity of further disturbing the congested ignorance of the bookish public by noticing Sir Walter Scott's misapprehension of the bovine temperament, as displayed in "The Lady of the Lake." You remember how the milk-white bull— "choicest of the prey we had, when swept our merry men Gallangad"— is depicted as fiery-eyed, fierce, tameless and fleet, to begin with.

> *"But steep and flinty was the road.*
> *And sharp the hurrying pikemen's goad;*
> *And when we came to Dennan's Row.*
> *A child might scatheless stroke his brow."*

Stockman will conclude either that the child would be an accomplished matador in disguise, or that Scotch cattle have some peculiar way of reasoning out a new situation.

Nor did the Goolumbulla brand entertain any Scotch idea respecting the advantageousness of southward emigration. A draft, started for Victoria, was like a legion of evil spirits evicted from their haunt. As they went through dry places, seeking rest and finding none, the frenzy of nostalgia, or home-sickness, aggravated by chronic insomnia, made them harder to hold than quicksilver. Their camp was liable to spontaneous eruption at any hour of the night; and then it would be as easy to steady a cyclone as to ring the scattered torrent which swept through the scrub, like a charge of duck-shot through a wire fence.

Drovers of superhuman ability and profane address had at different times taken away three drafts; but none of these professors had ever besieged the station for a second contract. Indeed, the last drover, though as vigilant, as energetic, and as prayerful as any on the track, had found himself with about forty head left out of two hundred by the time he had crossed the first fifty miles. His horses being completely played out in limiting the leakage even to this proportion, he had sacked his three or four men, and had sullenly escorted the remnant of his draft back to their beloved wilderness. The absconders found their way home in batches, franked by the boundary men of intervening paddocks, who willingly made apertures in their fences to speed the parting guests.

But now Goolumbulla had changed owners; and the new firm had authorised Mr. Spanker to get rid of the cattle at any price and stock up with sheep.

One of the Goolumbulla boundary riders was an old friend of mine. This Rory O'Halloran—better known as Dan O'Connell—was a married man. By nature dreamy, sensitive and affectionate, the poor fellow had a few months previously sustained a blow which left him in a trance of misery. His only child—a fine little girl five or six years old—had got lost in the scrub, and had been found too late. Rory had settled down patiently and submissively to his routine work again, but the memories and associations of his home, though precious while the sense of bereavement was fresh, had in time become intolerable. For such afflictions as his, there is no nepenthe, and the only palliative is strenuous action.

Hence Rory's nature, recoiling in unconscious self-defence from the congealing desolations of Memory, craved such hardship and distraction as would be limited only by physical endurance. And instinctively perceiving that the Goolumbulla cattle were quite competent to meet his requirements, he had talked the matter over with Mr. Spanker, and provisionally engaged to buy the brand for £100. He proposed me as an associate. Spanker, in seconding the motion, suggested John C. Spooner, professional drover, as a third co-operator. Seconded, in turn, by Rory, and carried on the voices. The station stockkeeper had then been approached on the subject, but he washed his hands of the whole business. He darkly predicted calamity to the enterprise and insolvency to the station, as a consequence of such "blanky, flamin', jump-up greed for a bit of wool."

Then followed hasty and copious correspondence between Rory, Spooner, and myself. Everything went without a hitch. The preliminaries were soon arranged. For my own part, not being blessed by Nature with the saving grace of thrift ("saving grace" is good), I had no cash reserve. Spooner was in a similar state of sin, for, in spite of his almost insulting efficiency, he was constitutionally unfortunate. But Rory had about £300 in the bank at Hay, and he was prepared to finance the undertaking.

The arrangement was this: Spooner was to enclose with a strong wire fence each tank from which the cattle were accustomed to drink, leaving the lower wire high enough to admit sheep. An open gateway would be left in each fence until everything was ready. Then the gaps would be closed, and the cattle, shut out from water, would hang round the tanks, tailed and humored by our party, till the whole brand was collected. Meanwhile, the three of us would jointly sign a bond for the £100—which, by the way, was merely a nominal price for the draft, and immediately make a start. The poor dumb beasts would certainly be thirsty to begin with, but this was nothing when you consider how much worse they would be by the time they reached the next available water.

No one had any clear notion of how many head might be collected, but we counted on something over four hundred—possibly up to five hundred and fifty, including calves and cleanskins. We intended to take them across the Murray, and dispose of them in handy lots at the agricultural fairs in northern Victoria, thus passing the trouble on a little farther.

But this was prospective. For the present, it had been arranged that Rory should meet Spooner and myself at Hay, on the next Sunday but one. Another week would take the three of us to Goolumbulla, with three or four hired men, and ten or twelve decent horses. Then, if we could not command success, we could do more, Sempronius, we would deserve it.

Again, we might fairly count upon favourable conditions. The route was familiar to Spooner and myself; there would be no disturbing moonlight for the first week or so; and we might expect reasonably cool weather. The trip to the Victorian border would be only about three hundred and fifty miles. So everything was propitious.

My own immediate business was to be at Yarrawonga on a certain day, there to take delivery of three horses, already purchased by Spooner with Rory's money; then I had to turn up at Hay on the Sunday above referred to. Meanwhile, Spooner, with a few more horses, would be converging from his native town of Wagga.

Of course, these details are nothing to do with my record; they are presented merely as a spontaneous evidence and guarantee of that fidelity to fact which I acquired early in life, per medium of an old stirrup leather, kept for the purpose.

I

I wol you tell a litel thing in prose.
That oughte liken you, as I suppose.
Or elles certes ye be to dangerous.
It is a moral tale vertuous.
Al be it told sometimes in sondry wise.
Of sondry folk, as I shall you devise.

—Chaucer's "Canterbury Tales."

Just as a bale of wool is dumped, by hydraulic pressure, to less than half its normal size, I scientifically compressed something like twenty-four hours' sleep into the interval between 9 P.M. and 7 A.M. Then a touch of what you call dyspepsia and I call laziness, kept me debating with myself for another swift-running hour. So it was getting on for nine o'clock when I sat down to breakfast with Mrs. Ferguson, the two servant girls, and the husband already glanced at. All the boarders had by this time dispersed for the forenoon.

However, scene and association presently recalled former companionship; and I varied the usual breakfast-table gossip by asking:

"Have you seen the Colonel lately, Mrs. Ferguson?"

"Not since a fortnight after the last time you were here; it's nine weeks today, and the other'll be seven weeks come Friday. There were two ladies here inquiring for him yesterday afternoon. One of them had a dark maroon, and a sailor hat trimmed with the same color; and the other had the new shade of brown, and a new tuscan with three black feathers. They wanted to know his address."

"Badly, no doubt. Had they little Johnny with them?"

"Go way. Well, I had just re-posted two letters that had come. They were both office envelopes; one of them was from Waghorn Brothers, who he was with three or four years ago fixing up them wire binders, and the other was from the agent he's with now. Most likely they want him again."

"Quite likely they do."

"That'll be it, then. But I wonder what they wanted him for. They were both strangers to me, and when they found I knew Mr. Rigby so well, I got them to come in and sit down in the front room in the cool.

They were very quiet-mannered and nice-spoken (I don't care what you say). They said they might call again before they left, and the one with the brown dress gave me her card. What did you do with it, Louisa?"

"Annie had it after me."

"It's gone," said Annie laconically. "That cardbasket's piled up; and I s'pose it got blown on the floor. Anyhow, I found Bibblims sitting under the front room table, eating it."

Bibblims was the baby.

"Do you remember what the name was?" asked Mrs. Ferguson.

"It's on the tip of my tongue," replied Annie. "Something like 'Tasmania.'"

"Tasman," I suggested, incredulously.

"No," replied the girl, "it was a long name."

"And where is Rigby now?" I asked.

"Why, he's at Yooringa, of course," replied Mrs. Ferguson. "Maginnis (late Waterton), Farmers' Arms, Yooringa."

"Just a nice stage for me today," I remarked; "and there's sure to be grass in Cameron's Bend. I'm going to Yarrawonga, and I'll take this side of the river. What is Rigby doing now? I thought he was running the vertical at Hawkins' mill."

"Only till they got properly going," replied the inspired woman. "He's taking pictures and writing for them American people now. He got started nine weeks ago. It's for a big book, all in volumes, on farming, and dairying, and vines, and fruit trees, and one thing or another, in different parts of the world. They've kept him on a string longer than they'd keep me, anyway. It's five months ago since he was engaged, and not so much as 'thanky' till he got orders to start in a hurry. It was the American Consult who recommended him; and well he might, for there's very few things that would take Mr. Rigby at a short."

"I'll be pretty sure to meet him at Waterton's, then?"

"Maginnis (late Waterton), Farmers' Arms, Yooringa. He'll be there today; and he won't be leaving till next Monday at the inside."

"Well, I think I'll be going now, Mrs. Ferguson. I'll just settle up with you, so as not to keep the horses saddled."

"Oh, Ferguson'll saddle them." That unobtrusive, but useful person hastily finished his coffee and glided from the room. "Just rest yourself while you can. I'm afraid you'll have a dusty day for travelling," and so the frivolous conversation went on till I shook hands with the three women, gave the two children a threepenny bit each, wrung Mr. Ferguson's hand in silent condolence, and took the track.

As I rode eastward across the town, followed by my pack-horses and kangaroo dog, the postman intercepted me.

"Morning, Collins. Jefferson Rigby's a friend of yours, ain't he? Any idea where he is?"

"Up the river, I believe—so Mrs. Ferguson tells me. I expect to see him tonight."

"Couple of ladies came to the post-office yesterday hunting him up. We sent them to Mrs. Ferguson. So they'll be right. Horses looking a bit hairy on it."

"Season's telling on them."

"Grand dog."

"Middling."

"So long."

"So long."

II

One azure-eyed and mild.
With hair like the burst of morn.
And one with raven tresses.
And looks that scorch'd with scorn.
But yet with gleams of pity
To comfort the forlorn.

—Charles Mackay

I went on, following the road up the river. I had cantered a mile, or better, and was hardening my horses with a long walk, when a buggy and pair overtook and passed me. Though grappling at the time with an exceedingly subtle metaphysical problem, I casually noticed that the driver was a boy of sixteen or seventeen wool seasons, and that there were two women in the buggy; a thinnish one sitting beside the boy, and a fatter one on the back seat, each sheltering from the blazing sun with her umbrella. The buggy went on its way.

My next spell of cantering took me past the vehicle, and my next spell of walking brought the vehicle past me again. This occurred time after time; it occurred till I was sick of it; and, when we had left Echuca twenty miles behind, it was occurring worse than ever. I had tried putting on more pace, and I had tried slacking off, but each expedient seemed equally to aggravate the evil, though the buggy horses kept up the same slow, uniform, slinging trot. Other travellers overtook and passed us, and were as though they had not been. We overtook and passed others, who similarly sank into oblivion. But we couldn't get rid of one another. Each time we passed I looked sternly ahead, and the women occulted their faces with their umbrellas, for the thing was becoming intolerable. I felt as if I were dogging them with some sinister purpose, and they obviously felt like people driven by the mere stress of circumstances into immodest conspicuousness.

My whole day's journey was thirty-odd miles, and I had intended doing it in one stage, but now altered my plan on account of that buggy. On reaching a place where the track branched, to unite about a mile ahead, I watched the boy diverge to the left, then I quietly dodged off to the right. Half a mile further on I stopped, pulled the pack-saddle off Bun-yip, and tied both horses in a good shade. Then I spent half-an-hour in carefully dredging Pup all over with insecticide, and another half-hour in the interminable work of carving a stock-whip handle. Having thus given the other party a fair start I resumed my way.

Passing the intersection of the tracks a few minutes later I saw the buggy standing in the shade of a tree, the boy taking the nosebags off the horses and the women putting things under the seats. They had been stopping for lunch, probably with a view to getting rid of me. Then I perceived that there must be something in it, and so resolved to let things take their course. I have seen too much of life to persist in shafting against destiny.

Still looking haughtily ahead, I passed at a walk within three yards of the party. The boy was now in his post of honor, keeping the buggy on the off lock. One of the women was taking her place beside him, while the other stood by, holding both umbrellas; then the latter climbed into the back seat. I had opportunity to notice that the first woman was tall, straight, and symmetrical, though rather spare than slight; and that her hair was of a glossy, changeable brown. The other showed large and Juno-like, black haired, fairly handsome, but by no means young; and I was further privileged to observe that a good deal of her had been turned down over the anvil.

By the foot, American, thought I, as my politely restricted arc of vision left the party behind—and you'll see by-and-bye how infallible that rule is. In fact, the foot of the American woman is a badge as distinctive as the moustache of the Australienne. However, there was a good expression in the foot now under notice; it was a generous, loyal, judicious foot, yet replete with idealism and soulfulness; wherefore, I became at once prepossessed in favor of the owner.

In a few minutes the buggy overtook me for about the fifteenth time, and the boy pulled up to the walking pace of my horses.

"Say, boss," he inquired, "do you know where Maginnis' Farmers' Arms is, if it's a fair question?"

"Yes, straight ahead."

"How fur?"

"Twelve or fifteen miles. That's where I'm bound for."

"Grand dog you got there."

"Fair."

"Not a bad style o' moke you're ridin'."

"Decent. He does me for poking about."

"Could you tell us what kind of place this hotel is?" asked the light—brown hair. "Are the people likely to have accommodation for us tonight?"

"Well, to tell you the truth, ma'am," I replied, "the house was nothing to boast of in Waterton's time. Grog business, pure and simple. The hotel itself would be no disgrace to Echuca; but the management, as I knew it, was not good; it was but so-so; and so-so is not good, it is but so-so. I trust it may be better now, though there are more promising names than Maginnis. I think I'd as soon chance Flanagan."

Both women smiled amusedly, but a perturbed expression soon gathered on the face of the brown-haired one. Whilst replying to her question, I had taken note of thoughtful, pure-grey eyes, a faultless nose (which is saying a lot), and a mouth of ideal perfection; altogether, a face of more than common beauty, but of such exceeding loveliness as to disarm criticism. A face with a history, so I immediately snapshotted it on a blank spot in my memory, with a view to working out the biography at some future time. I could get her name from the boy in the evening, and no other factor would be required.

Close ahead of us was a farm-house on the right-hand side of the road. A few full-grown cattle were in the stockyard; the portly agriculturist was there himself, ordering some boys about; and a long-legged, slow-moving man with a Robinson-Crusoe beard, was arranging a roping-pole. A bright chestnut horse, saddled and bridled, was hitched to the fence close by. It is easy to be mistaken in the identity of a man, but the horse is always a certainty.

"I'll likely overtake you again in a few minutes," said I to the boy, as I turned Cleopatra, and crossed the road to the fence. "At it again, Steve?" I called out. Steve laid down the roping-pole, and mounted his horse to ride the fifty yards.

"You gave me a start," said he, as we shook hands across the fence. "I'm busy now; but you had better stop with us tonight. We're camped in Cameron's Bend, down from Waterton's pub. Dixon's with me. I've bought a pair of steers from this cove, and we're going to couple them now, and let them civilise themselves in his paddock for a day or two. Save any chance of them sulking in yoke."

"Well, I won't keep you, Steve. Did you see Jeff Rigby at Waterton's?"

"No. Haven't seen him for five or six seasons."

"Well, we'll be able to hold a meeting tonight, with the Major in the chair. Now go back to your vile occupation."

When I overtook the buggy again, I was as jocund as a seeker after wisdom may permit himself to be.

"An old school mate of mine," I remarked graciously, as the three looked round toward me. "Steve Thompson, I've known him since we were each about as high as that middle rail. One of the straightest men in the country—though he's supposed to have a curse on him through a dubious transaction of ten or twelve years ago. He was owing fifty notes to a man that got lost in a shipwreck on the coast of New Zealand, and Steve failed to chase his friend with the money till the whole transaction adjusted itself at that, leaving a curse on Steve. I had little thought of meeting him today—thought he was a couple of hundred miles north. I was looking forward to meeting another very old friend, Jeff Rigby, a striking contrast to Thompson in many ways; the most conspicuous point about him being that he allows nobody to know anything except what he tells." The sentence seemed to die out to nothing; partly because it was impossible to finish the last clause without a solecism, but more particularly because I noticed both women's eyes fixed on my face, with a disconcerting interest in the casual gossip. It is humiliating when you feel yourself expected to say something good, and a swift reconnaissance of the subject shows you no opening for anything beyond what a nobleman might drivel. Moreover, I was fresh from the pastoral regions, where etiquette demands frank, unsolicited, and copious comment on the merits or demerits of some absent person; whereas these women were evidently civilised, and consequently regarded my conventional remarks as the exordium of some good anecdote. I therefore gave my earnest attention for a few moments to a mare and a foal, standing in the shade of a tree close by.

III

A still, sweet, placid, moonlight face.
And slightly nonchalant.
Which seems to claim a middle place
Between one's love and aunt.

—O. W. Holmes

P ardon my question," said the brown hair hesitatingly. She paused a
moment, then asked: "What countryman is your friend?"

"Australian, madam; born near Geelong. His parents are English."

"Are you sure?" she faltered, while the color faded from her face.

"Perfectly sure, madam. I'm as certain of his nationality as of my
own."

Then twenty or thirty seconds heaped twenty or thirty years on
that's girl's head. I hadn't noticed the faint wrinkles about her eyes till
now, but, riding close to her, and looking at her with puzzled sympathy,
I marked not only these footprints of the crows of Time, but here and
there a silver thread imparting unsought dignity to the beauty of her
sun-bright hair. And lapsing into my deplorable Hamlet mood I began
to calculate her age.

Ay, poor post-meridian! Under the searching analysis of some
mental confluent, the beauty was dissolving from her face, yet leaving
the loveliness intact. Enhanced, heightened rather, by unspoken
kinship in liability to the tyranny of Time—that pathetic kinship which,
clothed in poet's words carries more tenderness than any other touch of
nature. There is one grace of the rosebud; another grace of the expanded
blossom; and, to the enlightened mind, a more adorable grace in the
fading flower, which gains in fragrance as it loses in freshness.

When we liken women to glass—as we often do—the parallel rests
on fragility, on restorableness, on refractiveness, or some such property.
But there is a more touching similitude yet. Of all known glass the
most lovely is a collection exhumed some forty years ago at Idalium
in Cyprus. Science becomes Poetry in mere contemplation of these
relics. Take some excerpts from a description in Knight's "Dictionary
of Mechanics":—"Tints, positively outside of all experience, confuse
the most accurate observation. . . marbled with hues like those of

incandesence. . . sending light, pearly hints of variegated radiance from elusive depths fantastically pied with scales of iridescence on strong original coloration. . . defeating all sense of strict estimation and cheating the mind with the notion of a possible perfection. . . as if Turner had painted skies on them in his maddest mood, and had been allowed to use flames for colors. . . The general effect seems to suggest that all the sunsets that have glimmered over Cyprus since those vessels were lost on the earth had sunk into their hiding-place and permeated their substance."

The glass is perishing. Matchless, indescribable, inimitable in its beauty, yet it is a loveliness that comes only with decline, a passive response to the first tender touch of that inexorable hand which brings man and all his works to dust.

I wish I could stay to moralise on this, because our appreciation of women is a subject that seems to invite disentanglement and exposition. But knowing my own proneness to wander aside, plucking fruits of philosophy, I shall, for once, guard against disgression and confine myself to clean-cut narrative.

Two widely-divergent views of women are illustrated—one in "The Gowden Locks of Anna," by Burns, the other in Moore's exquisite paraphrase of St. Jerome "Who is the Maid?" The former paints the inherent sex-charm of Creation's fairest type; the latter pictures her attained sex-value. The former conveys passion; the latter, adoration. The former sees femininity; the latter, womanhood. And these are the two extremes.

The relative potency of these diverse influences depend, of course, upon the receptivity, sensuous or psychical, of the person subjected to their agency, yet it is worthy of note that, where controlling masculine minds are moved or biassed by sex-influence, the force is exercised by a woman, not by a female. And not till the peach-bloom of youth is gone can the woman dominate the female and her personality reach its maximum angel—loveliness or its most formidable devil-beauty. None but Kadijah, fifteen years his senior, could captivate the stormy soul of the Arabian prophet. Also, if the mature Josephine Beauharnais had cared for the Faubourg St. Antoine as she cared for the Faubourg St. Germain, Bonaparte might have been the brightest name in modern history; but we know in which direction her strong allurement led, and we know how he followed it to perdition. These instances, though multiplied by ten figures, could prove nothing; nevertheless, they exemplify how the world is swayed by women, not by females. And each man, be he king or beggar, is a little world of his own. If he be swayed by a female, as kings and beggars frequently are, he is an extremely little world.

But don't misapprehend me as identifying or confounding femininity with youth, and womanhood with maturity. Just as many a man, having outlived the boy's enthusiasm and ingenuousness, retains the boy's uselessness and self-conceit, so in the other sex, mere femininity too often accompanies maturity. When this occurs—in fact, when the case is one of incorrigible femininity—the subject is good for two things only: to suckle fools and chronicle small beer.

"I beg your pardon, sir," said the deliberate voice of the woman on the back seat, "were you speaking of Mr. Rigby, or of the other gentleman?"

"I was speaking of Thompson, madam. Rigby is an American. He came out here—let's see—just when Dunolly broke out; and our acquaintance began immediately after. Of the many friends he has made, my father, I think, holds priority in date, and I take precedence in intimacy."

My reply was, of course, addressed to the black hair, who had asked the question. Glancing then at the other, and perceiving that she had renewed her youth like the eagle, I thought to while away a few minutes by remarking, in my dry way, that Echuca was just then in a state of hungry curiosity touching two ladies who had been making inquiries after the very person under discussion.

"Speaking of Rigby," said I, "it was only this morning that I was a little amused by"—here, with a sudden flash of intuition, I loosely and tentatively identified my auditors with the mysterious scouts; whereupon, figuratively speaking, I flogged my tongue unmercifully, then gave it its head, and heard it continue in the same breath—"remembering what a hero he seemed to me in the days when the earth was young. I like to consider myself a Melchisedec in philosophy; but the conviction is often forced upon me that, in many ways, I have been a mere disciple of the Colonel's. In fact, we differ only on points where he's grimly and disagreeably right, and I'm comfortably wrong. I wouldn't take £100 a year and be as conscientious as he is. For instance, I'm a Conservative; and he is—well, not to mince matters, he's a State Socialist. In other words, I adapt myself to the times and the seasons, whilst he thinks the conformity ought to be on the other side." Rather disconnected, and altogether rudely confidential, but not bad for a desperate impromptu.

And the women, refined as they evidently were, listened as to the voice of a clergyman.

"What is Mr. Rigby's occupation?" asked the black hair, after a short silence.

"Second-rate photographer and descriptive writer, at present, madam. He has been a first-rate engine-driver, also mechanical expert, a third-rate journalist, and a fourth-rate builder. At various times he has ranked high up to ninth and tenth rate in something like a score of other and more menial occupations; but speaking with actuarial precision, he's a land surveyor. If there's any question of his identity, I may add that he was born at a place called Marathon, somewhere in the backblocks of New York State."

There was intense interest in the face of the brownhaired woman as I spoke, and evident relief as I concluded. Then another pause.

"This is a most happy coincidence," she said, with a frankness almost supplicatory. "Mr. Rigby and I were born less than five miles apart, and I knew him in America up to the time of his departure. Is—is he much altered since you know him?"

"A good deal, madam. The second twenty-five years of a man's life cover about two of the Seven Ages. In this instance, they have transformed the lover, sighing like the she-oak, to the mature egotist, full of wise fads and modern theories; but it would take an able reasoner to convince the Colonel that he has in any way altered for the worse. Physically, he's as strong as ever he was; he attributes this to his Puritan descent—I attribute it to my climate. For more than twenty years I have piously looked forward to the privilege of gracing him with the Earl of Morton's tribute to John Knox: 'There lies one who never feared the face of man.' But waiting is weary work, and hope deferred maketh the heart grizzle. He'll probably see me out. I fancy he'll be like Moses at the age of one hundred and twenty, his eye not dim, nor his natural force abated. He differs significantly from Moses, however, in respect of not being by any means meek above all men on the earth."

A subdued smile played over the face of the brown-haired women, leaving her eyes soft as velvet.

"He hasn't been successful?" she conjectured, almost timidly.

"Only in asserting himself, madam. Financially, he's a failure—like myself."

"He has served in your military forces?" she next suggested, with tacit apology in her voice.

I softened my negative down to a forbearing shake of the head, then perceiving a certain feminine deduction in the foolish surmise, I replied:

"You refer to the title of Colonel? The fact is that when I first knew him he seemed such an ideal Down-Easter that to deny him a title of some kind—military, naval, civil, or ecclesiastical, as the case might be—was to take from him that which not enriched me and left him poor indeed. The whole thing is merely a spontaneous concession to his nationality, carrying neither flattery nor sarcasm."

"Is he married?" asked the black hair casually.

"Oh, no," I replied. "So far from it that the incongruity of the idea amuses me."

"A woman-hater, I assume," she persisted, with uneasy boldness.

"Anything but that," I replied. "His demeanor toward women is partly paternal and partly reverential, and partly oblivious. I have always compared him with the earlier Benedick—one woman was fair, yet he was well; another was wise, yet he was well; another was virtuous, yet he was well; and if all graces had come into one woman, he would have congratulated that woman and passed on well pleased for her sake. I never met anyone else like him in this respect, but, knowing him as I do, his insusceptibility appears to me full of interest. I feel quite certain that it is owing to an early dis"—I checked myself barely in time, gave my tongue another flagellation, and heard it go on in its usual garrulous way—"cipleship of Epictetus, which had colored his whole life, endowing him with a form of selfishness that puts other people's generosity to shame."

I was in magnificent form and knew it, yet felt like a denizen of some cold country walking on thin, creaking ice. Who were these women with their reluctant forwardness and their wistful desire—tacitly expressed in tone and manner—to conciliate a mere passer-by, one whose character they could only conjecture, and of whose very name they were ignorant? Modest and cultivated they certainly were, but battling in some way with feminine inadequacy, the black hair struggling to carry off anxiety under cover of grave self-possession, the brown hair wilting under a helplessness so shrinkingly sensitive, and so sympathetically communicable that, stranger as I was, I could mentally feel her clinging to me with the mute entreaty of an ownerless dog. How did such people get through life? What business had they here? Why their interest in Rigby? Were they always like this?

"But pardon me, ladies," I resumed. "I ough to tell you that my name is Collins. In occupation, I change involuntarily, like the chameleon, according to my surroundings. At present I must stigmatise myself as a cattledrover. I'll feel very much honored if you avail yourselves of any information or assistance that it may be in my power to give!"

Whilst I was wondering whether this sounded courtly or impertinent, the brown hair bowed acknowledgment and, taking out her card case, replied with easy grace.

"Indeed, Mr. Collins, we appreciate your courtesy—Miss Artemisia Flanagan." I remembered my own rash witticism of a few minutes before, and raised my wideawake with extra solemnity. "I feel myself relying upon you already," she continued, handing me her card.

During the next minute I was a broken reed for anybody to rely upon. A good gust of wind would have toppled me off the saddle. To explain this seizure, it will be necessary to glance back along that rugged track which might have been travelled with something like comfort and profit if I had personally inherited from my forefathers a moiety of their sordid experience instead of the whole sum of their crude natural propensities.

IV

I loved Ophelia; forty thousand brothers
Could not, with all their quantity of love.
Make up my sum.

—"Hamlet," Act V, Scene 1

O n a summer morning, twenty-three years prior to this encounter, a Victorian ratepayer sent one of the arrows out of his quiver to muster some cows on the common, eight or ten miles from home. In the seclusion of the ranges this missile gathered as much wattle gum as he could eat; then leaving his horse to feed about with the saddle on, he lay down in the shade, and became immersed in a work of blood-and-thunder fiction, which his foresight had provided. After reading himself stupid, he took a swim in an adjacent water-hole, then basked in the sun for an hour, and finally dedicated his attention to a likely-looking place, where the age—abraded apex of a small rise showed abundance of shattered and weather—beaten quartz. This was his style of mustering cows.

Spare your scorn. The cloth-yard shaft left that rise with three specimens in his possession—one, showing a couple of colors; another, carrying a three-grain piece; and the third, a good half-penny-weight. Wearily returning home in the deepening twilight, our projectile reported the lack of success which had attended his exertions in mustering, and casually produced the specimens, which latter he had happened to notice on hastily dismounting to tighten his girth.

The ratepayer, being a man for whom digging had no fascination, just dropped a line to a young friend of opposite bent, then working a half—wages stringer on Pleasant Creek. A fortnight afterward, the digger arrived. A day or two more found the genial ratepayer, the enthusiastic digger, and the simple-minded arrow, on the spot where the latter had dismounted to tighten his girth—a spot known for years after as the Yankee Reef, and always more distinguished for promise than for fulfilment, even before the stone petered out into hungry leaders.

These details are merely introductory to the information I received from Rigby on the night we camped at the reef. We were lying, each wrapped in a blanket, around the smouldering fire. I was supposed to be asleep; in fact, I had been asleep till the sudden cry of a curlew roused me, and I found it worth my while to remain awake. For the accessories of the situation—soft summer moonlight, bush solitude, and one sympathetic auditor—had melted the Major's habitual reserve, and he was relating to my dad, in tones hoarse with emotion, the tragedy of his life. I muttered something in my sleep and rolled slowly over, face uppermost—a post hard to surpass in auricular advantages.

I soon discovered that a direful and ineffaceable quarrel with the girl of his choice had broken the poor Commodore's moorings, and left him rudderless, dismasted, derelict, at the mercy of wind and tide, and without the heart to rig anything jury. His sole consolation was in the certainty that his wrecker in ruthlessly working this havoc had marooned herself. She would never marry. She couldn't. He knew her loyal, lofty nature.

Here he stirred my depths with twenty minutes of steady panegyric, to the general effect that Miss Vanderdecken was beautiful, accomplished, gifted, amiable, beyond anything that imagination could body forth, or poet's pen turn to shape. Wherefore it warmed the very sickness of his heart to dwell on the misery she must be enduring. It was entirely her own fault. She was petulant and quarrelsome, frivolous and heartless, and the best thing that had ever happened to him was this quarrel, inasmuch as it had swept away all tawdry romance from his life, and laid bare its grand realities.

In describing this quarrel he was bitterly precise; yet I experienced disappointment, even injury, in failing to detect any blame attachable to the other party, whilst my dad's judicial mind could find no cause of misunderstanding whatsoever. But the Colonel quoted Byron, Tennyson and other excellent authorities, falling back at last on the solid though irrevelant fact that he had loved Kate too well, and it was her own sterling worthiness of that devotion which barbed the arrow that rankled in his heart. Then, again, the holy hush of Satanic tranquility (I can find no better expression) came, angel-winged, over the martyr's tempest-tossed soul, as he imagined the girl's irremediable despair.

Henceforward, however, their ways lay apart, and neither would ever know the other's fate. For the very short time that might elapse before he should shake the yoke of inauspicious stars from his world-wearied flesh, and the wattle blossom should wave above his lonely resting place, he would try to do as much good and as little harm as possible. He owed this to Kate's memory.

He had hardened himself in honor. Not one of his early friends knew whither he had drifted. He had no family obligations. His nearest relations were his step-mother and her children; and they were only too glad to see him out of the way. His sole tie to life was Kate, and when she was gone, chaos was come again.

He had looked back once, to see her standing in the doorway, with the snow-flakes falling on her head. When would that picture fade? Never!—till it dissolved with all earthly things. She was nineteen then, and he was twenty-five; she would be twenty-one now, poor Kate, and he was twenty—seven in years, but more than fifty in the iron stoicism which is bought only with blighted hopes.

And so on. Of course, I am only giving you an epitome. Yet this lugubrious ass was the sagacious, energetic, and self-reliant young citizen of the day before and the day after.

However, as twelve-year-old arrows of Australian manufacture don't notice or understand the discourse of their elders, this disclosure gave me something to ponder over in my own unsophisticated way; and thenceforward the Colonel appeared to me as one clothed in iambics, and spondees, and dactyls, and all manner of poetry. As years went on, my garnered knowledge of his life-absorbing infatuation provided a satisfactory key to his altruisms, integrity, and cynicism; and whenever the conversation of my adult associates tended to show that, in love as well as in other things, there was nothing but roguery to be found in villainous man, I had only to remember the Senator, and keep on believing.

I utilised him as an object lesson in fidelity, and it became my custom, whenever I saw him fall into reverie, to place myself, so to speak, en rapport, and thus enjoy a second-hand gloat upon the picture which I had learned to conjure up at a moment's notice—pine forests, wolves, and wigwams in the background; apple-trees, maize and pumpkins in the middle distance; and in the foreground, half-veiled by falling snow-flakes, the figure of a beautiful, though somewhat mynheer-looking sheaf of contradictions, standing in a doorway, and gazing out into the gelid desolation, whilst unavailing remorse, like a grub in the quondong, fed on her damask cheek.

In poetic keeping with his desolated life, the Judge ever afterward maintained perfect reticence respecting the unhappy stroke that his youth suffered. I have always been willing to acquire information and would therefore have welcomed his confidence at any time; but as he chose to keep the burden to himself, I had to content myself with the scrap I had picked up, remembering that all things come to him who philosophises.

At last the potato was cooked. The cryptic passage found its Rosetta stone in the card presented by the brown-haired woman, for the name thereon was "Miss Kate Vanderdecken." Also, the fate which had so sternly insisted on a conference between us was satisfactorily accounted for. Things will occasionally happen of themselves.

V

Gabriel was not forgotten. Within her heart was his image.
Clothed in the beauty of love and youth, as last she beheld him.
Only more beautiful made by his death-like silence and absence.

—Longfellow's "Evangeline."

The boy, perceiving the progress of our acquaintance, now threw out a suggestion:

"I say, miss, if this bloke's goin' to the same place as us, I wouldn't mind lettin' him take a spell o' drivin', and I'll ride. He needn't be frightened o' these yarramans. I got them like lambs."

"I have no objection, Sam. It rests with Mr. Collins. But don't imagine that we're tired of your company."

"I don't suppose you are," replied Sam, "but I want a smoke; an' I got too much manners to stink your clo'es with tobacker. I'd had a whiff when we stopped, on'y like a fool I forgot my matches in the hurry this mornin'. Wo, chaps! Hold the reins for one minit, miss." We altered the stirrups to his length, and he mounted: "Now, your matches, Collins."

"Do you want a pipe?" I asked.

"Let's see your pipe. That! No thanks! I got everything but matches. Well, we're right now. You go on ahead. Never mind me." Then the buggy horses resumed their steady trot, leaving Sam in the rear.

It was some minutes before the mutual constraint of passengers and driver wore off. The former—as I knew by my gift of intuition—were wondering whether I couldn't afford a new pair of boots. The latter—a poor arithmetician at best—was adding twenty-five to nineteen over and over again; but without being able to get the same result twice running.

But a reciprocal effort brought our gossiping apparatus into working order. It was a novel experience, to feel these educated and evidently exclusive women meekly endeavoring to stand well in my estimation. It seemed so like a restoration of the true Order of Things that I had temporary respite from the haunting consciousness of my entanglement with a Riverina lady who, in the slangy sense of the word, was too good for me. (But that is another romance.)

Rigby being our point of contact, the conversation leaned chiefly in his direction; and the women did most of the listening. Yet when a genial tact compelled either of them to contribute something, there was interest, as well as grammar, in what she said. I was not surprised to learn that, until four or five months previously, no one in Rigby's native region knew definitely the place of his self-exile. But Miss Flanagan's brother held some position in the publishing firm whose Melbourne agent had employed the prodigal; hence she had incidentally heard his name.

Miss Flanagan was a perfect stranger to the Colonel personally, though she knew his step-brothers and their families. The girls had been under her tuition a few months back. She was a teacher of mathematics, algebra and other inviting sciences in a ladies' seminary, and she and Miss Vanderdecken had been closely intimate for many years. She had taken a twelve months' holiday; and now the two were seeing what was to be seen in this right-hand lower section of the Eastern Hemisphere.

Each woman, in her own way, was profitable to me in spite of the prior soul-mortgage unhappily covering my moral securities; but, owing to a twenty-three years' contemplation of the snow-scape already described, my sympathy centred on Miss Vanderdecken. And though I had too much innate delicacy to go blurting out the General's nocturnal confidence to my pa, I felt deeply impressed by the concurrence which was bringing these two people together so felicitously, yet so involuntarily, after such long separation. At the time of that angry parting in the land of ague and dried apples the odds would have seemed a hundred millions to one against a purely fortuitous conjunction at the Farmers' Arms, Yooringa; nevertheless, this was coming to pass. Their lines of life must have been insensibly converging ever since, and yet the slightest dislocation in the tendency of event at any time during twenty-five years—one misfitting link in the chain of circumstances—and the parting would have held good for ever. Now I would make it my business to see that the connection was not missed at the last moment.

Presently a slight angle in the road brought into view the Farmers' Arms, two or three miles ahead and I pointed out the building to my passengers. From this time Miss Vanderdecken never spoke except in monosyllables, and though she was evidently on her mettle for firmness, there was something in her manner of breathing which made me wish I had given more attention to that branch of pathognomy which deals with the possible eccentricities of women who haven't seen their lovers for a quarter of a century. Miss Flanagan also looked perturbed, and I noticed that she was holding Miss Vanderdecken's hand. So I monologued with a fluent tongue and a speculative mind while we neared the pub, and drew up to a walk.

"Ah, there's the Colonel himself," said I, in an undertone, as we passed the house.

"No," whispered Miss Vanderdecken, with agony in her face, "there must be some mistake." And she averted her eyes from the figure of a bloated and sottish-looking, though decently dressed, old buffer who had just emerged from the bar door, and was slowly seating himself on the form on the verandah.

"In the parlor," said I. "You can see him through the window. I think he's reading a letter."

All her self-restraint could not repress something like a sob, as her eyes fell on the severely handsome profile of her countryman, framed by the open window. I drove on a few paces, and stopped at the gate of the yard. It seemed manifest that the women were leaving everything to me.

"Now, ladies," said I, "if this place is anything like what it was six months ago, you'll have to go on to the Royal, which is a traditionally respectable house, five or six miles ahead. In that case, I'll send Rigby with you; but I trust that I may feel justified in making arrangements for you here. Sam, just hook the horse on the fence, and take these reins."

"Thank you, Mr. Collins," murmured Miss Flanagan. "You're placing us under many obligations."

"Pray don't mention our arrival to Mr. Rigby just yet," added Miss Vanderdecken, in a quivering voice.

"I'll merely prospect the place. And let me repeat that if you fail to avail yourself of my further services, I must take it as a slight."

Both women bowed, without speaking. I entered the house, introduced myself to the bright young landlady, and saw at a glance that the government was much improved since Waterton's time. After making the necessary arrangements, I returned to the buggy, and Sam drove into the yard.

With the air of a Castilian noble, I assisted Miss Vanderdecken from the buggy. Meanwhile, Miss Flanagan had disembarked herself. The landlady received them with overflowing respect, and led the way into the house, while I followed, carrying two portmanteaux.

I had placed the luggage in the passage, and was wondering what was the proper thing to do next, when Miss Vanderdecken with a gesture of polite deprecation, stepped past the landlady, and detained me by a glance. The pathos in her appealing eyes and paled lips was heightened by the seven hours' deposit of dust on her features—nothing being clean about her but the whites of her eyes.

"I have no scruple in adding to my indebtedness, you see, Mr. Collins," said she, in a barely articulate voice, "but I should like to speak to your friend while I am here."

"Indeed, Miss Vanderdecken, apart from the pleasure of meeting your wishes, I shall be delighted to confer such a happiness on the Senator. A message from you at any time will find me in the parlor." And so I withdrew.

VI

O if thou be'st the same Ægeas, speak.
And speak unto the same Æmilia!

—"Comedy of Errors," Act V, Scene 1

W ell," said Rigby to me as we left the bar, "my waggonette is down beside the waggons. Get your horses ready, and we'll follow Dixon and cast our lines in the river too."

"In the river of Time, Colonel?" said I dreamily. "Our lines are cast therein already, foolish one; and our business is to—Oh, now I know what you mean! But you should either qualify your river by its distinguishing adjective or call it by its strikingly appropriate name—for 'murrey' means dark red. If the people who frequent its banks don't know its proper title, I wonder who does; and they never speak of it loosely and indefinitely as 'the river'; they always call it the crimson river. Please bear this in mind, Major. It's the king of Australian rivers, and I naturally feel a little nettled to hear it shorn of its title. However, we're not going yet. Come into the parlor. There's a surprise in store for you. I providentially met an acquaintance of yours today—Miss Kate Vanderdecken. She knows you well, and has been the whole afternoon looking forward to meeting you. She's here now, taking her ease in her inn—the only way in which she resembles Sir John. She intends to stay all night; so I suppose you won't be down at the Red River till late."

"Ah! what did you say her name was?"

"Miss Kate Vanderdecken. Here's her card. She comes from your own blizzard-smitten land, and the unerring law of Happenology—the very law that moulds marbles to a spherical shape and controls the apparent vagaries of our planetary system—has landed her here, to give you an evening momentous enough to date from. How is that for lofty?"

"You bewilder me, Tom."

"I expected nothing less, Sheriff. By the way, there's another lady with her—Miss Artemisia Flanagan, and a calculator by profession as well as by nationality. Hence I'm glad to see you so clean and presentable, though, to do you justice, I knew your habits, and was under no apprehension. I'm as proud of you as if you were one of my own. Turn round, till I see if there's any grass-seed, or horse-hair, or whitewash on your back. No, you're humanly perfect; you would pass for a married man of the upper middle classes. You know a married woman always keeps her old impostor trim and tidy, even to the inner ply of apparel, so that in case of him getting killed off a horse, or in a railway accident, there will be no damaging discredit reflected upon the widow."

"I feel like a man in a dream, Tom," said Rigby, absently. "You haven't told me how you came to—"

"Mr. Collins," said the low, soft voice of Miss Flanagan, who paused in the doorway, then glided into the room, acknowledging the Deacon's presence by a slight bow and a penetrating glance.

I introduced the two Down-Easters, and at the end of three minutes desultory conversation perceived that Rigby was weighed in the balance and found genuine. Such is the inconceivable despatch of feminine judgment.

Then Miss Flanagan led us to the private parlor, where, with a couple of nicely-turned phrases, which I had rapidly concocted and committed to memory, I presented the long-severed friends to each other. Miss Vanderdecken, exquisitely lovely in a simple dress of creamy white, betrayed no trace of her former agitation. Her face, always sweet and engaging, was now transfigured, glorified, by the emotions of woman-hood at its best; and, indeed, I never saw Rigby appear to such advantage as under the inspiration of her presence. Of course, there was no crash, nor was there any embarrassment on either side, nothing but a graceful interchange of courtesies and polite solicitude, and presently the Senator, according to his custom, settled down into the leading part. Still, I could detect, under the grave tenderness of his manner, a certain abstraction, easily accounted for as things stood.

I remained only five or ten minutes. Then, promising to call on my new friends in the morning as I went out, I retired with some ceremony, readily pardonable when you consider everything. I had furnished the epilogue to a drama of thrilling interest. Alone I did it, and therefore felt morally and socially uplifted.

VII

Whilst re-saddling Bunyip, I got into conversation with Sam, who was making friends with Pup, obviously with a view to his seduction, the latter being no difficult matter by reason of the strong spiritual affinity always existent between a boy and a kangaroo dog.

"Fond o' scenery, ain't they?" remarked Sam, as he passed me the girth from the off side.

"Who?"

"Them shemales I fetched. That's what they come for. Dashed if I could see any scenery about. I say, which o' them do you fancy most?"

"Both about equal. Which is your choice?"

"Well, I ain't at liberty. I'm ordered. But I should say Arty. I like them a good size."

"Which Arty?"

"Miss Flanagan. Her with no feet."

"How far are you going up the river?"

"No furder. Back tomorrow or next day. They jist hired the buggy for a couple or three days to come on this fur. My word, they was in luck to git me for takin' charge of them. Touch-an'-go. Happened to be out o' work, on account o' my boss havin' to clear, with a warrant after him for biggany."

"For what?"

"Biggany. Havin' two wives, both to the fore. Rotten contract, ain't it? Wheelwright by trade. Me an' him was getting on grand together, only for this bust up. I got another place to start improver, soon's I git back. Wheelwrightin' ain't a bit stinkin' for a trade—is it? Got a few new idears ripenin' ready for when I git on my own. See, most o' the wheelwrights is imported beggars; an' they can't be expected to have the best quality o' brains. Wish I had that dog."

"What use would he be to you, Sam?"

"Well, a feller must have a dog, an' he may as well have a kangaroo dog. Where you clearin' off to?"

"Down to the river, to camp with some chaps I know. Come and have a drink of soft tack before I go."

"Not this time, thanks. We fetched a dozen bottles o' lemonade, an' each o' the shemales drunk two bottles, an' you drunk one, an' I polished off the other seven or eight—not to speak of a gorger before we started. That'll do me today. My inside's all furmentin' now. You could hop a marble off o' my stummick."

"You'll soon get over that, Sam. So long."

"So long."

The sun was still half-an-hour high when I repassed the pub, and turned down the reserve. Half a mile along the line of fence, and just where the latter ran into the river, I found the two waggons, and, near them, Rigby's covered waggonette. By Dixon's directions, I took my horses across a dry billabong, and, mindful of the escaped thirty-pounder, brought a fishing rod back with me. I had hooks and lines in my swag.

Whilst cutting this rod, I noticed a curious thing. Close beside me stood the shell-stump of a freshly-felled hollow tree; and about twenty feet along the prostrate trunk was a newly-cut aperture that a middle-sized man could nicely creep through. And straight above the stump, in mid-air, was a little stationary dark cloud easily resolvable into a multitude of bees. The loud, menacing hum hinted that they were by no means in the best of temper. They had come home from all quarters to find things not merely disarranged, but vanished entirely, like the early cloud and the morning dew. Here a phrenologist would think it strange that an organ of locality, perfect enough to guide its possessor through the undiversified air, should be so poorly balanced by perceptive and reflective faculties that the subject, in the first place, couldn't see what had happened, and, in the second place, couldn't reason out the certainty that its tree must be somewhere, and that the best way to find it would be to look for it. But the case appeared to bear out my theory that we are all specialists. And it seemed to clash with Lubbock's hypothesis, namely, that the bee has no intuition of locality, but steers its course by sight alone. At all events these bees, being like myself, conservative in tendency, were lost for lack of a precedent. Hard work and no play had tied Jack immovably to the fine "old moorings"—had, in fact, paralysed his reasoning faculty and extinguished his initiative, thus making him a model wealth-producer and a never-failing text for the Thrift-homilist.

Yet the lack of this perceptive shingle on the thought-dome of a docile wealth-producer sometimes upsets the calculations of the wise and prudent. For instance, an intimate friend of mine was a most able and accomplished theorist. Like Columbus, he was a man with a fad; and this fad was the common domestic hen. He maintained that women, owing to a constitutional dearth of enterprise and understanding, were incompetent to manage these birds. But, having worked the thing out scientifically in his own mind, he saw his way to fortune in a flock of judiciously-crossed Black Spanish and Brahmapootra, stiffened by a strain of the Dorking, with, perhaps, a blend of the Orpington for fertility, and just a suggestion of the Wyandotte, as a precaution against pip.

Under this impression, he sold out his grocery business and bought a small farm. Here he supervised the erection of ten hen-houses, to begin with. Each little edifice was fitted with nests, ladders, roosts, etc., and was mounted on four low block-wheels. Next he obtained a supply of hens, and allotting twenty-four of these unassuming producers to each caravan, he spent a week in training them to consider themselves at home. Then at the dead hour of the night he hooked a steady old horse to each hen-house in turn, and distributed them, with their sleeping tenants, over paddock No. 1. During the ensuing day, the hens, spreading out like sheep, fared sumptuously on locusts, grubs, seeds, etc.; and in the evening they retired—not to their houses, but to the vacant spots from whence those abodes had been shifted.

There was nothing for it, of course, but to carry each slumbering imbecile to her proper address—a work which occupied half the night—and this task had to be repeated every evening for a week. By this time, according to the system so elaborately worked out, commissariat conditions necessitated a removal of the caravans to No. 2 paddock; and for six or eight nights each former site in No. 1 was pathetically indicated by the globular forms of two dozen somnolent hens. Nor did this innocent contumacy admit of any remedy; for the whole physical construction of the feathered races, particularly their external finish, clearly indicates that Nature has not designed them to be cowhided with satisfaction or profit. Anyway, the enterprise ended ignominiously; and now, if you want to make an enemy of that most amiable experimenter, you have only to introduce the subject of hens.

"Just set down an' wire in," was Dixon's salute when I returned to the camp. "Soda bread, an' bacon, an' honey, ad (adj.) libitum. Dunno whether you like mustard mixed up or not. We always eat it dry. Ain't got sich a thing as a swappin' book on you, I s'pose?" he continued, as we settled down to the provender. "One o' Nathaniel Hawthorne's here, waitin' for a new owner. Can't suffer that author no road. He's a (adj.) fool; too slow to catch grubs."

"Haven't got a book to my name, Dixon. Flying as light as possible this trip. What are you reading now?"

"Bible," replied Dixon, with a touch of self-righteousness, whilst indicating with a sideward glance the noblest compilation on earth, where it lay in a kerosene-box, together with a supply of tobacco and matches, a large dictionary, and well-worn pack of cards, and the insufferable Hawthorne. "Got her in a swap for one o' Ouidar's," he continued. "Ignorant galoots, they'll tell you she's a passel o' nonsense; but strikes me very forcible the bloke that wrote the Bible he had forgot more'n them other (sceptics) ever learned. An' as for it bein' true—why, Jerusalem's to the good now, large as life, for anybody to see. 'Spect you're a bit o' a ringer on Scripture?"

"I only wish I was. Certainly, I had to read a good deal of it when I was too young to understand."

"That's on'y yer misfortune," replied Dixon gravely. "It ain't yer fault. That's where my main (adj.) hold is—graspin' what I read. Never knowed no more about the Bible three monce ago nir I knowed about my gran'mother. Matter o' course, I thought hell was on'y a man's own conscience; thought the divil was only a sort o' byword; thought God was nature; an' so on. But I foun' things a (adj.) sight different. No (adj.) shinnanigan about the Bible. It ain't frightened about offendin' people; an' it don't give one stick o' tobacker difference between Abraham on his throne an' the (derelict) at his gate, loafiin' for the manavelins off of his table. That's what I like her for. Straightest book ever wrote. But she gave me a (adj.) fright," he continued, in an altered tone. "A (sheol) of a (adj.) fright," he repeated thoughtfully.

"But surely you didn't find it all discouraging?" I argued, contemplating with a listless interest the fine forehead and engaging face of the bullock driver.

"Dunno," replied Dixon dubiously. "Most of it's (adj.) frightensome. But mebbe things'll work roun' all right by the time a feller dies. Sneak

JOSEPH FURPHY

in some (adj.) road. Anyhow, I'm glad I ain't a Scribe, nor yet a Pharisee, nor yet a hypocrite."

A minute of sombre silence, for our parallel forecasts had reached the confines of that void whereinto no ray of science may penetrate, to dissolve the hundred shapeless, flickering wisps of Dogma.

VIII

> Yea also, when he that is a fool walketh by the way, his wisdom
> faileth him, and he saith to everyone that he is a fool.
>
> —"Ecclesiastes," X 3

B ut the fascination of a new book was on the receptive mind of my
companion; so, judiciously waiving the unpleasanter features of the
work, he gave his harmless pedantry its fling.

"Samson, he was the strongest (individual) ever lived," he remarked,
in a careless tone; "an' Solomon he was the wisest—an' who do you
think was the foolishest?"

"The man who built his house on the sand," I suggested.

"Ain't come to that bloke yet," replied Dixon; "but I'm thinkin' Moses
could give him about halfways an' lick him (adv.) bad. Yes, Moses
was the foolishest (person) ever lived. Bible cracks him up, mind you,
because he was a decent feller in his own sort o' soft-headed way. But
he didn't know his road roun'. Cripes, if I got slants like him I'd shift
things a bit! My (adj.) oath!"

"Israelite, wasn't he?" I hazarded. "Perhaps I've been mixing him up
with somebody else."

"Ought to guard agen that," replied Dixon kindly. "No; he was a
Hebrew. Properly speaking, Israelites is Jews. But Moses cottoned to
the Israelites. That was his first bit o' foolishness after he got on his
own hook. When he was quite a young feller his brothers sold him for
thirty bob to some Ishmaelites merchantmen on account of him always
dreamin' he was goin' to be cock-o'-the-walk an' not bein' able to keep
his (adj.) dreams to his self. Anyhow, he foun' his road into Egypt, an'
there he dropt across the Jews. Seems, so fur as I can make out, a feller
name o' Parryo was bossin' the whole show in Egypt; an' he had some
sort o' (adj.) purchase on the Jews; an' he kep them making bricks and
druv them most unmerciful; an' they didn't know what the (adj. sheol)
to do about it; so natural enough, they cried unto the Lord.

"Well, them ole times, the Lord used to mix Himself up a lot with
people an' take no end o' trouble tryin' to keep things a bit straight; and
He looked roun' for the foolishest bloke He could find to take on such
a (adv.) dead—horse racket as gettin' the Jews out o' this perdicament,

an' the (person) He picked out was Moses—a feller that might 'a' bin a swell among the Egyptians if he'd knowed when he was well off."

(If the student of this simple memoir should thoughtlessly impute anything like irreverence to Dixon, I hereby warn her that she does so at her own risk—at the gravest of all risks, namely, the risk of doing injustice. The comrade of nature, unconsciously profane, is rarely irreverent, never flippant. For instance, though Dixon habitually uttered the name "God," without the slightest mitigation or remorse of voice, the pronunciation of "the Lord" was unaffected, grave and devout. Briefly, the worst you can say of this wild-flower of the plains is that his Jahvistic idea was anthropomorphically on a level with that of the writers of the Pentateuch, and that his phraseology was governed by his vocabulary.)

So, innocently paraphrasing the sacred narrative he continued:

"Accordin'ly, Moses went an' barracked with this Parryo to let the Children go. (They're always alluded to by the name o' 'children' on account o' their (adj.) uselessness, an' pigheadedness, an' frightenedness). Fust go off, Moses on'y ast, quite simple like, for all hands to get a couple or three days' spell, an' fetch their live stock, an' flittin', an' tucker, an' every (adj.) thing they could rake up to sacrifice to the Lord in the wilderness.

"'Rats!' says Parryo. 'Gorstruth!' says he, 'did you think you'd come Paddy over me? Won't wash no (adj.) road. Jist you (adv.) well scoot back,' says he to Moses, 'and tell the Children to buck into their work a bit livelier, or, take my (adj.) word for it,' says he, 'I'll straighten the (malingerers) up!'

"But the Lord He backed up Moses, an' sent locusts, an' pleuro, an' Scotch greys, an' all manner o' curses on the country. Some sort o' oversight, seemin'ly, for it was the people that fell in, and Parryo never turned a (adj.) hair. Anyhow, after no end o' disturbance, the Jews got clear; an' Parryo he rallied up the Egyptians an' sooled 'em on to foller. Then a thing took place that no livin' man would believe, without he seen it for his own self, or read it in the Bible. Seems when the Children come to the Red Sea the water formed up into a (adv.) great bank on both sides, an' they walked across, quite unconcerned. Then when the Egyptians follered, the water walloped together, an' the Egyptians was (adv.) well had. Course, it ain't our place to say the wrong people was wiped out by mistake. I s'pose it was to be.

"Well, Moses he knowed the track to the Land o' Canaan, an' he went with the Children to show them the road. This was a land flowin' with milk an' honey, but there was some middling rough stages across a bit o' country called the Wilderness o' Sin. Anyone would think they'd put up with a trifle o' hardship, considerin' what was behind them and what was in front, but they begun to growl at Moses for fetchin' them into the wilderness to die. That was always their (adj.) chorus—'fetchin' us into the wilderness to die.'

"Then when the Lord foun' this was the sample o' thanks He was gittin' for all the trouble He'd took, He said He'd let them die and be d—d to them on'y for a promise He'd made to Aminadab years and years before. So he sent quails an' mannar, as much as they could (adv.) well tuck into them. No go. They was like some new chums that's bin halfstarved at home, an' jammed together like fleeces in a bale; an' these is the very blokes that can't find a good word to say about a country where they got any gosquantity o' room to look roun' an' a slant to be their own boss if they (adv.) well like. So, accordin' to accounts, they murmured agen Moses, sayin':

"'What the (adj. sheol) did you want fetchin' us out of Egypt, where we had as much meat and vegetables as you could shake a stick at?' says they. 'You (adj.) rotten (charlatan),' says they, 'seems like's if you was workin' some little point fetchin' us into the wilderness to (adv.) well die.'

"Then the Lord—He was fearful hot-tempered them 'ole times—He says, 'Stan' clear, Moses.' Says He, 'I'll destroy these (adj.) varmin, promise or no promise; an' you can make a fresh start with yer own kids.'

"Slant for Moses. Fact, you couldn't propose anythin' softer—but what d' you think the (adj.) fool done?"

"Snapped at it?" I suggested.

"Prayed for the (adj.) weeds," responded Dixon, emphatically. "Prayed for 'em. Well, I be—," he paused to select some adequate self—imprecation, culled a suitable one, and delivered it with a vigorous rattle of consonants. . .

"'Well, I'll only jist thin 'em out a bit this time,' says the Lord. 'Must stop their (adj.) jaw some road.' So He sent swarms o' snakes into the camp; but whether the snakes picked out the individuals that growled, or whether they bit anybody they could ketch, the Bible don't say. Anyhow, Moses rigged up a brass snake on a pole, an' stopped the poison actin.' It ain't as clear as it might be, but things was different in them ole times.

"Well, these Jews they sort of verbed along through the Wilderness of Sin, till they come to the Land o' Canaan; an' Moses he sent twelve spies on ahead to spy out the nakedness o' the land, an' these emissaries fetched back a sample bunch o' grapes, as much as two o' them could stagger under. The account they give of the country was that a land flowin' with milk an' honey was no name for it; but the Canaanites, an' the Rechabites, an' the Mammonites, an' all the other (adj.) ites looked like as if they was able to take their own (adj.) part agen anybody that come foolin' roun' with the idea of shiftin' 'em.

"'We'll (adv.) soon see about that,' says Moses. 'We're on for possessin' that land, no matter if we got to take a couple or three (adv.) good lickin's at the start. Audaces fortuna (adj.) juvat,' says he. 'All in favour o' this dart will please signify the same in the usual manner,' says he. An' what do you think the Jews done?"

"Gave three cheers," I suggested.

"Yes. Vill you buy a vatch? They lifted up their voice an' wept. Lifted up their voice an' (adv.) well wept.

"'To (sheol) with you an' yer (adj.) Land o' Canaan, you blatherin' morepoke,' says they to Moses. 'This comes o' you fetchin' us out o' Egypt, where our hides was whole, no matter if we was welted up to our work now an agen. We gone quite fur enough,' says they, 'so we'll stone you to death for makin' a (adj.) fool of us, an' off back to Egypt before we die o' fright.'

"'Stan' o' one side, Moses,' says the Lord. 'I ain't goin' to put up with this sort of (adj.) nonsense one minit longer. No use argying with a certain class o' people. I'll jist wipe out these (adj.) soojee (cravens), an' make a great nation out o' you an' yer own picaninnies.'

"Slant number fifty, or so, for Moses; an' what does the (adj.) fool do but he prays for the apostates again. Prays for 'em.

"'Have it so, then,' says the Lord, but they got to go back into the Wilderness of Sin an' do another perisher. Sin by name an' sin by nature.'

"'Hold on,' says the Jews. 'We're on the (adj.) job. We'll go an' possess the land.'

"'Not if I know it,' says the Lord. 'You should have thought about that before. Too late now. You're like the Portigee divil—when you're good, you're too good. Back you go to the Wilderness an' think the (adj.) thing over for a matter o' forty years. We'll have another confab about it when you got some o' the stiffenin' took out o' your (adj.) necks.'

"Course, this druv the Jews to desperation, an' they roused up all hands an' went to hunt the old inhabitants out o' the land. Moses, he argied with 'em an' told 'em the Lord was departed from them, but they only ordered him off. Six rails an' a cap wouldn't hold 'em. Fair bustin' with false pluck an' bluff an' blatherskite.

"Best instance of Moses's foolishness. One time he was away on some business with the Lord, an' the Jews they scraped up all their jewellery an' melted it, an' made a golden calf, and was holdin' a corroboree over it an' goin' on with their (adj.) childishness, as usual, an' up comes Moses, ropeable—an' what d'you think he done?"

"Confiscated the calf?" I suggested.

"Not his (adj.) height. He seized it, like a case o' tobacker at the Customs, an' groun' it into powder, an' mixed it with water, an' made the delinquents drink the water—an' so good-bye to as much as would have kep him independent for life. Fair chased with every (adj.) description o' slants, an' never froze on to one o' them. Got worse as he got older, an' died at last on top of a mountain, like some pore swaggie—a man that might hav bin at the very top o' the tree if he'd collared half the slants that come his road. I got no pity for a feller like that. Fact, I got no pity for anybody that crawls after Jews. Bad eggs, the Jews. When them temporisers was commanded to do anythin' good they used to forgit, or buck, or dodge out of it some (adj.) road; but when they was commanded to stone anybody—whoop! they was there quick an' lively. My (adj.) oath."

"Much the same with ourselves at the present day, Dixon," I remarked, with the magnanimity of one who has dined well. "Think over it every time you hear of somebody getting hanged."

"Moke of a different color," replied the bullock driver gravely, as he began to pack away his primitive table-service. "The world's a (sheol) of a sight better now nor it was in them ole times, an' the main reason is because there's a fair mixter of other people stead of Jews, Jews, Jews runnin' the whole (adj.) contract. Another thing's got a lot to do with it"—he paused, then continued with marked reverence—"there's a (adv.) great improvement in the Lord's way o' workin'. Eased off a lot—ain't He?" Another pause, then in a wistful tone, whilst suspending his domestic labor. "Now, onna bright, Collins, do you think the fear of the Lord will save a person?"

"We're led to believe so."

"But is that what you was taught, or is it only yer own (adj.) idea?"

"It's what I was taught, and taught by professing Christians!"

"My strong point," responded Dixon, with ill-concealed relief.

"Grand (adj.) holt—ain't she? Spes tutissima (adj.) coelis." He lit his pipe on the strength of her. "Hello, here's Rigby. More the merrier. Plenty a tea in the billy, anyhow." And he proceeded to relay the spread corn sack with his frugal store.

IX

The stranger's hand to the stranger, yet—
For a roving folk are mine—
The stranger's store for the stranger set—
And the camp-fire glow the sign.

—Henry Lawson

Rigby met my glance of surprise with a faraway, dreamy look; then, with the same preoccupied air, he walked across to his waggonette, and drew his tucker-box from beneath the seat. Whereupon Dixon became so frankly offensive that Rigby put the box back, and took his place at the bullock driver's ocean-bounded table.

"I didn't expect you so soon, Colonel," he remarked.

"I can't stay long," he replied. "Nice evening." The latter observation was addressed to a flash-looking young man, who came up with a rod and a line in his hand.

"I've seen worse, an' at the same time, I've seen better," replied the young fellow. "Whereabouts was it that your mate caught that thirty-pounder?" he continued, turning to Dixon.

"Sit down and have a drink of tea," replied the bullock driver. "Who was tellin' you about that (adj.) fish?"

"What's that got to do with you? I want to know where he caught it?"

"Well, you kin jist (adv.) well find out," replied Dixon with dignity. "Polite sort o' (person) you are," he continued as the other strode away. "Bin dragged up anyhow, seemin'ly."

"Who is he?" I asked.

"Kangaroo hunter, supposed to be. One (adj.) horse an' no dogs. Nothin' but a rifle. Camped over there, aside the big log. Look out for yer dog tonight, Collins."

"More sacks to the mill," I remarked, as another man approached us with a fishing-rod in his hand. A little, puny, mild-looking man this time.

"Good evening, gentlemen. I believe Thompson hooked a fine fish this morning somewhere here?"

"Who was tellin' you?" asked Dixon.

"That foreigner up at the pub."

JOSEPH FURPHY

"Well, yes; he got a thirty-pounder this mornin'," replied Dixon suavely. "Landed her after a (sheol) of a (adj.) struggle, but when he thought she was safe, away she goes slitherin' down the bank an' into the (adj.) river agen. Have a drink o' tea. There's a (adj.) pannikin."

"I've just had supper, thank you."

"What're you baitin' with?"

"Bit of roasted 'possum—can't beat it," replied the visitor, as he retired towards the river bank.

"Decent little (fellow)," commented Dixon, without waiting till the other had got out of hearing. "Londoner, by profession cockney, with no inside. Name o' Furlong. Scrats out a (adv.) good livin' 'possumin' in the winter, when the skins is good. That's his (adj.) spring cart over there. He on'y come this forenoon; an' now he's got dozens o' sheepskins in the lagoons, fishing' for leeches. Gits the raw pelts cheap at the wash and sen's the (adj.) leeches to Melbn' wholesale. Great little (fellow) Stuff any (adj.) thing, from a emu to a tomtit. Best (adj.) bee-hunter in these parts, too. Got a eye like a (adj.) hawk. Got a bee-tree this afternoon, that I'd bin walkin' past a dozen times, an' he collars that (adv.) great treacle can an' he fills her full o' honey for me, an' no compliment."

While imparting these biographical notes, Dixon had taken from an adjacent hollow stump an old billy half-full of live mussels, in water; now he laid three of these in front of the fire and replaced the billy.

"Allowed to be the best (adj.) 'possumer on the track," he resumed; "an' he tells me he wasn't worth a (courtesan's) curse at the trade he was brought up to."

"A familiar experience, Dixon," remarked Rigby, partially rousing himself from his reverie. "Non omnia possumus omnes—which may be freely translated, 'We can't all of us be 'possumers.'"

"Hum," replied Dixon, warily. "Anyhow, me an' him got acquainted campin' together on the Island two years ago. That (man's) got a blessin' on him, jist the same's Thompson's got his (adj.) curse. Spends mostly all his spare time readin' the Bible an' prayin'. Puts the (adj.) stuns on me how some chaps kin be so good. Roughest contract ever anybody took on is to do everything to the glory of God, but that (fellow) manages it. Can't you eat no more, Rigby? Well, I'll pack up the (adj.) jewel'ry-box, an' we'll go an' have a shake for this thirty-(adj.)-pounder."

Meanwhile, I had rigged up my fishing-tackle. Rigby, having finished his meal, glanced at his watch, hesitated a moment, then walked to his waggonette, and returned with a jointed fishing-rod. Dixon's tackle was already prepared. Each of us took one of the gaping mussels and baited his hook with the naked mollusc, now shrunken and toughened by the slight roasting which had opened the shell.

"My intentions ran on another kind of fishing," remarked Rigby to me, as we made our way down the bank. "However, I may combine the two forms for a very short time, since the circumstances are so contributory as almost to amount to compulsion."

He was right. Better conditions could not have been supplied to order. Three large red gums stood on the edge of the river ten or twelve yards apart, and their roots, washed clean by the stream, afforded seats and foothold anywhere on the steep slope; while before us the faintly-swirling water seemed full of promise. The kangaroo-hunter and Furlong were already seated, watching their floats. The fascination of the thirty-pounder was over us all.

It was a beautiful evening—dead calm, with just that flavor of sultriness which, at a later hour, matures into temperature so perfect that the most accomplished tippler wouldn't know whether he wanted his refreshment iced or mulled. Any person whose smelling apparatus was not debauched by smoking would have found the air fragrant with scent of pennyroyal and rich with aroma exhaled from countless tons of eucalyptus leaves. Best of all, no annoying hum of mosquitoes marred a concert of evening sounds, made up by the homely clatter of myriad frogs, and the tangled melody of a dozen bells, copious in range of tone and timbre. And from time to time, like a drunken Welshman talking in his sleep, came the guttural discourse of a 'possum, or perhaps the mumble of a bear; while at shorter intervals some solitary mopoke solemnly announced himself by name, eliciting occasional response from two or three faraway friends, who seemed to call themselves "pope-pope"—certain sound-waves of the note being exhausted in transit. Three hilarious kookaburras, sitting side by side on a dead branch close by, did their best to liven things up before retiring for the night; while now and then some dejected curlew yelled his probably imaginary woes on the sympathetic air; and away in different directions the monotonous and foolish barking of several dogs might lead the thrifty soul to meditate on the unpreventable leakage of Energy in this world of ours.

Behind where we sat, a sheep-proof fence, running down from the pub, terminated in one of the three big trees I mentioned. The east side of this fence was a grazing paddock, consisting of frontage land, purchased or stolen by a squatter in the good old times, and now rented by a local boss—cockie. The pub was part of the same property, all belonging to some indefinite person in Melbourne. Just behind us, a section of charred ruins, overgrown with nettles and variegated thistles, showed where the old out—station had stood in the corner of the land. The place was known as Cameron's Paddock, from the name of the second last, and longest—bleeding, tenant.

The west side of the fence was river frontage, the red-gum flats coming southward to the road, while the river itself swept away miles to the north, and again approached the road about two miles westward, thus forming a fine bend, mostly inaccessible to loafing sheep, by reason of billabongs, lagoons, and swamps, and therefore much valued by such bullock drivers as knew its geography, and could avail themselves of its resources.

Here I may remark that, as a rule, the trans-Murrumbidgee bullock driver, like the emu, is more inclined to follow water conservation northward through the back blocks than to drift down into the distracting civilisation of the Murray. But Thompson, Dixon, and a few others, being Victorians and familiar with many desirable spots along the Border River, sometimes condescended—condescended—I say, to put in a month or two on their native territory when the grasshoppers began to starve on the plains through which the Lachlan ought to have run. Victorian trips were too degradingly short, and Victorian wheat too abominably heavy handling for these aristocrats; but, as Falstaff says, young men must live and seasons are not unknown when—to use a composite metaphor for which Thompson is responsible—the rat who refuses to leave the sinking ship will be reduced to live on the boiled tongues of his own dead bullocks. Thompson had been that rat.

Whilst we were selecting comfortable seats and throwing our lines into the river, the rhythmic pattering of a cantering horse came faintly on the air, followed by the jangle of a bell at the waggons on the bank above us, and the shrill neigh of a liberated animal, starting in search of his mates. Then Rigby, mentally shaking himself up, turned toward me and murmured confidentially:

"By the way, I was just going to ask you—"

"That you, Thompson?" shouted Dixon.

"No," replied Thompson, appearing on the bank. "How are you, Rigby? I'm glad to see you. All hands fishing? Any luck?"

"Stacks of it, so fur," replied Dixon, "only it ain't the proper specie. Layin' wait for that (adj.) thirty-pounder you lost here. Ole Parley-voo told us about her."

"Ah, I remember I mentioned it to him this morning. And there's five of you on the contract, like the five foolish virgins in the Bible. However, I'll keep you company, if anyone can shout me a bait."

"Plenty mussels in the ole billy in the holler stump aside the (adj.) fire," replied Dixon. "Don't roast none but the one you want. Keep the molluscs fresh. Letter for you in the pocket o' yer (adj.) waggon— forrided from Hay."

"Only somebody sticking me up for damages, or claiming one of my bullocks, or threatening me with seven years for passing a bad cheque, or perhaps some new style of misfortune," replied Thompson wearily, as he turned back to prepare his fishing-tackle.

"Swore off smokin' a fortnit ago, an' he naturally gits as miserable as a bandicoot when night comes on," observed Dixon. "Reckons to git his (adj.) curse shifted through knockin' off his bad habits little by little. Hard to say. Worth tryin', anyhow."

While we mused over this suggestion—each in his own way— Thompson joined us, threw his line into the river, seated himself on a root, and sighed deeply.

"I get melancholy every time I see this camp," he remarked. "I knew the people that lived here, where the house is burned down. Old associations of ten years ago. Now everything's changed, and changed for the worse. The people are gone—gave up the place three or four years back, and selected away towards the Coolaman. The waggon I had then is at the bottom of the Murrumbidgee, the bullocks are gone, every scrap of tackle is gone, the horse is gone, even the dog is gone; my youth is gone; my hopes are gone; and I'm neither use nor ornament in the world. It would take a smarter man than myself to tell what I'm living for."

"Sic transit gloria (adj.) mundi," observed Dixon, as if to himself.

"What was her name?" asked Rigby.

"Agnes," replied Thompson sadly. "Their house stood on the bank behind us here, where you see the thistles growing now. Her father was a hard, strict, religious Scotchman, with fierce eyebrows. His name was Cameron—Lyon Cameron."

"I came across a sheep-drover name o' 'Swearing Cameron,' three seasons ago," remarked Dixon, thoughtfully. "Might be some relation. These things often runs in the blood."

"I'll tell you the whole story," pursued Thompson, "and you'll see what it is for a man to live in the position that I'm in. His whole life is just composed of retreats from Moscow, one after another. Sometimes it seems to slacken off a bit, and you think the infernal thing has sort of exhausted itself, but it's only gathering strength for a fresh spring; and before you know what you're about, it's on you again. I'm not a superstitious man myself, but I can't help noticing that ever since I cheated that dead man Providence seems to go clean out of its way to have a clip at me. Now, this instance of Agnes Cameron is a proof of what I say."

During this confession the little trapper, leaving the butt of his rod jammed among the roots, had picked his way along the water-scarped bank to the speaker's side.

"I beg your pardon," said he, in a low, eager voice, "were you camped about two miles from Mathoura, four years ago—four years on the third of March last?"

Thompson pondered. "I don't remember—Oh, yes, that's all right."

"I was sure I knew your voice," replied Furlong. "I just camped here today." A pause. Then the two shook hands, and the trapper returned to his line.

X

For rustic youths could I a list produce
Of Stephen's books, how great might be the use;
But evil fate was theirs—survey'd, enjoy'd.
Some happy months, and then by force destroyed
So will'd the Fates—but these, with patience read.
Had vast effect on Stephen's heart and head.

—Rev. George Crabbe—"The Learned Boy."

Yes, boys," continued Thompson, sadly. "She was the only girl I ever was properly in love with, and one Sunday I took her out in a canoe—"

"This won't do, Steve," I interrupted, with some severity. "You must tell us how you met her first, and what induced you to fall in love with her; also what sort of a canoe it was, and who you stole it from—and, in fact, all the details."

"I can tell you exactly what caused me to fall in love with her, Tom. It was yourself that did it—indirectly, of course. I'll tell you how. It was in January, '73, that I camped in this bend for the first time, to have a few months' spell before the next wool. Now, you remember that I met you at Deniliquin in the spring of '72, and we spent a Sunday together at my camp on the common? Do you remember telling me then that there were ten masterpieces of poetry that nobody on earth except yourself had ever read clean through, or ever would? I took a list of them at the time, if you remember, but, in any case, I'm not likely to forget the names. Let's see—'Paradise Lost' and 'Regained,' counting the two as one; Goethe's 'Faust,' especially the second part; Dante's 'Divine Comedy,' Spenser's 'Faery Queene,' Thomson's 'Seasons,' Cowper's 'Task,' Tennyson's 'In Memoriam,' Edwin Arnold's 'Light of Asia,' and, lastly, any poem of Walt Whitman's.

"Well, being young and flash at the time, I began to think how I would shine if I had those books at my finger ends, and you know the sort of lunacy that comes over a man when he fancies himself good enough to go through with a thing that everybody has shied clear of. I seemed to look forward into the future and hear people saying: 'See that cove! that's the man I was telling you about—that's Thompson—best-educated fellow on the track.' And this ambition got possession of me till at last I wrote to Cole for the price of the best rough-and-ready editions delivered at the Melbourne Railway Station. The end of the matter was, that the parcel was waiting for me at Echuca when I crossed the river on my way to this bend to spell for the next wool. Of course, the ten books included a lot of reading that wasn't properly in the contract, but I wanted to be on the safe side, and I was game for anything in the way of reading.

"I camped on a little sand-hill, half-a-mile across there. I had nothing to interfere with my reading except to boil the billy about once a day, and make a damper about once a week; and between my natural laziness and the strain on my mind, I got too feeble to do even that much properly. But I stuck to my studies, though I'm a slow reader at the best of times. When I got so disgusted with one book that I couldn't face another line, I used to take a spell and then tackle some other book, and so on—always marking the place where I knocked off, and never slumming a word."

"But we want your love-story, Steve," interposed the Major.

"This is my love-story, and I'm telling it according to Tom's specifications. Better decide whether I'm to study your taste or his. Or, if you like, I'll drop it altogether."

"Ne Jupiter quidem (adj.) omnibus," observed Dixon, sententiously.

"Are you to the fore?" growled Thompson. "You ought to be yarded, without water or tucker, till you learn to speak English again."

"Didn't mean no (adj.) offence," replied Dixon, scoring heavily with the ostentatious mildness of his tone. "I only shoved in a word, as a amicus (adj.) curiae in a manner o' speakin'."

"We all apologise; myself foremost," said Rigby. "Go on with your story in your own way."

"Very well," replied Thompson. "After I had been camped about a month I went across one day to enquire about a roan steer that had taken up with my bullocks, and there I saw Agnes for the first time. She was a fine lump of a girl, no doubt; but my mind was so disordered and stupefied by the class of books I had been reading that she seemed like a bird of paradise, and she'll have that appearance to me, as long as I've got a head on my body." He paused, and sighed deeply.

"Well, I bought this roan steer off Cameron, and that started a sort of acquaintance. Agnes was just twenty, and she had two brothers of sixteen or seventeen. Mrs. Cameron was a nice, fat, easy-going sort of woman, frightened to death of Cameron. Everybody was frightened of that man, and no one worse than myself. Most God-fearing man I ever knew. But the boys were great disciples of mine. Many an evening the three of us have sat fishing here, where we are now. And many a Sunday morning I've dressed myself as like a Presbyterian elder as I could come to, and sneaked across here, to fawn like a dog on Cameron, and go mooning about the place like a harmless lunatic. By-and-bye I got a letter from my sister that fairly knocked me. Cameron happened to be a townie of my father's next neighbour (that was old McFarlane, Tom), and it seems he had written to this cove for particulars about me. Not much to build upon, of course, but I fancied that Cameron afterwards talked to me in a tone that I could imagine him using to the son of a respectable man, and I caught at the hope as the drowning man catches at—"

"Not at a straw, if you please, Steve," interposed Rigby.

"Well—at an anvil. However, time passed till I began to think about starting for Hay. Mind you, I was in a curious position. Agnes and I understood each other, of course, and we felt that nothing short of death would shift either of us, but then again we seemed to have very little say in the matter. We were both in such bodily fear of her dad that we were sort of paralysed. It's all very well for you to say that you'd have done this, or that, or the other thing. You'd play (sheol). So would I. But if you were withered up with the course of study that I had gone through, and had old Cameron to deal with, you'd do just as I did. You see, I didn't know what value he put on me—in fact, I didn't know what value I put on myself. Sometimes I seemed a fine, promising young chap; and other times I seemed about on a level with a Chinaman. It was those infernal books that did it. I think Mrs. Cameron stood to me. At all events, one day Cameron made me tell all my affairs, and then brought in Agnes' name, and finally told me that if I could give a good account of myself in another year he would allow me to write to her. But I must turn over another leaf in the matter of thrift. Of course, I promised anything and everything, and began to feel like a respectable, right-thinking citizen, never considering the thing that was on me.

"This happened on a Saturday morning. Cameron had a habit of finding some work of necessity for Sundays to keep the family out of mischief. He was starting away down the country that afternoon with the two boys to meet some store cattle, not expecting to be back for four or five days, and as I was to start for Hay on the Monday morning we weren't likely to meet again for six months. In the meantime, I was to write to him, but not to Agnes. You'll understand that I had been loafing in the bend for four or five months, and by this time it was well on in winter.

"Now, you'll see what comes of doing things on Sunday that ought to be done the night before. On Sunday morning I went to the smiddy that used to be a mile up the road here to get some keys I had ordered, and I was coming back along the frontage with the keys in my hand, and when I struck the river about half-a-mile above here the first thing that caught my eye was a canoe, with a couple of oars in it, sailing along on its own account. She was a heavy wooden concern about four feet wide and twenty feet long—just a hollow tree, with the right bend dressed into shape, two or three boards nailed across for seats, and a couple of irons like spurs stuck one in each side for you to work the oars in.

"She was travelling within a few yards of this bank, so I peeled off and slipped in and snaked her ashore with a bit of clothes line that was hanging to one end. I tied her up while I went back after my duds. Then I got on board, and came rowing down here, like Trickett himself, and stuck her snout among the roots, just about where Rigby's sitting at the present moment. Of course, the river was twelve or fifteen feet higher than it is now.

"After dinner, nothing would do me but to take Agnes out for a pleasure trip in the canoe. She was on, but her mother was dubious. However, I argued so hard, and lied so fluently about my skill in handling boats that Mrs. Cameron gave in at last, and off we went. It wasn't the first time I had been in a boat, but it was the first time I ever had an oar in my hand, and the new-chum flashness was strong on me. This was about two in the afternoon, and we were to be back in a couple of hours. Of course, I knew Cameron wouldn't allow such Godless recreation if he was at home, but I quieted my conscience with the thought that what the eye never sees, the heart never grieves for."

Thompson paused, sighed heavily, and mechanically felt for his pipe. Then, even in the gloaming, I marked his form assume a resolute, almost arrogant, bearing. The haughty consciousness of self-subdual was more grateful, after all, than even a soul-satisfying smoke; it threw boldness on his forehead, gave firmness to his breath, and he looked like some grim warrior new risen up from death.

XI

But now secure the painted vessel glides.
The sunbeams trembling on the floating tides;
While melting music steals upon the sky.
And soften'd sounds along the waters die;
Smooth flow the waves, the zephyrs gently play.
Belinda smiled, and all the world was gay.

—Pope's "Rape of the Lock."

T hompson resumed. "I just let the boat drift, dipping the oars in a light, off-hand way, to steady her along; and the time passed as pleasantly as time can pass, and quicker than it ever did before, or ever will again. Agnes was even happier than I was, for the whole transaction just came up to her poor little idea of devilment. As it happened, the sun wasn't shining that afternoon, and my watch had gone cronk some weeks before; so I could only guess at the time. But we wanted to be on the safe side, so presently we agreed that it was time to be getting back. Just then we saw a boy putting a night line in the river, and I says to him:

"'I say, sonny,' says I. 'How far back is it to Mr. Cameron's?'

"'Well,' says he. 'I donno how fur it is by the road you come, but you won't do bad if you pad it in five miles. Ain't that Agnes Cameron you got with you?' says he. 'Wonder how they let her come out. I seen Cameron half-an-hour ago.'

"'No,' says I, 'you couldn't. He went away yesterday!'

"'I know he did,' says the boy. 'I seen him and Billy and Malky goin' away yesterday, and I seen him comin' back today by his own self. Ought to be home about dark.'

"We were travelling so fast just then that the boy had to yell out his last remarks after us, and by this time we swooped round a point, and lost sight of him. Of course, Agnes began to cry, and, of course, I kissed her; and I remember to the present day that the taste of the poor girl's lips reminded me of dead leeches. But there was no time to be lost, so I welted away with one oar for about a quarter of an hour till I got the boat turned, and then started to send her up against the stream. But she was over a ton weight and she took such a terrific hold of the current that I could hardly gain an inch while I was rowing my best; and, at every fourth lift or so, I used to miss the water and turn a back summerset; and then, while I was getting into position again, she would get the speed on her, and by the time I had steadied her I was heels over tip again. And all this time we were going round one bend after another and evening was coming on full speed. Then I could see that there was nothing for it but to get ashore and walk home, and I told Agnes so. And to make matters better, the poor girl had chilblains, and her Sunday boots punished her so that she had taken them off soon after we started, and now she was tugging and panting and half—swearing to get them on again, but all to no purpose, while I was tumbling over the top of her, and nearly capsizing the boat.

"However, I aimed for a good landing-place, and hit a steep, greasy bank about fifty yards lower down, where Agnes couldn't get out; and altogether by the time we got landed, the night was fairly on us, and it was beginning to rain. When we were landing, I held on to some roots and kept the boat jammed against the bank while Agnes crept out on her hands and knees. Then I let go, and stepped ashore. But clumsy as the boat was, it was lively enough to swing out while I had one foot on the edge of it and the other on the bank. Of course, I plopped into three or four feet of water; and, before I had cleared myself the boat was well out into the main current, and off full tilt for Echuca, with Agnes' boots and shawl and umbrella on board. There was a curse on that boat." The narrator paused in gloomy abstraction, then resumed.

"When we got up on the bank, things looked worse than ever. No appearance of a light anywhere; not even the bark of a dog to be heard; no sign of population; nothing but a wretched red-gum flat, most likely miles across, and cut up in all directions with creeks. However, the first thing to be done was to get out to the main road, so I cheered Agnes up, and gave her my coat and boots, and we made a start together. Naturally, a couple of hundred yards brought us block up against a billabong. We ran it along to the left for a quarter of a mile, and found it joined on with the river. Then we turned back, and ran it half a mile to the right, and found it stuck on to the river, there, too. Of course, we were on an island, and by this time it was pitch dark, and raining cats and dogs. Then I could see that the infernal thing had roused itself, and was fairly on the job. So I was thankful for the very small mercy of a hollow tree, with just enough room in it for Agnes to pack herself as scientifically as a chicken in a clocked egg.

"Next consideration was a fire, so I groped under logs for dry leaves, till I got enough for a commencement. It was a close shave for matches. I had just three left, but they were dry, for the box was a waterproof one. My fingers were numb with cold, so I managed to drop the first match and lose it; but the next was a success. I got the handful of leaves lit, but I had to supply the fire in its infancy with wet stuff, and in spite of all I could do, it dwindled and flickered and died out."

"I'd a give five bob to hear you dealin' with the (adj.) subject," remarked Dixon, complacently.

"You'd have lost your money. I had another match left. I spent a quarter of an hour groping out more dry leaves and twigs. Then I got Agnes' handkerchief for kindling, and made a final attempt. But the match turned out to have no head. I didn't come out. I was past that. I was crushed. It wasn't the hardship, for I've had worse nights, and I expect to have worse still before I die, but it was the troubled mind along with it. And in cases of this kind a girl is as foolish as a foal, so there was Agnes crying and blowing her nose all the time, and wondering whatever she would do; and there was me walking back and forward, with my teeth going like a chaffcutter, and the fine rain for the farmer coming down wholesale where there was no thanks for it. I wouldn't go through it again—not for Father Peter. The hardship was as bad as Dante's Inferno, and the trouble was a lot worse than Milton's Hell."

"Hear, hear," said I, rattling my feet on a root. "Wasn't it worth while to be led into all this unpleasantness by those books, when they repaid you with the power of illustrating it in such a scholarly way?"

"Case of vigilate et (adj.) orate, when a man's in such a (sheol) of a (adj.) st-nk," interjected Dixon, with good-natured emulation, as the last syllable left my lips.

"Go ahead, pile it on!" retorted Thompson, maliciously. "I don't know any surer way of falling in the fat—and I ought to be an authority."

"Let them fill up their measure of iniquity, Steve," remarked the Deacon. "Go on with your story."

"Well," resumed Thompson, "after about three months daylight came, and the rain cleared off. Agnes hadn't felt the cold much, for she had a layer of fat all over her, and her clothes were dry; so she had dropped asleep at the drowsy time in the morning. As soon as it was light enough to see, I had explored the billabong and found one place where the current was middling strong. I tested this spot from bank to bank to make sure of the bottom, and found it was only three to four feet deep. So I got the loan of my boots for the trip, and took Agnes on my shoulder to keep her out of the water, and a good pole in both hands to prop against the current; and I made the passage with about two ounces of strength to spare, for she was 11st. all out—and I was anything but fresh.

"By this time the sun was out nice and warm, and the rest of our journey was easy. We came straight in this direction, thinking to get a shorter cut than the main road. Besides, we felt modest about showing off before the public, for I was bare-footed and bare-headed and wet and miserable—looking, and Agnes' face was dirty and her hair all wild, and her clothes torn, and she was lame with her chilblains, and altogether she looked as if she had been on a bad drunk; and the terror of old Cameron made us both look as if we ought to be in jail, and knew it.

"When we had gone a little better than a mile, we saw a farm house in front of us, and we knew where we were. Agnes was acquainted with the people of the farm, so we decided to give them a call. It was Quarterman's place—two or three miles from here by the road. He's a pompous individual in his own little way. He took on himself to cross-examine me about our misfortune, and he ended by writing a note to Cameron over it. But Mrs. Quarterman did all she could for us, and presently we started off home in a spring cart, with a half-grown lump of a girl to hammer the old moke along. Of course, this girl had to carry the note for Cameron. But now that the adventure was drawing to an end, I found a peace of mind that all the old fogies on the river couldn't disturb. I was as happy as Larry."

"I don't perceive much opening for self-felicitation yet," observed Rigby. "The figure of Cameron seems to loom large in perspective."

"Now, I've told this yarn to three different women, and they all saw the point at a glance," replied Thompson. "But we're dense beggars, the cleverest of us. Anyway, if the idea had struck me before, I would have been proof against all the misery of the night. It just occurred to me that this bit of a mishap would grow into a very good scandal, and that nobody else would have Agnes at any price. My old mistake, forgetting the thing that was on me.

"However, after we got started, I whispered to Agnes, so that Jim couldn't overhear (Jim was the girl's name), 'Agnes,' says I, 'it's a dead certainty that I won't be allowed about your place for some time to come. Now listen and remember. In six or eight months, if I'm alive, I'll come in the night and blaze that big red gum, with the lot of mistletoes on it, just opposite your bedroom window. When you see the fresh blaze, you'll know that I'll be waiting for you that evening at sunset, in the whipstick scrub, at the right-hand lower corner of your calf-paddock. I'll wait there every night for a week.'

"I impressed this on her mind, and cheered her up, and we jogged along to about half-way home, when up comes Cameron behind us on horseback, as savage as a bull-ant. He ordered me out of the spring cart, and I obeyed like clockwork, after giving Jim a half-sovereign for herself. Then, whilst the spring cart went on, Cameron stayed a few minutes, and told me what he thought of me. I took it like a poor man with a large family. I could afford to take it in that way, for I seemed to have a grip that couldn't shake. When he had finished, I went down to my waggon, yoked up, and camped that night twelve miles beyond Quarterman's, and in less than a fortnight I was at Hay, still gloating over my mortgage on Agnes."

"And the books I had recommended—did you master any of them?" I asked.

"No, Tom, I didn't. They mastered me. I gave them to the Public Library at Hay. They reflected a glimpse of credit on me in the end; but, as I told the secretary when he was writing my name and title in the front of each, and complimenting me on my choice of reading—'Stephen Thompson, Esquire,' says I to him, 'has never been the same man since he tackled them!'"

Again Thompson sighed hopelessly, shoved his hand half way down his right-hand pocket, then slowly withdrew it, whilst his whole attitude and demeanor showed that he was vividly realising how sublime a thing it is to suffer and be strong.

XII

This is the state of man; today he puts forth
His tender leaves of hopes; tomorrow blossoms,
And bears his blushing honors thick upon him;
The third day comes a frost, a killing frost;
And—when he thinks, good, easy man, full surely
His greatness is a-ripening—nips his root.

—King Henry VIII, Act III, Scene II

D id you keep your appointment with the girl?" asked the Colonel, after a pause.

"Well, Providence took a hand in the arrangement, and I'm not rebellious enough to complain," replied Thompson, with the diseased humility of a self-pitying egotist. "I'll finish the story. It was in June, '73, that I left here, and I came back in February, '74. I had made a splendid season of it—the best I had ever had. The squatters were coining money, and there was no end of new country fresh stocked with sheep in place of cattle; and the grass was good, and I had one of the best teams that ever travelled Riverina. We'll never see such times again. Before Christmas I had cleared 210 notes beyond expenses, and my team nothing the worse. Full loaded both ways every trip, and me grabbing the monish till I could feel my nose growing big and hooked, and my eyes taking the appearance of black beads. I was a man to be avoided.

"During the season I wrote two letters to Cameron, apologising for the other affair, and reporting progress in a modest, off-hand way, but he never answered. So, as I was telling you, I got back in February. I camped about a mile below here and that evening I swam the river with a tomahawk in my teeth, and blazed that big tree—there it is, just opposite. Next evening I was at the corner of the calf-paddock, and who should come pushing through the scrub but Cameron himself.

"'Now, let me hear what you have to say, Thompson,' says he, in an awful voice. 'I'll represent my daughter this evening, if you've no objection.'

"Nothing for it but to face him square, though, in a manner of speaking Agnes seemed to have gone over to the enemy, and I felt like a tree suddenly stripped of every leaf in a hail-storm."

"A vicious combination of metaphor and simile, Steve," remarked the Senator, critically. "Also, the latter seems somewhat exaggeratory. A man with a first-class carrying plant and £210 might be regarded as relatively umbrageous."

"I agree with you there," replied Thompson, bitterly. "However, I found myself able to speak to Cameron in a manly way, and he took it in such good part that I began to think he was making allowance for the purchase I had on Agnes; but it was the old mistake of not allowing for the thing that's on me. So there we stood, while I told him the whole story of my wool season, and when I had done, he canted his head to one side, and says he, 'Do you expect a man of my experience to believe a yarn like THAT?'

"'Well,' says I, 'it does sound a bit hollow, but that's not my fault; the story's true, post to finish.'

"'And it is a fact,' says he, 'that you're got no plant now except nine skeletons and a waggon?'

"'Gospel truth,' says I. 'If you have any doubt about it, you can come to my camp, and see for yourself.'

"'And how much cash have you to the good?' says he.

"'I'll conceal nothing from you, Mr. Cameron,' says I. 'I've just got three-and-fourpence in hand, and I'm about 12 notes in debt; but, against this, I have 36 notes coming from M'Culloch.'

"'Look here, Thompson,' says he, 'if ever I catch you in sight of my place again, I'll put the dogs on you,' and he wheels round and walks off."

"I don't blame him," observed the Major. "Can't you perceive that it requires a higher order of mind than yours to make one substantial structure out of two thin ones, without showing the joint? In fact, your composite style of architecture, though it may make the Washington laugh, cannot but make the Munchausen grieve. Just stand off and look at your two-story yarn. One moment you're clothed in property and cash; the next moment you're sitting at your own slip-panel, full of indigence."

"However, that's my love story, and short as it is, it covers my whole life. No more romance for me. Certainly there's an oldish girl in Moama that I could fall in love with if I let myself loose, but that would be madness for a man in my position. Anybody else might live in hope, but I don't; for the Providence that knows how many hairs a man's got on his head will take thundering good care I don't get off so cheap. I'll live and die on the wallaby. I'm like that character in the Bible—I forget who he was—always going to and fro on the earth, and walking up and down in it. I've got the satisfaction of knowing that I deserve it all."

XIII

Enter Lucifer as a priest.

—Longfellow's "Golden Legend."

Mournful is thy tale, son of the car," I observed, thriftlessly using up a good quotation from Ossian. "But you're only passing through the cycle of adversity that every novelist-hero has to fulfil. You'll meet your antithetical affinity yet—some woman with the curse of prosperity on her; and such a woman's alkali, chemically combined with your acid, will fill the goblet of life with a delectable fizzer. Why, this afternoon, when old Fritz spoke of your catching a thirty-pounder, I thought at once, from what I knew of you, that he was referring to some heiress. You'll be a shire—councillor—possibly a churchwarden—before you're done; and one that knows the Law, go to; and a rich fellow enough, go to; and a fellow that hath had losses, go to; and one that hath two gowns, and everything handsome about him. You'll be a man of acres—like Binney, over there—with a good-natured toleration for the lower classes."

"I don't thank you for the compliment, though Binney's a ten-to-one better man than I am," interrupted Thompson, contentiously. "I'm Berryite to the bone; and Binney's tarred with the same stick as yourself—with this difference, that he's a sound Conservative, and you're a rotten one. He's a good, honest pillar of Conservatism; and you're a sepulchre, whitewashed with Conserv—"

"Is that you, Thompson?" inquired a cheerful voice from the top of the bank.

"What's left of me," replied the bullock driver.

"Stay where you are, Thompson. All fishing? You'll have company, Harold. Why, Collins, is this you?"

"No," I replied, and shook hands with the two-cloud-dropped visitors. Binney was a special friend of mine; a farmer, living just beyond the pub. Harold Lushington, a young Methodist minister, was Binney's brother-in—law. I introduced them to the Colonel, inadvertently omitting to mention Lushington's profession.

"I heard this afternoon that you were camped here," said Binney to Thompson, "so I just came over to tell you that I want to sent away a couple of hundred bags of barley if you'll take it at the current rate. Will you call round tomorrow morning? Right. We'll leave it till then. Harold is on business, too. When he was down at the post this afternoon, the old German told him some fish yarn, and it takes a very small touch to put him off his head on that subject."

"What bait are you using, Collins?" asked Lushington. "I have supplied myself with sheep's lungs."

"No good," remarked Thompson. "Dixon'll give you a roasted mussel if you don't mind going up to the fire for it."

"Thanks," replied the young clergyman; and he hastily climbed the bank.

"Now, I don't want to disturb you, boys," said Binney, who had seated himself on a root. "Go on with your conversation, if it's not private. You were talking of Conservatism, I think."

"The subject of politics was casually glanced at, I remember," replied the Major, "but our topic was the romance of life—the love-story. We had been listening to a most interesting experience of this kind, and my mind had just reverted to a speculation touching a very worthy, though somewhat profane, friend of ours—now gone to prepare a bait. I was busied in conjecture as to what phase the grand passion would be likely to assume in his case. For we must by no means suppose that his unconventional address and seventh-century moral culture, have emancipated him from the common thraldom or tended to make him the exception which is erroneously supposed to prove the rule."

I noticed the respectful air which Binney unconsciously assumed under the glamor of the Judge's perfect enunciation and measured rhetoric. But Thompson nagged in reply:

"You're doing the chap a great injustice, Rigby. Though, to be sure," he added sadly, "there's so much injustice in the world that a little here or there makes no difference. Anyway, Dixon's not to blame for being rough—and-ready; and he lives up to his standard as well as you live up to yours, and better than I live up to mine. And he's no such half-savage as you want to make out. Willoughby could tell you that."

"You must know," I explained to Binney and the Colonel, "this Willoughby was a whaler of the scholarly-aristocratic type, placed by an inscrutable decree of Providence in the position of understudy to Dixon during last wool season. Dixon and Willoughby must have got on well together, Steve?"

"They did, indeed," replied Thompson. "They were together for over three months, and their friendship grew stronger every day."

"This accounts for Dixon's smattering of the classics?" I suggested.

"Ay, he's a bit aggravating that way," conceded Thompson, reluctantly. "He's mad on it. He has a dictionary in his waggon, that he bought for the sake of the Latin phrases at the end. Willoughby used to be posting him up day and night, and everything he learned stuck to him—not like me. It was the fun of the world to Willoughby. Dixon naturally washered up his phrases with a 'bloody' or two to make them sound sort of free-and-easy, and Willoughby made him believe it was exactly what was wanted. However, at the present time, if you were to ask Dixon who, of all his acquaintances, stands highest in his liking, I'll wager anything he would say Willoughby, and if you were to ask Willoughby the same question he would say Dixon. Strange, isn't it, when you come to compare the men? But they were both open-minded chaps, and each found a lot to respect in the other. I can speak positively about this, for Dixon and I travelled together from Nalrooks to Hay, just before Willoughby left. Willoughby's one of the nicest coves I ever met; and he can no more help his own infernal uselessness than Dixon can help his own infernal ignorance. I've seen the two of them lying on their backs for hours together, looking at the stars, and Willoughby trying to learn Dixon astronomy. Then, again, I've seen Dixon doing all he could to make a man of Willoughby; but they both had too many rings on their horns, and the teaching glanced off. However, if there had been any nastiness about Dixon, or any super—super—dash it! super—"

"Say manager, Steve," I suggested.

"'Ciliousness," proffered the Colonel.

"Yes, that's the very word—any superciliousness about Willoughby, they would have quarrelled and parted the second day instead of living like brothers for three months, and then parting with real regret. I went with them to the railway station to see Willoughby off. Worst thing about it was that, though they couldn't improve one another, they infected one another. Willoughby took Dixon's style of swearing with him for a keepsake, and left Dixon his style of slapping Latin in people's faces. Hanged if I know which habit is the worst."

"Where did Willoughby go?" I asked.

"To Sydney. He's in an insurance office now. Dixon persuaded him to write respectfully to a Mr. Wilcox that he knew; so a friendly correspondence grew up; and this Wilcox offered him a billet where, according to his own account, his duty consists in being the nephew of an English baronet. Wilcox is one of the directors. So Willoughby went back to Sydney with some éclat, and no need to deny himself any of the little requirements of a gentleman. It cost Dixon over forty notes to put him through."

"Does Dixon advertise this?" I asked.

"Now, wouldn't it be like him? Don't judge everybody by yourself. I'm pretty intimate with him, but I wouldn't know anything about that part of the business only for reading a long letter he got from Willoughby, as we came through Echuca the other week."

"And you read Dixon's private letter?" said I austerely. "O, you skunk!"

"Simply because Willoughby writes such a scholarly hand that Dixon doesn't know which is top or bottom, though he has learned himself to make out any sort of plain writing, if the words are not too long. I'm not justified in telling all this, but you fellows drove me to it. And I don't see why Dixon shouldn't have a romance in his life as well as anybody else. Now that I come to think of it he HAS one. The scene of it was on the Goulburn, twenty or thirty miles from here, and the girl was a State School teacher. She was boarding at the farm where Dixon paddocked his bullocks when he was pontooning logs five or six years ago. I don't know how it ended, but the beginning was romantic enough for anything."

"You whet our curiosity, Steve," remarked the Major, as Lushington came down the bank and selected a convenient seat.

"Your friend kindly gave me the bait he had prepared for himself," explained the clergyman to Thompson, as he drew his line into the water.

"Of course," replied Thompson. "However, as to this love story. It seems that one Saturday when there was no school, this Miss Coone— that was the girl's name—was out with the youngsters of the farm gathering flowers."

"Gathering flowers is good, but hackneyed," interposed the Colonel critically. "It dates from the abduction of Persephone."

"—and Dixon was drawing up the river with a log, but not in sight of the girl, on account of a belt of whipstick scrub, when suddenly he heard a scream."

"Decency, Steve," said I. "That scream is older than the Iliad. Behold, it is written in the Book of Jasher."

"Have you done?" asked Thompson coldly. "As I was saying, he heard a scream."

"And saw the girl struggling in the grasp of two bushrangers," rejoined the Senator. "Yes, go on."

"No, I'm d—d if I do. Tell the story yourselves to your own satisfaction."

"Well, you ARE a polite pair," remarked Binney.

"It was a most remarkable thing, and a good deal talked about at the time," continued Thompson, turning toward the last speaker. "There was about an acre of smooth tableland, ending in a steep bank, and the river below. Not a safer looking place in the country, and this Miss Coone and three or four youngsters were scattered about gathering flowers, and they had a basket pram with the youngest kid asleep in it standing in the middle of the open. It was a beautiful calm day, I believe, but a sudden gust of wind caught the hood of the pram and whirled the whole concern, baby and all, straight for the steep bank. Of course, the teacher gave a scream and after it full lick. Providentially, Dixon was close handy, and, in spite of these unmannerly animals, he heard the scream and went. He could do his hundred yards in eleven or twelve seconds those times, and I don't suppose that trip took him much longer, boots and all. He just saw the pram toppling over the bank, and he overtook the girl, and flung her back, and the next moment he went head foremost into the river. It was a fat baby, like they generally have on farms, and it floated like a cork, so he had it out in no time. Then he snaked out the pram and pillows and things, and went back to his team. The people at the farm made a hero of him for the time, but whether Miss Coone actually fancied him, or whether it was a sort of gratitude, or whether she was taken with him as a novelty, I can't say. I believe she was a city-bred girl, and polished at that."

(Faint praise. She was a poem. I met her afterwards. But that, saving your patience, is yet another romance.)

"And in good time here comes the noble duke," said I. "We'll make him finish the story."

"Very well," replied Thompson, "and though I know no more than I've told you, I venture to say the to-be-continued is as much to his credit as the beginning."

"Good evening to you," said Binney civilly, as Dixon passed him, descending the bank.

"Same to you, boss, if you was the divil hisself," replied the bullock driver with equal courtesy. "What's on the (adj.) blackboard now?"

"Well," replied Thompson, "we were talking about that schoolmistress of yours over here on the Goulburn, and wondering whether she was gone on you or you on her."

"Case o' mutuus (adj.) consensus," returned Dixon genially. "Six o' one an' half-a-dozen o' the other. Used to fancy myself a bit then. Used to be the gaudiest man on the (adj.) river. Non sum qualis (adj.) eram. Gittin' a sensible ole person now."

"In the name of incongruity, Collins, what have we here?" whispered Lushington, whose seat was adjacent to mine.

"Knowledge ill-inhabited, worse than Jove in a thatched house," I replied. But the young clergyman's unappreciative silence showed that he regarded my answer merely as ungrammatical and heathenish.

XIV

Ursula, thy words may shame us.
Yet we once were counted famous—
Morituri salutamus!
Au victurite!

—Gordon's "Ashtoreth."

Tell us the yarn, Dixon," said Thompson. "Well, there ain't much yarn about it. Sort o' (adv.) well missed fire. Grand bit o' goods she was, too! Knowed grammar, and jography, an' sums, an' every (adj.) thing. Gosh! she was facilis decensus—no, that ain't it; but it's on the tip of my tongue—she was facile (adj.) princeps. Well, as I was tellin' you, it didn't come off. Couldn't hit it, no (adj.) road."

"What broke it off?" asked Thompson.

"A (adj.) dance."

"You wanted her to go to a dance, and she wouldn't go?" conjectured the Sheriff.

"Yes; she did go. I wanted her to go, an' she (adv.) well did go."

"And you parted on that?"

"Yes; you see, I got a black eye."

"What did she hit you with?" I asked.

"Hit me? That wasn't her (adj.) style. Tell you how it come. I goes into a (adj.) township, and strolls into a billiard room, an' the marker he was playin' billiards, or bagatelle or some (adj.) thing with another feller; an' the other feller he was a (adj.) weed to look at; an', in the course of conversation, he says:

"'Cannon!' says he. An' the marker he says.

"'No, it ain't,' says he.

"'Yes, it is,' says the telegraft feller."

"Which telegraph feller?" asked Thompson.

"Which would you (adv.) well think? How many telegraft fellers was in the contract? Why the (sheol) don't you lis'n? An' the telegraft feller he turns to me, an' says he.

"'Ain't it a fair cannon?' says he.

"'No, it ain't,' says I. (Course, I didn't know a cannon from Adam.)

"'O, yes it is,' says he.

"'You're a (adj.) liar,' says I.

"'WHAT!' says he, an' with that he hauls off. Puts the (adj.) stuns on me."

"Where did he get you, Dixon?" I asked.

"Smeller," replied the narrator. "Well, I ain't used to sich rough (adj.) company, an' I never bin hit but once before this time, an' once since. Anyhow, my principle is to take the meanest (adj.) advantage I kin git— an' to take it quick, for the sake of peace and quietness. But this little (individual) seemed to want spankin' more nor squashin', so I goes for him bare-handed, and he fetches me right (adv.) bang on the peeper. I follers him up ropable—gosh! he was like a (adj.) eel; an' he lands me fair on the point; I drops like a cock, jumps up agen, an' goes for him like lemons. No (adj.) use. He gits home on the butt o' the log this time. I drops agen, an' rolls under the (adj.) billiard table.

"'Come out o' thet, you dem scoundrel!' says he.

"'I'll see you in (adj.) pandemonium fust,' says I. 'I ain't comin' out till you clear off,' says I. 'I give you the (adj.) scon,' says I."

"Big man in small compass," suggested Binney.

"Fair science frowned not on his humble birth," I rejoined.

"Deceivin'est little (person) ever I dropped across," continued Dixon, with a touch of enthusiasm. "Grand thing to be a (adj.) snag like him. Sort o' gift. Gosh! he was there. Volens et (adj.) potens."

"And this painful incident disqualified you as a suitor?" conjectured Rigby. "You and the lightning-jerker were rivals, I presume?"

"None but the brave," I suggested.

"He never seen the gurl in his (adj.) life, so fur as I know. But we parted that night through a (adj.) dance. Fond o' dancin', Rigby?"

"Any man who wants a run for his money must prefer any other folly," replied the Deacon disagreeably. "I have some little toleration for drunkenness, and gambling, and so forth, but one must draw the line somewhere, and I draw it at dancing."

"And do you think," said I, "that, because you are vicious, there shall be no more 'promenard,' and 'change partners?'"

"Oh, shut up, both of you," growled Thompson. "Never mind them, Dixon. Go on with your yarn."

"They ain't annoyin' me. But as I was tellin' you, it was on'y a sort o' silver-weddin' dance at the 'joinin' farm; an' the whole (adj.) lot o' us was ast; an' her ladyship was lookin' forrid to it like goin' to heaven— flyin' round like a dog off the (adj.) chain."

"And you wouldn't go?" suggested Thompson.

"Yes, I would go (verb) you. Didn't I scoot to the (adj.) township to git a new set o' leadin' harness, an' when I come back, says she.

"'What the (adj.) Gehenna have you bin doin' with yer eyes?'"

"Were those her words, Dixon?" asked Furlong gravely.

"Well, it's five or six years ago, an' I don't s'pose a man kin make sure of bein' ipsissima (adj.) verba, as the sayin' is."

"Very true," I interposed. "That's all right. How did you account for your eye?"

"Well, I just told her, plain an' straightforrid, I told her three Cousin Jacks manhandled me in the (adj.) township, an' while I was beltin' two o' them, the other (fellow) he hove a brick an' landed me on the (adj.) eye."

"And you told her you couldn't take her to the dance on that account?" prompted the Judge.

"Wrong. It was her spoke. She said she didn't see what the (adj.) Avernus I wanted goin' in such company."

"But, Dixon," I remarked, "you see, your own excuse laid you open to that retort. You might, for instance, have told her that you saw a fellow morticing posts, and you goodnaturedly took an axe for a few minutes, and omitted to dodge the core."

"Or," said the Deacon, "you might have told her you saw a woman winding a bucket of water from a well, and you gallantly offered your services, but she let go the handle before you had a proper hold."

"Well, Satan'll have a hard choice among you three," muttered Thompson. "But how did things go then, Dixon? What did you say to her?"

"Well, I up an' says, 'O, it's no (adj.) odds,' says I. 'I kin see to dance anyhow.'

"'Like Tophet!' says she. 'Why, d——n my rags,' says she, 'you ain't fit to be seen at a (adj.) dog-fight. Think I'd go with you?' says she.

"'Do the other (adj.) thing, then,' says I, gammonin' to fire up. 'Stop at home,' says I.

"'I'll see you in (adj.) Plegethon fust,' says she. 'I'll jist go.' An' so she did. She went."

"Dear, dear," murmured Lushington. "This is dreadful."

"You're right, young feller," replied Dixon cordially.

"How the (adj.) Abyss could I go when she told me not to? My feelin's is a (adj.) sight too fine for that lot. But I'll tell you what (verbed) the (adj.) contract. I'd jist bin through 'Jane Eyre' along of another feller, name o' Jack Whitby, an' I'd come to the (adj.) conclusion that clever, edicated gurls doesn't believe in a (adj.) walk-over. They want a bit o' bullyraggin'. They (adv.) well like it. I read a book once, where a toff-gurl name o' Florence, used to nag at her bloke, o' purpose for him to show her she wasn't goin' to wear the (adj.) breeches. Let a man be a man not a (adj.) monkey that's their idear. On'y, sometimes it don't work properly. Varium et mutabile semper (adj.) foemina." He paused and sighed. "Anyhow, I was moochin' about the door, waiting for her when the corroboree was over, an' our people they walked on ahead, an' me an' her we follered in the dark, an' not a word out o' me till we got half-round; then it was hammer-an'-tongs."

"You expostulated with her?" suggested the General.

"Not me. That ain't my (adj.) style. But I argied like (Acheron). Fust she says:—

"'Well,' says she, 'done actin' the (adj.) goat?'

"'You ain't goin' to no more dances, jist for this (adj.) lot,' says I.

"'Indeed, says she, 'an' who the (adj. Townsville) do you think you're talkin' to?' says she.

"'Ain't you gone fur enough?' says I, lettin' on to git wild. 'Ain't you (adv.) well frightened?'

"'Tartarus sweat the frightened,' says she. 'Strikes me, you're the person that's in the (adj.) crush. You ain't my boss; so you needn't be gettin' yer (adj.) wool off,' says she."

"O, dear, dear," moaned Lushington.

"'Who the (inferno's) gitting their (adj.) wool off?' says I. 'Not me. But you ain't goin' to no more dances,' says I.

"'I'll go if I (adv.) well like,' says she.

"'Say that agen,' says I.

"'Think I ain't game, you (adj.) morepoke?' says she. 'Well, I'll go if I (adv.) well like.'

"So with that I ketches hold of her by the arm, an' fetches her a couple o' picaninny kicks—not enough to hurt a (adj.) musketeer. Mere matter o' form."

"Had again," muttered Thompson resentfully. "You uncivilised animal; you're just about fit to associate with remittance men."

"Jis' so," replied Dixon, with a touch of bitterness, most unusual in his tone. "Course, you know a (adj.) sight more'n the blokes that writes books. So do I—when it's too late. You know a (Hades) of a lot about edicated gurls."

"He thinks he does," said I. "But what did Parthenia do when you admonished her?"

"Ain't hardly fair to give her the name of a race-horse, Collins," protested Dixon, with spontaneous delicacy. "What did she do? Well, she sort o' sulked. Gurls is (adv.) pig-headed if they take the notion, an' when she took the notion twenty bullocks wouldn't shift her. We'd a got on beautiful if I'd stuck to my own (adj.) idear—but it wasn't to be. I always said it was cowardly to be nasty to a woman or a kid, an' I consider the stinkin'est (adj.) thing a man kin do is to welt a woman. Dunno how the (adj. Malebolge) he kin ever look hisself in the face agen. Ain't that your idear about it, Collins?"

"Depends on the woman herself," I replied judicially. "I agree with you in respect of the thin, bony subject but a plump, cushiony woman seems to invite beating."

"I am surprised that you should justify such a barbarism in any case, Collins," interposed Lushington warmly.

"Any how," continued Dixon, "I should a backed my own (adj.) fancy, an' let Mister (adj.) Rochester go to Cocytus with his bullyraggin'. Too late now."

"Nusquam tuta fides, Dixon," remarked Rigby, sympathetically.

"Hum," replied the bullock driver, in non-committal acknowledgement of the comment. "Gosh! I could a said prayers to that piece, like a Jew to a graven image, only I wouldn't bemean my (adj.) self. So, as I was tellin' you, we walks on home, an' never another (adj.) word we speaks, from that day to this. Never as much as 'Good-bye' or 'Go to Niffelhem' when I was comin' away for good. Hated the (adj.) sight o' me. Aut amat aut odit (adj.) mulier. That's the (adj.) conclusion I've arrove at, Rigby. Think I'm fur out?"

"You have the key to the situation, Dixon. But you hove many a sigh when the disappointment glode across your memory?"

"Most unlikely," said I. "My impression is that he merely wunk the other eye, and smole philosophically whenever he thunk of his escape from bondage."

"Ever hear what became of Miss Coone afterwards?" asked Thompson.

"Well, yes," sadly replied the unfairly penalised life-racer. "I'm always sort of foxin' round for news about her, in a careless (adj.) frame o' mind, an' now an' agen I hear how she's gittin' on. Yes, she'll be (adv.) well gittin' married to some member of Parliament yet. I shouldn't wonder.

If things had went middlin' right between me an' her, I might a bin that (adj.) member o' Parliament myself."

And so Dixon's romance petered out to a lame and by no means logical conclusion.

XV

Name her not now, sir, she's a deadly theme.

—"Troilus and Cresida," Act IV, Scene V

All individual meditations on Dixon's story were forestalled by the Senator, who straightway opened an address, speaking in that oracular style which Thompson and I recognised as portending a steadfast resolution to inflict counsel on everyone within range. My own thoughts had already reverted to Miss Vanderdecken; hence I listened with some apprehension, for the masterful intonation of Rigby's deep voice was gone, and the faultless accents were low and sad.

"Romance everywhere, hardening into tragedy, as the real supersedes the fanciful; for the real is always tragic," said he gravely. "Comedy is tragedy, plucked unripe. Farce is the grimmest of all tragedy; it is the blind jollity of an Irish wake, with the silent guest none the less present because unassertive. There are eight of us here tonight, and probably seven of the number are more or less abject and trashy heroes of romance—romance which has ended, or will yet end, in tragedy."

"Don't talk like that, Colonel," said I, with an involuntary shiver, as my thoughts flashed two hundred miles northward.

"You're not the odd man out, I'm most happy to remind you," said Thompson aside to me.

"The Lord reward you, Steve."

"He means himself, right enough," suggested Thompson.

"Not he, his mind is full of his own romance. I only hope it won't overflow in an unbecoming way."

During this whispered colloquy, the deacon continued speaking in an even graver tone. "I was much impressed this afternoon by the last act, though not the last scene, of a saddening life tragedy which long ago on the other side of the globe opened as love's young dream." (Now, after all, thought I, is he going to entertain a random audience with such a story as that for the sake of pointing a moral?) "All the details of the drama happen to be within my cognisance," he went on. "It is not for your entertainment that I shall unfold them now, but in order that you may be set thinking for yourselves and thinking in the right direction."

"O, give the love-story a rest," I broke out with pardonable rudeness. "Let each of us tell the meanest thing he ever did, or the wickedest, or the silliest—anything but a love-story with a sermon hooked on behind."

"Let Mr. Rigby go on, Collins," said Binney. "Don't change the topic while you can keep up anything like Dixon's standard!"

"Don't pay any attention to Tom," remarked Thompson. "He only wants to follow suit himself. His love-story is a live one—not like Dixon's or mine. You'll hear some version of it from anyone you meet in Riverina, and the only point they all agree upon is that the other party clings to Tom like a mortgagee, though she's the haughtiest subject on the plains."

"Probably that's as near the truth as a man of your moral dimensions can get, Steve," I replied severely. "But if I happen to be the somewhat measly object of a woman's misplaced devotion, am I to parade her loyalty publicly, and make it the text of my homilies? Of course, this doesn't touch your case, nor Dixon's, but would it be the right thing for me? Why, I couldn't even bring myself to pronounce her name before all hands. It would seem like sacrilege." There, thought I, surely that's broad enough.

"I apologise for the whole company, Mr. Rigby, as I had a share in interruption," said Binney. "A story that you think worth telling must certainly be worth hearing."

"O, don't expect anything sensational," replied the Major. "Moreover, the fact that the leading character is not more than half-a-mile from us at the present moment brings an objectionable element of personality into the story; hence it must be taken as related, so to speak, under protest, and only for the sake of the moral which will become apparent. Experience is said to be the best school, and if you can avail yourselves of the experience of others, there is certainly a point gained. Further, though each of you may appear old to himself, you all appear young to me in a mental sense, and I feel it incumbent upon me to give you something to carry away from this accidental foregathering." (Hopeless, thought I. One never knows where this class of moralist may break out. Why, already that woman with her lovely face and truthful eye is holy even to a promiscuous acquaintance like me, and what should she be to him?) "Very well," continued Rigby, "picture to yourselves a young—"

"Hang it, I don't mind if I do tell my love-story, after all," I interrupted, too hastily to get out of the rut of my reading. "About a year ago, riding along a track through one of the belts of scrub on Runnymede, I heard behind me the clatter of hoofs blended with a woman's scream, and the next instant a lady on horseback passed me like a bird on the wing. I was startled to notice that the bit was out of her horse's mouth, and a chill of horror came over me as I thought of a tremendous precipice half-a-mile in front. I darted forward at full speed, gaining stride by stride, till at last by a desperate effort I drew abreast. Then with one hand I lifted the lady from her saddle, and with the other I wheeled my horse round in his own length. The edge of the precipice crumbled away under his feet as he turned, while the lady's horse went over. I heard the dull, sickening thud as he found bottom far down in the gorge, after I had pulled up. It was a near thing, but—"

"That'll do," interposed Thompson with chilling unresponsiveness. "Goliath himself couldn't carry out such a contract, and a bolting horse always looks after himself, unless he has a vehicle behind him; and there's not six inches deep of a precipice within a hundred miles of Runnymede. That's the sort of yarn you'll tell when you get into your dotage."

"This is hardly fair to Mr. Rigby," protested the mild voice of the trapper.

"So say I," rejoined Binney. "What's the matter with you, Tom?"

"Now, Collins, like a good fellow," added Lushington.

"Go on, Judge," said I, perceiving that the whole conclave had fallen under the fascination of Rigby's palaver. "I won't interrupt again. Nor will I listen."

And I didn't listen. The experience of monotonous church services and interminable sermons in my boyish days, and of noisy huts in maturer life, had trained me to enlist at pleasure Falstaff's faculty of hearing without marking. So whilst Rigby's measured monologue went on I switched off my auditory nerve system and heard only the soft, sweet voice of the woman for whose sake I had ineffectually acted the hog. It needed no effort to recall her enchanting face for every lineament was photographed on the retina of my memory. Then, by a sequence which it would be curious to trace, my mind drifted round to Mrs. Beaudesart. The women were in no way alike, save that both were attractive to the eye, and both bore evidence of that social cultivation which is every woman's birthright, and would be every woman's inheritance if men in name were men in reality. But Mrs. Beaudesart, though probably the younger of the two, had already gone through three husbands, and now the most obscure member of her little circle of friends was living in a state of perturbed speculation as to whose turn would come next.

"You're doing it grand, Collins," said a low voice beside me, and I felt that the Colonel had lived too long, for it was Sam's hand that was laid warningly on my knee. "Sh-sh, I don't want to let on I'm here," he continued, settling himself comfortably in a hollow. Evidently the boy was solicitous only to avoid Rigby's observation, for almost any other member of our party might have perceived him in the dark if his presence had been worth noticing.

"Didn't I hear Miss Vanderdecken say she wanted you tonight?" I whispered, mentally crossing myself as the tergiversation passed my lips.

"So she did," replied Sam, "but I'm on her business now. Sort of aidy—conk, K.C.B. Rigby's got the flute, I notice. Don't baulk him agen. He's worth a bob an hour to lis'n to, judgin' by his style."

XVI

O blest effect of penury and want—
The seed sown here, how vigorous the plant;
No soil like poverty for growth divine.
As leanest land supplies the richest wine.

—Cowper's "Truth."

—takes a pride," continued the deacon, "in tracing his ancestry back to the third generation, where baronial bastardy links his human nature with Olympian preeminence. He comes of a decayed family."

"Takes after 'em a bit, poor fellow," murmured Dixon complacently. "What's his other (adj.) name?"

"Wetterliebenschaff. A good name; and Fritz inherited the pride of his forefathers, along with the untiring purpose of his race. It has long been the custom in Germany to train all boys to (more or less) useful trades, so that as a rule every German is a specialist. Fritz, therefore, on leaving school, served an apprenticeship of seven years; then his term of military service—"

"What (adj.) trade did he learn?" demanded Dixon.

"Belt-maker," replied the sheriff unsatisfactorily. Dixon, though badly in the dark, was too well acquainted with the guileful inveiglement of sells to seek further information. Rigby resumed, "Then three years in the standing army left him, according to the German idea, fit for anything on earth. At what time he met with Wilhelmina Rottendammer, I don't exactly know—"

"Gosh! It was about time for her to get spliced anyhow," whispered Sam, somewhat shocked.

"—but the romance was no doubt heralded by a scream on the lady's part. At all events, they loved each other with that calm, devoted, exclusive affection so much less liable to satiety and re-action than the restless passion which, I take for granted, each of you fellows has experienced. Their position in life conduced to love and fidelity. The bulk of the German people, for sufficient reasons, are far from rich; and Fritz's family was poor in Manasseh. His trade was his fortune, which, in the language of the Fatherland, means that he could eke out an existence by working 12 hours a day, with a half-holiday every

JOSEPH FURPHY

second Sunday; and they have a proverb to the effect that if a man can't do a day's work in 12 hours he can't do it at all. Mina, whose face was her fortune, made a much poorer living by working 16 hours a day in a carpet factory, though she also had each alternate Sunday afternoon to herself. Therefore, she not only adored Fritz for his high descent, but reverenced his relative opulence."

"Steady, steady; don't gloat over anybody's poverty," grumbled Thompson. Whilst he was speaking, a half suppressed sigh broke from the little trapper. Rigby resumed, with marked complacency in his tone—

"Profit by their experience, boys. There is not a country on earth competent to support its whole population in easy comfort, nor is there a country able to sustain a section of the community in extravagant luxury, and the rest in bare decency. This applies to all ages, to all lands, and to every degree of civilisation. The chapter of history which records the suppression of the starving Jacquerie by Gaston de Foix contains also a significant item to the effect that this gallant gentleman kept 1,600 hunting dogs for his own private delectation. Can you trace any connection between the French packs of hounds and the French packs of paupers? No; you have nothing to do with history. Very well. Can you trace any connection between British packs of hounds and British packs of paupers in your own day? No; it's none of your business. Very well. Then as surely as Touchstone's figure of rhetoric is impregnable— to wit, that drink being poured out of a cup into a glass by filling the one doth empty the other—so surely shall you, in due time, be called upon to trace a connection between Australian packs of hounds, and Australian packs of paupers. How often must I repeat that if Job be permitted to own 7,000 sheep and 3,000 camels, with other property in proportion, the overwhelming majority of his fellow—sinners will have to pluck up mallows by the roots and juniper bushes for their food— as per text. No State, no territory, however bountifully endowed by Nature, however ably administered by man, will yield a superabundant dividend all round. Excess will be balanced by deficiency, which is bad for both poles of society, and therefore inimical to the progress of the race. Suppose you are told that there is a famine somewhere, but your informant has forgotten the locality, don't you at once conjecture India as the scene of the trouble? And yet you know that India has been a current proverb for wealth through more than 2,000 years. Well may you sing of India—strictly, of Ceylon, it amounts to the same—as a place where every prospect pleases and only man is vile. Vile he undoubtedly is, and vile he will certainly continue, while his attitude invites despoilment—a proviso which escaped the well-bred contemplation of Heber. Of course, you're not responsible for India; but, by Heaven, you're responsible for Australia!"

"Lis'n!" whispered Sam. "This bloke's an artist."

"So there was evident and ample reason for the poverty of Fritz and Mina, but, like yourselves, they concerned themselves only with the effect—letting other people attend to the cause. They were happy enough, as each alternate Sunday afternoon left them at liberty—in winter to walk through the public galleries, or in summer to go on the spree in some cheap pleasure boat."

"Can't rise any pity for young couples with sich a (sheol) of a (adj.) thirst on 'em," interposed Dixon, who, being a strictly temperate man, naturally damned the sins he'd not a mind to.

"Socio-political questions didn't trouble these soul-wedded lovers much," pursued the Colonel, politely ignoring Dixon's comment. "They went on their way, rejoicing in the true wealth of mutual affection, and earnestly discussing the great German problem."

"I understood you to say they didn't trouble themselves with social politics?" remarked Binney.

"I say so still. The great German problem is black bread and sauerkraut—just as the great Australian problem is rapidly resolving itself into mutton and damper."

"To hear you talk," I observed, "one would think the great Australian problem was coming perilously near yam and 'possum."

"So it is, Tom. Any more objections impending?"

"None. Proceed, good Alexander."

"Cripes! ain't he quick on the trigger?" whispered Sam.

"Our lovers had much to rejoice in," continued the Major. "Apart from youth, health, and hatred to France, they always had the satisfaction of seeing people much poorer than themselves; so, like Paul, they thanked God, and took courage. Moreover, the Providence which kindly divides the responsibilities of life, so as to attain the greatest good—"

"Summum (adj.) bonum," suggested Dixon, modestly.

—"allotting extravagance to one section of the community, and thrift to another—had met the interests of both classes by pouring on Mina's head the negotiable blessing of a superb crop of that pale golden hair which never goes out of fashion. Altogether, the world went very well then."

"But as far as making a living's concerned, Mina might as well have been bald," remarked Thompson, cautiously.

"So she was—periodically," replied the Judge. "But a few small silver coins go a long way towards tempering the wind to the shorn girl. Try it. Bestow your own unlucky hand, and your lacerated heart, upon some other and more trustworthy Agnes, and the time will come—it will assuredly come, if not prevented—when your daughters (to quote from the Song of Solomon) will be 'like a flock of sheep, that are even shorn.' They will learn to cheerfully forego every branch of culture except the eternal tillage of their own heads, the harvested crop being of course, thriftily reserved for the thin-haired members of your plutocracy."

"Not while I can see along a gun-barrel," muttered Thompson.

"But you won't be able to see along a gun-barrel, Steve, after you've been bound hand and foot, and shunted into outer darkness, on account of misconduct as a bailee of your Lord's money. And your daughters—barring intervention—will humbly regard your plutocracy as a divinely-instituted sponge for the absorption of every desirable thing the world can produce. Consider how many people hold this view now."

"Mr. Rigby, Mr. Rigby," protested Lushington, "you do the plutocracy an injustice. In point of fact, its office is to spread the blessings of wealth."

"And how is this distribution to be carried out?" asked Rigby, turning courteously toward the last speaker. "If paid away as the wages of wealth—producing labour, the tendency of our hypothetical capital will be to multiply itself by itself, thus aggravating a social-economic discrepancy, already existing, and tacitly apologised for. If distributed by donation, the effect will be infinitely worse. Any wealthy man, impelled to benevolence by human sympathy, love of popularity, fear of hell, or what not, will tell you—as several have told me—that 90 per cent. of the money so apportioned does more harm than good. Now, I am not impudent enough to dictate a course of action for the man of wealth, nor a rule of reasoning for you, but I wish to point out a remedial principle which has its root in the moral constitution of our race."

"So like you, Commodore," I murmured.

"See here," pursued Rigby, unconsciously preserving that insidious inflection of voice which gave his dogmatism all the sweetness of flattery, "any act toward another person has within it a soul, a certain idea or import, and it is upon this idea, not upon the act itself, that the parties come in touch. Aside from 'presents,' betokening esteem, or affection, or congratulation (see how tactfully we select the term, Mr. Lushington), most recipients, and some donors, are rightfully sensitive respecting the idea which may inspire an act of benefaction. If the idea of sharing can be preserved, the parties are brought abreast and mutually elevated by the primitive virtue of the principle. Whereas, the eleemosynary idea, interpreting a similar act, brings the parties into contact vertically, not laterally, and the benefaction, materially good, is poisoned by its implication. Philanthropists should learn the ever-true proverb that 'a gift destroyeth the heart,' and engineer their work accordingly. The idea of sharing, of participation, admits of indefinite extension, and never comes out amiss. Applied, in spite of Individualism, to historical memories, to national aspirations, to religious beliefs, to literary and other ideals, it constitutes a bond stronger than actual kinship. And how eagerly you avow this principle when an enemy is at the gate! Therefore there is ample reason why sharing, not giving—irrespective of quantity in either case—should be the sentiment of bona fide Christianity, and that it is so none but the most inveterate churchgoer will deny—"

"Confine yourself to the case before the court, Sheriff," I interposed, shocked by Rigby's unconscious personality, and dreading worse. "You were giving evidence in re Fritz and Mina."

"And you may rest assured that our female descendants' coiffures are in no danger," added Lushington, with clerical humor.

XVII

Wal, it's a marcy we got folks to tell us
The rights an' the wrongs of these matters I vow;
God sends country lawyers, an' other smart fellers.
To start the world's team when it gits in a slough;
For John P.
Robinson, he
Sez the world'll go right ef he hollers out Gee!

—James Russell Lowell

L et us see to it in time," replied the General, after a pause. "We know that other populations were once as pompously free as we are now; and we know that through ignorance and neglect of their own responsibilities and slavish toleration of class encroachment, the wool of their female descendants is in the market today. We know that, broadly speaking, the Russian peasant of the 17th Century was a freeman, and we know that his descendant of the 19th Century was a serf; and this without foreign incursion. There was a time when 'Frank' meant 'freeman,' just as definitely as 'negro' meant 'black man,' but another time came when the Frankish widow gathered nettles for her children's dinner, and the perfumed seignior—also a Frank, bear in mind—had an alchemy whereby he extracted the third nettle, and called it 'rent.' To come nearer home, we know that the English peasant in Chaucer's time was much better off than his descendant in Cowper's time, though four centuries of material and intellectual progress lay between. One thing, however, we don't know—we don't know where unbridled aggression would voluntarily pause."

"And yet our British freedom has broadened down from precedent to precedent," remarked Lushington.

"I fear it will be found," replied the Colonel, deferentially, "that the freedom to oppress is the only growth of socio-political organisation which, in any race, at any time, or under any form of government, has of its own accord broadened down from precedent to precedent. Even in the Hebrew theocracy, authorised levy and authorised dominion broadened down to the devouring of widow's houses and the grinding of the faces of the poor, while the graces and concessions of the

Sabbatical and Jubilee years narrowed down until they went the way of all unguarded popular privileges. My own remote ancestor, the free Saxon barbarian, who voted his chosen leader to the chieftainship, was represented in the time of Ivanhoe, by a descendant wearing a brass collar, inscribed: 'Gurth, the son of Beowulf, is the born thrall of Cedric.' How was this? Why, Cedric's freedom had broadened down till it absorbed not only Gurth's freedom, but Gurth himself."

"You're forgetting the Norman Conquest, Mr. Rigby," suggested Lushington.

"A matter of indifference," replied the Major. "If the Gurth of 1066 had been a freeman, Senlac would have been a Marathon. Do you think Saxon England fell unwept, without a crime? No more than Poland, and the crime was the same in each instance. What did it matter to Gurth whether Saxon earl or Norman baron kept him making bricks without straw? What will it matter to your own grandchildren whether they toil and starve and cringe under the Australian flag or any other? There was no Norman Conquest in France or Germany, but there also Gurth relaxed his vigilance, and so bequeathed perdition to his descendants. You see, I decline to take advantage of the conspicuous fact that Cedric was as hopelessly Saxon as Gurth himself—and heaven knows he was Saxon enough for anything. By the way, the manual-labor Saxon was helpless enough and servile enough under the Saxon earl Leofric, a few decades before the Conquest. But he hadn't always been so. There was a time when he didn't polish up his brass collar to captivate the girls. Now I want to draw your attention to a carefully-slurred truth, which is, that in the interval between the 11th Century and the 19th, between Senlac and Eureka, your human rights didn't broaden down by any process of easy evolution into your present limited citizenship. By no means. Each inch of recovered ground cost a hundred lives, and very often you paid the lives without recovering the inch. In obedience to that grand law which guarantees the sure recoil of any redeemable race against aggression which has broadened down to the insufferable stage, you rose from time to time, making some incoherent demand for restoration of certain privileges which had strangely disappeared. You were hanged for your trouble. You rose under Wat Tyler, and you were hanged; under Cade, and you were hanged; under Ket, and you were hanged. You rose again and again under various interested agitators of more or less ignominious memory—never demanding anything beyond partial restitution of your own stolen rights, and you were promptly and cheerfully hanged every time; but some inch of lost ground was recovered with certain martyrdoms."

"Might draw it a bit milder," protested Dixon. "Ain't hardly fair to allow that any of our (adj.) posterity was ever hanged."

"True, Dixon. The honor is in reserve. Your posterity will be hanged upon every slight pretext, as a punishment for your present sin. Can't you see that the mere toleration of a growing inequality is treason in the first degree, and that some one must soon or late swing for it? Why should you spend your life and your labor in tenderly rearing a vampire to batten on the big toe of future generations?"

"Well, what the (adj. Sheol) can we do?" asked Dixon, good-naturedly.

"What could my ancestor, the free barbarian Gurth, do? What he did was exactly what you're doing now. He obediently contributed his human birthright to the building up of Cedric's monopoly, and therefore succeeding Gurths were hanged, mutilated, flogged, branded, and slaughtered wholesale, merely for thinking they had any rights at all, and thinking too audibly. There, I challenge all the orthodox clergy of Christendom to adduce a more striking incidence of the sins of the fathers visited upon the children. What the expletive can you do?—You ask. Why, simply be a Christian. Let your whole life be a protest against the system which aims at leaving a coming generation the miserable option of serfdom, suicide, or Sicilian Vespers. But no, you prefer to follow the line of least immediate resistance, Dixon. A mess of pottage—sawdust pottage at that—and away goes your birthright. For this choice, Paul calls you a 'profane person,' and do you think—"

"Well; he's barkin' up the wrong (adj.) tree," protested Dixon. "I don't deny I'm a sort o' plainspoken (person), but I ain't profane. I know where to draw the (adj.) line."

"And do you think he regards your own perdition as a feather in the scale, compared with your treason against unborn generations. I tell you that from the present social system of pastoral Australia—a patriarchal despotism, tempered by Bryant and May—to actual lordship and peonage, is an easy transition, and the only thing that can prevent this broadening down is a vigorous rally of every man with a clear head and a heart in the right place."

"There's no denyin' that (adj.) lot," remarked Dixon, in wise acquiescence. "Anythin' for a quiet life. Shove ahead with Fritz an' Minar. We're follerin', all right."

"Very good. I must endeavour to guard against these discursions. Where was I? Yes, the course of true love was running smoothly. Presently appeared a cloud in our lovers' sky, but in the strictest sense of the word, it was one with a silver lining. I think I have mentioned that Mina's face was her fortune. A very good fortune it proved to be. An old financier, Herr Moses Isaacstien, transgressed the injunction of his namesake and lawgiver by making her an offer of marriage. She, of course, thought of Fritz, and claimed a fortnight for consideration. On the two available Sunday afternoons, as well as on other occasions stolen from sleeping-time, the lovers discussed their future prospects in the new light emanating from the Herr's proposal. Here they found themselves confronted by an alternative which involved the greatest of all principles. Both hearts rang true to the touch, and their resolution was bravely taken. What says Emerson?"

So nigh is grandeur to our dust.
So close is God to man;
When Duty whispers low, "Thou must."
The youth replies, "I can."

Like Costard, they smelt some envoy, some goose, in the enterprise. In a word, they felt it absurd to love so much, loved they not honor more. And their conception of honor was as old as the economic disparity which Socialism seeks to redress.

"So when Herr Isaacstien and Mina were joined in those holy bonds which effectually cancel any little element of impropriety associated with such unions, Fritz had no thought of hanging either his harp or himself on a willow tree. But with a Continental instinct of utilising things that other people would waste, the young fellow availed himself of the old fellow's jealousy to obtain a free passage to Melbourne. And so they parted—Fritz leaving his heart with its idolised queen, while she sent hers across the ocean with its incomparable king. Not even the consciousness of duty nobly performed could make that parting otherwise than heart-breaking. They knew that to each of them the time had come when the prayer of morning would be for night, and the nightly prayer for morning. Their only happiness lay in the backward glance of memory, and their only hope lay beyond the grave—the grave in question being, of course, that of Herr Isaacstien. In fact, poor Mina's feelings might have found expression in a fine Scotch song."

"'Auld Robin Gray,'" interposed Thompson, with that bookish

affectation which should have been cured by his experience of the Standard Poetical Works. "I know the song, it's by Lady Anne Lindsay—

"'Young Jamie lo'ed me weel, and he sought me for his bride.'"

"Tut, no," interrupted the Colonel, in turn. "I mean,"

O, an ye were deid, Gudeman.

Wi' a green turf on your heid, Gudeman.

That I micht ware my widowheid

Upon a rantin Highlandman.

"However, the rantin' Highlandman—such as he was—reached these shores during that severe depression which gradually lifted on the opening of the lands in '65. The poor fellow had a hard enough time of it for the first year or two. It is no light thing, let me tell you, boys, to be a stranger in a strange land—ignorant of the language and at your wits' end to find any sort of work by which you can earn your salt."

"But you said he had served a long apprenticeship as a belt-maker," objected Thompson. "Couldn't he tackle snobs' work?"

"He knew less of the process of boot-making than any other man ever did. His experience lay entirely in soldiers' belts."

"Then surely he might have got work in a saddler's shop?"

"He had never seen a stitch put in. His trade was cutting-out. I think I spoke of him as a specialist. But he had one solace that no hardship could take away. Through the assistance of a friend in Berlin, he kept up a correspondence with Mina, who faithfully furnished him with bulletins of her husband's health. Independently of this, Fortune seemed at length to smile faintly on his meek persistence. He obtained permanent employment as gardener's off-sider on Tartpeena station, in the south-western district, and began to save money. But Herr Moses hung out still."

XVIII

"O let me safely to the fair return.
Say with a kiss, she must not, shall not, mourn;
O let me teach my heart to lose its fears.
Recall'd by Wisdom's voice and Zara's tears!"
He said, and call'd on heaven to bless the day
When back to Schiraz' walls he bent his way.

—Collin's "Hassan."

It happened that at this time I was in charge of a small survey party," continued the Deacon; "and on Tartpeena station I met Fritz for the first time. I had spent a few months in his native city when I was a boy, and had afterwards made a futile attempt to learn the German language; hence there was a silken thread of fellowship in the intercourse which sprang up between us. During the few months that gave us occasional opportunity to enjoy each other's society, I noticed three excellent qualities in Fritz—one was his simple fidelity to Mina, another was a capacity for thrift, unparalleled yet within my observation, and the third was a patient, unwavering trust in Providence, though Herr Moses was worth twenty dead men yet.

"In the spring of '65, as some of you may remember, all the unalienated portion of Tartpeena was thrown open for selection by lottery, and the pastoral tenant, Mr. Goodfellow, made every effort to secure as much of the run as possible. He lavished drinks and civilities on all the employees of his various stations, and as many other presumably reliable vermin as he could rake up. He sent these jackals forth, thoroughly posted in the lion's interest, and equipped with the lion's money, to seek the luck of that roaring specimen who is said to look after his own. It is difficult—from a strictly moral point of view—to imagine a shadier transaction, but easier to account for it. Thrift, thrift, Horatio. Mr. Goodfellow wished to provide for a rainy day."

"Now, you or I would have done the same thing, under the same circumstances," protested Binney.

"I deny your major," replied Rigby. "But if we had done it we would certainly have deserved to be jailed for life, as enemies to the human race. Apply the final test—the test of results. Look at the south-western district now—partly unpopulated, partly rack-rented, and all alike unprogressive. What a collapse for Mitchell's well-named Australia Felix—the potential garden of the province. Better be with the forgotten dead, Mr. Binney, than be alive and sharing in the responsibility for such a far-reaching abuse of the national heritage."

"I wonder that you will still be talking, Signior Benedick; nobody marks you," said I, coldly. Not that I cared, of course. But it was well-known to most of the audience that, in time past, my Conservative principles had escorted me through the somewhat devious and dirty ways of land—dummyism. Moreover, it was bad form on the Judge's part to censure spoliation, or fraud, or corruption, in the presence of an avowed Conservative.

"It will remind Tom of old times," continued the Colonel, blandly, "when I explain that Fritz—armed with an area-map whereon the allotments were numbered consecutively, according to their desirableness, and also with £32 in cash for a first instalment—got the third call, and secured the mile—square block numbered 1 on his map. The two first selections had been made by bona fide men, who hadn't money enough to pay the shilling an acre on this full-sized lot. As Fritz left the office, Mr. Goodfellow greeted him with enthusiasm. Fritz received his congratulations with freezing formality. Goodfellow mildly reminded him of the understanding that existed between them, and produced a blue paper about two feet long, which he requested Fritz to sign. Fritz didn't remember any understanding, and preferred to reserve his signature. This transaction, in point of shadiness, hotly rivals Mr. Goodfellow's own record, and is to be accounted for in the same way. Thirft, thrift, Horatio. Fritz also wished to provide for a rainy day—particularly as Herr Isaacstien was proving, like Major Bag-stock, tough, sir, and devilish sly.

"It is a big undertaking for an exceptionally useless man to make a start on 640 acres with barely £50, but Fritz did it. How he did it, heaven only knows. Certainly, Providence, per medium of Mr. Goodfellow, had franked him for the first half-year—a good illustration, by the way, of Mr. Lushington's contention that the office of the plutocracy is to spread the blessings of wealth. I often went out of my way to see Fritz during the steady progress of that Herculean labor, and always recognised in him the stuff that millionaires are made of. When I complimented him on this—as I frequently did—he almost fell down and worshipped me. However, two or three years passed, and Fritz received a letter which seemed to prove beyond controversy the existence of a divinity that shapes our ends, if we rough-hew them judiciously. Herr Isaacstien had taken his departure to another, and, let us hope, a better, world. But you may be sure that the question where Moses was when the candle went out didn't trouble Fritz much. His interest was centred on the large fact that, with the exception of a trifling fire-insurance premium, bequeathed to the local synagogue, Mina inherited all the old gentleman's accumulations, amounting to 15,000 thalers, or £2,200 sterling. Owing to some recent transactions of Herr Moses with an American firm, this sum was only about one-half of what might have been expected; nevertheless, the splendid sacrifice of our lovers was by no means unrewarded. Indeed, as a set-off against their cash loss they had the knowledge that the worry of those transactions had materially hastened the good man to his recompense.

"Germany being the only country fit for a man of fortune to live in, Fritz offered his selection to Mr. Goodfellow at a price, and, after the usual nibbling and coquetting, the squatter paid him £4 per acre for his title. This would amount to £2,560, or £360 more than Mina's contribution, but Love is too blind to notice such discrepancies. At all events, with this tidy little evidence of his thrift and intelligence, Fritz returned to the Fatherland, arriving, I think, in the end of '68 or the beginning of '69. His whole soul went forth in Lutheran appreciation of the Providence which had moved in such a trustworthy way, and which now seemed to be giving virtual guarantee of continued fidelity to his interests.

"That is the end of the first chapter, boys. You may discuss it while, with Dixon's permission, I prepare one of his mussels for its appointed service in the scheme of the universe." And so saying, the Major climbed the bank, and disappeared.

We were silent for a minute or two—not thinking over the story, but listening to an intermittent sound which, ever since the meeting opened, had been inviting attention. Sometimes it resembled the shrill appeal of a pig caught in a garden fence; then it would, perhaps, die away altogether, and presently rise like the melancholy dirge of a disobedient child shut up in a store-room; then again it would swell forth like the epithalamium heard by the awakened sleeper in the dead, unhappy night, and when the cat is on the roof. Sometimes it seemed to come from the waggons behind us, and sometimes from the opposing bank of the river.

"What the (sheol) 's that?" queried Dixon at length. "Gettin' sort o' satis (adj.) superque."

"Cattle-pup," replied Thompson. "Millbank's people gave him to me today. Stumpy-tailed breed. Poor little chap's lonely; I'll fetch him down here." He went up the bank and shortly returned, resuming his seat with the pup on his knees. "Makings of a good dog, if I could only keep him," he remarked sadly. "But I can't keep anything now. I've had five dogs since that infernal thing came on me; and they're all gone. Wonder how long I'll be allowed to keep this little cove?"

"Always easy to lose a good dog," remarked Binney.

"Any owner of a kangaroo dog will endorse that," I sighed.

"The fidelity of some dogs is marvellous," observed the trapper.

"See how a dog'll shepherd a drunk man," added Dixon. "Wonder if the (animals) has souls?"

"The Jewish abhorrence of dogs seems rather strange to us," remarked Lushington.

And so for five or ten minutes we discussed dogs in a manner too trivial to be worth reproduction here.

XIX

Hear you this Triton of the minnows—
Mark you his absolute "shall."

—"Coriolanus," Act III, Scene 1

Now, boys," said the Colonel pleasantly, as he came down the bank and resumed his rod and line, "what is the result of your discussion? What moral or morals have you derived from the first chapter of my story?"

"Well," replied Dixon frankly, "the thing's only sub (adj.) judice yet in a manner o' speakin'; but we was jist wonderin' among ourselves how sich a perseverin' strong-stummicked bloke as Fritz got down to what we see. Should a' bin in the Upper House by this time, you'd think."

"Time and chance happeneth unto them all, Dixon. Now, Steve."

"I say he proved himself an all-round varmin if you ask me anything about it," replied Thompson, sullenly acquiescent in the Judge's expanding ascendancy. "Bad blood, I suppose."

"Transparently right in the predicate and conventionally wrong in the inference," commented the Major. "Next."

"The man is below criticism," remarked Binney, somewhat coldly.

"Manhood conceded, Mr. Binney, the subject cannot be below criticism, nor above. Every man has his place and his use in the world. Nothing walks with aimless feet. Fritz's vocation is to point a deduction or adorn a narrative. A suppositious case would have been open to the imputation of falsity. Fact is authoritative. Next."

"The land transaction seems to me a very ordinary and vulgar piece of roguery," observed Lushington. "But I cannot even apprehend the sentiment which must have actuated the lovers in their strange decision."

"I endeavoured to make it understood that in their case sentiment was subordinated to principle," replied the Deacon, forbearingly.

"The story seems to me more unpleasant than instructive, Mr. Rigby," remarked Furlong. "What can we learn from the disgraceful fact that two lovers, with all the possibilities of life before them, deliberately sold their birthright?"

"We can learn one great lesson," replied the General, "to wit, that the person who loves a fellow mortal more than the bawbee is not worthy of the bawbee."

"But, after all," I said, "we've been most exercised over the fact, so happily set forth in your yarn, that an almost inevitable corollary of poverty is the violent itching to get rid of it at any price. The demand of the footsore beggar is identical with that of Richard at Bosworth; but supply him with a horse and, according to the wisdom of our forefathers, he rides to the Evil One. From a moral point of view it's a hopeless tangle. Fritz, in spite of his strictly legal efforts, doesn't seem to have attained any permanent exaltation, mentally, morally, or socially. Alcoholically and temporarily, no doubt, he has often been so elevated that his feet scorned the earth."

"Human nature at large is the beggar you speak of," replied the Deacon gravely. "We're all beggars and—"

"Not this (adj.) infant," muttered Dixon resentfully.

"—and the difference between the mounted beggar—hereditary or otherwise—and the pedestrian beggar is merely the difference between the devil's recruit actual and the devil's recruit potential. The tangle is before us, right enough, Tom. It's a moral tangle certainly, but a material tangle in the first place, to be sorted out by material agency; and seeing that we know of no avoirdupois intelligences in the universe except ourselves, will you tell me who is to perform the sorting? For performed it must be, and the sooner the better. Disorder from its very nature cannot be eternal. Now, approach this moral tangle inductively—a posteriori, as Dixon would say—and you'll find it based on the temporal considerations which must underlie every ethical problem in a world where daily necessities and anxious forecast make us men primarily, and only secondarily rogues or loafers. Here, at the very outset, you're confronted by the immovable fact that superfluous wealth in one class is always synchronised by corresponding poverty in another class. That fact, as a fact, is of neutral morality. But to bring the material and moral questions into relation you will now inquire whether this disparity is for the best or for the worst. And to arrive at a true answer, you must imagine yourselves as gracing the very lowest walks of life, hearing in mind that the thing hostile to your own higher interests is equally hostile to the higher interests of your fellow—weed. You have answered. Then, if there's any force in deductive—or, for Dixon's better understanding, a priori—reasoning, we may be sure that while the individual is encouraged to hold rights as against society; while to the economic perdition of the many, the few are allowed to amass; while private wealth carries the honor attached to the divine right of aggression, misguided pedestrian beggars in great abundance will be found to offer their kingdom for a horse, generally losing their kingdom and getting no horse after all. Aggression is the divine right of the mounted beggar, but, mark you, aggression is strictly limited by the point of recoil on the opposing side, and by nothing else on earth. And the line of human progress—carrying within itself the redeeming point of recoil, is advancing toward the frontier of absolute right. That boundary, by the way, will never be reached. Mundane administration cannot attain perfection. The line of perfection and the line of human progress may be taken as representing a moral asymtote."

A non-committal grunt of acquiescence masked the dignified mystification of our synod. We had forgotten Fritz by this time, and the Colonel, like Satan, was leading us captive at his will.

"That is about as near as we can come to it," he continued after a reflective pause. "But in case that any of you should not fully apprehend the illustration, I may remind you that the asymtote is a mathematical paradox, consisting of two converging lines which never intersect each other. Let absolute perfection be represented by a straight line of unlimited length, and human progress by an approaching curve, with its convexity towards the straight line. Extend this curve indefinitely, at the same time expanding its arc to approximate, but never to reach, your right line; and you may continue it for ever, always approaching, though never blending. This, I think, is as closely as we shall be able to work out the fulfilment of our hackneyed petition, 'Thy will be done on earth as it is done in heaven.' Take the avowal as a concession to your individualism. The new order can well afford it."

"You must have a moral revolution first," observed Binney.

"And isn't this moral revolution in progress now?" rejoined Rigby. "The vile snobbery of that axiom relating to the beggar on horseback unmistakably stamps it as the coinage of a former generation—a generation that might as well be hanged for stealing a sheep as a lamb. Our pedestrian fore-fathers, my dear boys, were hanged wholesale for stealing lambs, and the very thought of accusing their equestrian hangmen of riding to the devil was their notion of the unpardonable sin, vide the current literature of that day. Haven't we reformed this indifferently? And, for the first time in history, isn't there a widespread movement toward reforming it altogether? The moral revolution that is imperceptible to you will appear to future ages as a gigantic leap."

"But if things are working out their own cure, there's no need for us to make trouble," objected Thompson. "And this doesn't agree with your own preaching about the danger of some new style of slavery that'll bring us a trifle below the level of dogs."

"Has the tendency of abuses been to work their own cure, Steve?" asked the Senator, with a mildness almost pompous. "Isn't history full of relapses? How often has the ripe fruit of threescore years been blasted in a day? Wasn't the Promised Land in sight 18 centuries ago, and weren't our forefathers, from age to age, forbidden to enter in, because of their dense unbelief, and their lack of moral enterprise, and their incurable hankering after the congenial debasement of their fathers? Isn't the Promised Land always within one day's march—if the pilgrims are worthy to occupy it? We are nearer to the border now than ever before, but we may yet be sent back in the wilderness to die off out of the way."

"Wilderness of Sin," interjected Dixon. "Stick to that (adj.) argyment, Rigby. Can't better it."

"Your aptitude encourages me, Dixon. But, Steve, will you assert that we now stand at either the base or the summit of that toilsome ascent which leads upward from palaeolithic savagery to the sixty-fifth chapter of Isaiah, or the Fourth Eclogue of Virgil? You will not. Then, since there is no safety-racket on the wheel of Progress, the mere arduousness of our upward road implies a corresponding facility in the descent to a state worse than the first. Now, what prevents relapse? Do you know that, wherever old abuses are giving way, and new abuses are disallowed, and citizen rights are being conceded—there the pick of humanity are battling for every inch of ground won from their unduly-privileged fellow-men? Do you know that it is the nature of oppression to intensify wherever resistance slackens? Do you know that all popular progress is conditional on the untiring exertions of men who must practice the self-sacrifice they preach, and whose only hope and aspiration is to pass on the torch to the next generation?" The Major paused a moment, then resumed—

"What cause do you suppose has operated to keep up the sun's light and heat since life first appeared on this earth, Steve?" he asked.

"Well, so long as we get the light and heat," replied Thompson, guardedly, "we needn't concern ourselves about how they're manufactured. Likely they produce themselves, some way."

"Exactly," rejoined the Colonel. "However, the most approved theory is, that the sun's power is maintained unabated by the concussion of meteorites, which are swallowed up and absorbed by the solar mass. You would imagine these meteorites lost, yet they serve the purpose of making life possible on the planets. So the Spirit of Freedom demands absolute self-surrender of certain individuals, as the price of light and warmth to others. And where history shows periods of that national declension, that all-round fitness for wiping-out, which inevitably follows on class—degradation, it merely signifies that the meteorites of those periods are rare and sporadic, or have ceased altogether; whilst a recorded influx of moral light and an awakening glow of hope indicate a shower of these erratic bodies, reinforcing the central source of vitality. Ay, and as times go, the personal renunciation here implied is better worth assay than anything else can be. This magnificent virgin continent is amply worth it—and the time is opportune. The service is more than expedient; it is imperative. For just fancy a community composed entirely of well-meaning and self-centred men like you, and of equally well-meaning and self-centred men like the squatters you work for. What would be the inevitable outcome—in view of the social-economic handicap now current? Why, your grandson, ear—marked and branded on the off ribs with his owner's initials, would work out his damnation with fear and trembling, arrayed in a skimped form of the Hindoo breech-clout; while your granddaughter, cent. per cent. more despicable still, would think herself honored if the local demi-god condescended to exercise his droit de seigneur."

"What's that?" asked Thompson, inadvertently.

"Literally, 'landlord's right.' Jus primae noctis is the legal term. It is the peasant bride's tribute to the landed gentleman who virtually holds the power of life and death over herself and her bridegroom. Read Beaumont and Fletcher's 'Custom of the Country.' O, your ancestresses, for many succeeding generations, knew all about it. So did mine, of course. See how pleasantly the Tory, Scott, refers to the usage in his 'Ravenswood.' Well, the prerogative is not dead, but dormant, pending a future broadening down of vested rights. What is to prevent its revival, under favorable conditions? Orthodoxy? Rot! Did orthodoxy prevent it before? Did the orthodoxy of any governing class ever stand in the way of the interests or appetites of that class? Does orthodoxy stand in the way of capitalism, of usury, of profit-mongering, of land monopoly, or any other monopoly, of royalism, or of anything that panders to class-domination? Where is the limit to human aggression upon humanity, unless that aggression be sternly checked—and what appeal to oligarchy has ever proved operative, except in an appeal to its fears? Well, Steve, in the natural sequence of events, the institution I have modestly hinted at will be restored—not by statute law, of course, but by social-economic pressure—in the time of your granddaughters, if you have any."

"No, I'm d—d if it will," muttered Thompson.

"There you are," replied the Judge, complacently. "That is precisely what the free barbarian Gurth, said 1,300 years ago. See how history repeats itself." The Senator paused and lit his pipe.

XX

Divinity of hell!
When devils will the blackest sin put on.
They do suggest at first with heavenly shows.
As I do now.

—"Othello," Act III, Scene 2

B etter if we had died when we were kids," remarked Thompson bitterly. "Better be dead than making trouble. But I don't give a hand," he continued, finding relief as the abstract moral question dissociated itself and drifted out beyond his own personal horizon. "Most of the squatters are fine, straight men—a lot better than we are, if it comes to that."

"Be it so," replied the Deacon, with ominous pliancy. "David may be a good king, as kings go; but his successor, Solomon, makes the burdens grievous, and chastises the bearers with whips; his successor, Rehoboam, whilst frankly acknowledging the hardship, avows his intention of making the burdens more grievous, and chastising the bearers with scorpions; and so the thing broadens down smoothly and spontaneously. Time will sanctify any encroachment and petrify any grip; hence the tendency of classes is to congeal into castes. Freedom comes back in strong convulsions, often accompanied by hemorrhage, never without strenuous battle in field or senate, waged under terrible disadvantages. Nothing is easier than for Pompey to laugh away his birthright; nothing is harder than for him to weep it back again."

"God looks after all these contracts that's too (adj.) heavy for us chaps," observed Dixon, piously.

"A popular mistake, Dixon, and to some extent, a pardonable one, but a mistake nevertheless. At what point does God interpose? Think over that. God cannot interpose in this matter, except by miracle; and the age of miracles is past. The Lord of those servants is gone into a far country, leaving them in charge of his vineyard, with a guarantee that, while the earth remaineth, summer and winter, and seed-time and harvest, and day and night, shall not cease. The rest is ours. A fine allegory—reiterated, evidently, for emphasis, in the guise of Pounds or Talents entrusted for augmentation. Bear in mind that we are responsible caretakers of the vineyard, not freeholders, or even lessees. So also with the Many. Here the Eternal is a Usurer, and an Austere Man. Now, there you have the grandest hypothesis ever presented to mankind. We need look no further for a Scheme of the Universe. Observe that there is one demand upon us, and only one—to wit, consistent effort toward progressive betterment of this planet, for the—for the—what shall I say in lieu of that parrot-phrase, 'Glory of God?' But how is that for an Increasing Purpose? Can you improve upon it? And now tell me, boys, in what conceivable way you think you can glorify God, except by working toward the elevation of the human race, as a whole?—a movement which carries with it all subordinate interests of the earth. To be sure, God has been very considerably glorified since man differentiated himself from the apes. But we are only on the threshold of progress yet, and it is manifestly incumbent upon each one of us, freeman or slave—"

"Now, Mr. Rigby," protested the clergyman, rousing himself from the sorcerous spell of the Senator's rhetoric, "pray remember that you are speaking to Englishmen. The distinction of master and servant we cheerfully recognise; but slavery is a different matter."

"True," replied the Sheriff, gently. "And the grade of the 'servant' is, in reality, much lower than that of the 'slave.' At a time when slavery was not the exclusive badge of inferior races, but stood fairly on its merits, the slave looked down on the wages man, and was entitled to do so. You will find this statement supported by all the evidence available. 'Hireling,' or 'hired servant,' in our translation of sacred and classical literature, is always a term of reproach; whilst 'servant'—which, in every instance, means either bondman or vassal—carries the idea of servitude without ignominy. You may remember that passage in the 'OEdipus Tyrannus' of Sophocles, wherein a slave plumed himself upon belonging to his master: 'Born in his house; no hireling I,' he says. And you're all familiar with the parable of the Prodigal Son—"

"Feedin' pigs?" interposed Dixon, in genial assent. "Yes (sheol) of a comedown for that bloke; an' served him (adv.) well right. Heard a sermon on it, a couple o' year ago; an' the parson he fetched it out red-hot."

"No doubt," replied the Judge wearily. "But did he invite your attention to the fact, just as the whole resources of Oriental hyperbole are exhausted in the degradation of the prodigal to a swineherd—lower than which, in Jewish estimation, no man could possibly sink—so his humiliation touches the conceivable nadir of abject submission. 'Make me, I pray thee, as one of thy hired servants.' The author of the parable could cite no depth of penal servility beyond that. We speak of the labor market, and rightly too; well, the vast majority of our fellow-citizens are chattels in that market. Playing it pretty low down on the reputed image of God—isn't it? But whether the scheme of human life includes personal service to a personal master or not is immaterial. The Man Friday may be a permanent institution. The amended Antony of the future may have his unpurchasable Eros; the ameliorated Timon, his Flavius; the improved Uncle Toby, his Corporal Trim. And if an immeasurably higher grade of civilisation should still produce anti-types of the men who fought and died for Charlie, these will certainly find somewhat worthier objects of personal devotion. But there will be an end to that ghastly dislocation of order which occurs when the personal service is one of ignominious necessity, not of self-respecting fidelity. However, to return to my story—with apologies for this digression—

"It is worth while to bear in mind that man was, and is, made upright, but he has sought out many inventions. And, to avoid all ground of offence, let it be understood that, in speaking of the man who is made upright, I refer neither to the gardener of Eden nor to the pithecoid gentleman of Science; but simply to the everyday infant, mewling and puking in the perambulator. Unfortunately, this peculiarly human faculty of invention, or initiative, is turned by its possessor to an account which always obscures, and generally extinguishes, the manifest purpose of his existence. Like Falstaff's boy, he hath a good angel in him, but the devil outbids him. In a civilised state, he must have an aim of some sort; and his first mistake is to accept St. Paul's halting metaphor of the life-race, with a prize for the winner, and devil take the hindmost. His next mistake is to set up one of his pet inventions as a prize, and to qualify for the race by pawning the god-like element in his nature. Remember that, whether he wins or loses the prize, he inevitably forfeits the stake. Now I want you to notice how faithfully Fritz and Mina pressed on toward the mark of their high calling, namely, that invention known as the 'medium of exchange.'"

XXI

These lips are mute, these eyes are dry.
But in my breast, and in my brain.
Awake the pangs that pass not by.
The thought that ne'er shall sleep again!
My soul nor deigns, nor dare complain.
Though grief and passion there rebel;
I only know we loved in vain—
I only feel—farewell! farewell!

—Byron

The Colonel resumed: "Mina's last letter was five or six months' old when Fritz reached Berlin; and that period had been an eventful one. A Jewish lawyer had found an informality in Isaacstein's will, which rendered the instrument invalid, and thus brought into force a former will, made in a sulky fit, a year previously. By the provisions of this disruptive document, three-fourths of the old gentleman's assets passed to a distant relation, and Mina was placed under a complication of liabilities and obligations deliberately calculated to eat up her legacy. The poor, outwitted woman had desperately disputed this will in court, with the result that a week or two before Fritz arrived to claim her as his bride, she had returned, destitute and friendless, to her 16 hours' shift in the carpet factory.

"Mina's misfortune was a terrible blow to Fritz, especially as he couldn't regard it in the light of an impediment to their marriage. An impediment is an entity, an actuality, a thing to be grappled with, or outflanked, or outlived. Herr Moses, for instance, was an impediment. But here was an evanishment, invulnerable to any weapon or any tactics. Just imagine a man trying to overcome, or circumvent, or weary-out, a vacuum! The great gulf fixed between the well-to-do and the poverty-stricken is quite as impracticable on this side of the grave as on the other; and Fritz felt as one standing on the edge of that plummetless abyss, looking across the yawning depths into Mina's pleading, haunting eyes. This, of course, is figurative, for the lovers literally mingled their tears as they sat together in her poor apartment. But murmured vows, and clinging kisses, and the mutual retrospect of youthful aspirations could never bring back those 15,000 thalers—the absence of which merely made the heart grow fonder. That long heart-sickness of hope deferred by the tenacity of Herr Moses was now to become a chronic ailment. Fritz clothed himself in sackcloth and went softly; he metaphorically attired himself in this fabric because his hopes were dead; he literally went softly because the Fatherland—then furtively preparing for war with France—was likely to give him a cheap uniform and a soldier's grave. In the end, he tearfully embraced the doubly—widowed Mina, and tore himself away, after giving her, as a farewell present, the sum of 1,000 pfennings—"

"He ain't my idear of a (adj.) man," observed Dixon. "Same time, I give him credit for whackin' the (adj.) spons after that style."

"—equal in value to exactly eight-and-four-pence of our money—"

"(Sheol)" breathed Dixon, in moral collapse.

"—and so they parted for ever. Orpheus and Eurydice over again. A cruel mockery of restoration, serving only to add poignancy to the final severance. Mina returned to her carpet factory, to revel in the luxury of despair—the only luxury she could afford—while Fritz slipped quietly away, and took his passage to Melbourne. His love for Mina was intensified to distraction by a forecast of her desolation in the coming years, when he would be pursuing his own career, feet uppermost in a foreign land; but there was a balm for himself in that antipodal Gilead, if he could only be on the spot in time to secure it. Everybody on board noticed his impatience during the voyage; and, on reaching port, he was the first to skip ashore and hurry to the railway station."

XXII

The broken box of ointment
We never need regret.
For out of disappointment
Flow sweeter odors yet.

—Frances Ridley Havergal

Within sight of Fritz's selection, on Tartpeena," continued the Major, "there had stood a roadside pub, doing a rattling business under the management of a licensee, whom I remember merely as a full-shaved man, with 10 days' growth of iron-grey stubble always on his face. Diligent in business—as per Apostolic precept—this Mr. Maginnis had in course of time surrounded so many hogsheads of tanglefoot that his career of usefulness seemed rapidly drawing to a close. Mrs. Maginnis was an abstainer, a fine, dashing woman, blithe and frolicsome, and about a hundred years younger in wisdom than her good man. She had fairly pestered the reticent, melancholy selector with her courtesies and confidences. Her autobiographical narrative was simple. Dazzled in her girlhood by Maginnis's wealth, she had married him, only to find that she didn't love him. Her ideal was a fair man, of quiet demeanour; and her heart told her she could love no other. She knew that Maginnis wouldn't long be spared to her; and she would remain a widow for the rest of her life. She would still have little Jimmy left, and Maginnis's will secured her a lot of property in her own right."

The Major paused. I was glad to notice a tinge of compunction showing through the habitual cynicism of his tone and words. He mastered this weakness, however, and continued:

"Such had been the burden of the young matron's song only half a year before, so there was good reason for Fritz's impatience. It even occurred to him that Maginnis's clothes would be about his size. He crossed the couple of hundred miles of country between Melbourne and Tartpeena in record time, and presented himself at the door of the Travellers' Rest, with a fluttering heart, for the sign intimated that a person named Algernon Sidney was now authorised to dispense the hospitalities of the bar. Here Fritz learned that a couple of months after his own departure for Europe, Maginnis had gone to join his brother-blockader, Isaacstein, in the Elysian fields. Mrs. Maginnis—sole legatee of her husband's extensive Melbourne property—had gone to the metropolis, to watch her interests. The Travellers' Rest was already let, on lease, by the executors, on behalf of Jimmy, to whom it had been bequeathed by his father.

"Back to Melbourne fled Fritz, sickened with apprehension, maddened by the coquetry of Fortune, and invoking the milk and water curses of his complicated language on his own want of prevision. But zeal and persistence seldom fail in the end—a fact which each of us would do well to bear in mind—and, on reaching Melbourne, Fritz obtained from the late Mr. Maginnis's solicitors the address of his cynosure."

"What the (adj. sheol's) that?" demanded Dixon inadvertently.

"Literally, 'dog's tail.'"

"Hum, had (adv.) simple. Well, I give you credit."

"No, no Dixon; you mustn't take me in that way. It's the Greek name of a star in 'Ursa Minor,' or the Little Bear—a northern constellation, invisible to us here. Rather an anomaly in astronomical nomenclature, that the dog's tail should be an appendage of the Little Bear. However, it's the poetical name of the Polar star."

"Political name o' the poler Star," mused Dixon. "No (adj.) savvy."

"Not your height," said Thompson, ill-naturedly. "But Rigby's always correct in his dic., no matter how rotten his arguments are. He has Milton to back him for using 'cynosure' in that sense. Let's see—it's in Comus, I think, yes:

"And thou shalt be our star of Arcady.

Or Tyrian cynosure."

"What's your opinion of that?" I asked Lushington, aside. (As a matter of fact, the 12 Standard Works comprised about one-half of Thompson's aggregate reading, hence every book had left its impression on his mind, like a replica in copying ink. Indeed he afterward told me that he had committed to memory this particular passage, thinking it might come in handy for courting purposes.)

"It takes my breath away," murmured Lushington. "I've been strangely misinformed respecting the erudition of bullock drivers. Latin and Milton. Are they all like this?"

"Certainly not. Other branches of knowledge are no less ably represented. They excel chiefly as linguists. But there goes the Colonel again."

"Fritz presented himself to Mrs. Maginnis at the hotel where she was temporarily residing. He called upon her again and again, daily escorting her to some place of popular resort. If he was delighted to find her unchanged, she was no less gratified to learn that her image, engraven on his heart, had compelled him to repulse a young German heiress, and perforce return to his Australian enchantress, like the weary dove to its gin case. This was by far the happiest era of his life. Let me explain that I hold Shakespeare's audacious insistence upon Romeo's fascination for Rosaline, up to the very moment of his meeting with Juliet to be one of the most masterly strokes within the range of Plays. A man's first love never scores. Metaphorically, the first love is a mere encounter with the cushion, which, however, produces a recoil; and it is this recoil that scores. We have already wept with Fritz over his rebound from Mina's unprofitable side, where, in the nature of things, it was impossible to pocket; we shall presently see how the tangential impulse coincident upon this resilient projection—"

"Not this (adj.) time, ole feller," muttered Dixon.

"—enabled him to register the highest score allowed by the laws of the game. Moreover, if the saying be true, that love goes by contraries, what could be more natural than that the quiet, offensively blonde German and the mettlesome, black-eyed Irish-Australian should reciprocate? Still, no bliss is without alloy. There were times when the ghost of a dead past rose unbidden, throwing its chill shadow across the sunny present, and into the fairyland future—times when Mina's desolation recurred to Fritz, and his heart was wrung with anguish as he mentally totted up the expenses of his fruitless voyage. But Louisa would box his ears and tickle his ribs when her quick eye detected the fit coming on. 'Money gone, you goose,' she would say. 'Ain't I better than money?' You will observe that Fritz was scoring.

"Not only was she better than money, but she had the latter in abundance. Her property consisted of about a dozen cottages, two shops, and an hotel; and her rent-roll—as she casually remarked to her lover—varied from £15 to £20 a week. He, after verifying the information by private interviews with some of the tenants in the bar-parlor of the hotel, spent his own money with a somewhat freer hand, and about six weeks after his arrival, the solemnisation took place. I gave the bride away."

Again the Deacon paused and sighed. Then the ice of carefully-cultivated cynicism closed over the inadvertent thaw, and he continued:

"I happened to be working on a Melbourne daily at the time, and having met Fritz a fortnight before the happy day, we renewed our old intimacy, when he forced upon me, in a rather boastful way, the details I have recalled for your instruction. Only up to the date of the ceremony, of course. The sequel to his marriage he told me about a year afterwards, sobbing on my neck, and smelling like a brewery in a good way of business. At that time he was keeping a shanty on Spring Creek, and I was working out an excellent little industry in connection with a carpenter in Sandhurst and two carriers on the track. We used to buy empty weatherboard houses at Sandhurst, and sell them, re-erected on Spring Creek. Then, of course, you remember how the second flood of '70 swamped every claim on Spring Creek beyond remedy; and the last great alluvial diggings of Victoria was snuffed out. Nineteen-twentieths of the people left Spring Creek immediately, and among the exiles were Fritz and myself." The General paused, as if losing himself in retrospect.

"That was 13 years ago," he continued, meditatively, "and I never met him again till this afternoon. Jimmy Maginnis tells me his mother died two years back. Poor, vivacious, mercurial woman. To this favor she has come. Merely the common lot. She would have died hereafter. There would have been a time for such a word. Probably she was content. While the future extends in front, death seems a calamity; when the past extends behind, the same event becomes an acquaintance. Thackeray, revelling in that purposeless cynicism which is his leading characteristic, has a remark to the effect that 'if you would die regretted, you must die young.' Ah, boys, it is a cheerless element of truth that gives point to this ruthless apothegm, for we instinctively know, though the impression is not formulated, nor even apprehended, that a lifework in the elevation of humanity is open to the young, while this task has already been fulfilled, or evaded, or repudiated by the old. Still, the bare truth is cruel. Indeed, it is difficult to conceive how any man can be a cynic, seeing that he himself is frail fallible and ephemeral, as the subject of his misplaced derision."

XXIII

Come, Disappointment, come!
Though from Hope's summit hurl'd.
Still, rigid nurse, thou art forgiven.
For thou severe wert sent from heaven.
To turn mine eye
From vanity.
And point to scenes of bliss that never, never die.

—Henry Kirke White

B ut hold on," said Thompson, circumspectly, "you led us to think that Mrs. Maginnis had houses to the value of 15 or 20 notes a week?"

"Such was my frank intention, Stephen."

"And this didn't continue?"

"Nothing continues, my boy. But this terminated with dismal abruptness. Immediately after their marriage, Mrs. Wetterliebenschaff mentioned to her husband, in a tacitly apologetic way, that a slight error had crept into her statement of assets—though rather an omission than a mis-statement. Here we must glance back a few years. The late Mr. Maginnis, rightly calculating the effect of the Land Act, had mortgaged his city property to build and furnish the Travellers' Rest. Then, desiring to remove the encumberance as quickly as possible, and remembering how he had originally enfeoffed himself of the Melbourne property by unloading Koh-i-noors and Golden Fleeces on the very crest of the great mining boom in '64, he turned his attention to El Dorados, Pactoluses, Great Golcondas, and other certainties, intending to repeat the operation. But the other fellows had gone out on the tide this time, and there was a stony glitter in the eyes of the public. Meanwhile, so spirited and enterprising were the directorates of these Dead Sea apples that his own city rents, along with the surplus profits of the Travellers' Rest became, in the literal, though by no means in the accepted sense, a sinking fund. At last the time came when Maginnis stepped over to consult Isaacstien on the retention of the unretainable—the only question that had occupied either of the worthy men here, and, by every rule of growth and continuity, the only question that can interest them whilst individuality holds good. But compound interest had undermined the city property before Mrs. Maginnis came into possession, and, of course, she was fooled to the top of her bent by strictly practical jokers of the Civil law. Excellent lent client as she was, she never could make out how it happened; but, by the time of her second marriage, somebody was impounding her rents as the agent collected them, whilst offering the property for sale by private contract, with a reserve price which merely represented the aggregate encumbrance, inclusive of liberal pickings for the learned gentlemen who were so dexterously piloting the lady through her little proceedings. By the way, the Hebrew word for usury—neshek—signifies 'to devour.' The poor woman, on mentioning the matter to her husband, went on to asseverate that the loss of property didn't cost her a second thought, as she still had Fritz, and indeed she had him to perfection.

"It was about 36 hours before he came to, and even then he went on like one that hath been hocussed. He fancied himself standing on the deck of a 'Frisco steamer, with a small portmanteau in his hand, whilst a peculiar sensation of coldness on his upper lip seemed to convey the reminder that his moustache was amongst the sweepings of a barber's shop. The consciousness of a foreign accent also appeared to weigh upon what was left of his mind, and he heard himself remarking to the bystanders in a hollow voice that he was a Norwegian gentleman travelling for pleasure and that his name was Bjornson—Mr. Henrik Bjornson, of Sondre Trondhjems. Then, in pitiless response to this ingenuous admission, one of his auditors seemed to draw him aside and show him a blue document, at the sight of which his heart became as water. Everybody appeared to take an interest in him as he accompanied his new friend ashore, whilst a marine officer's flippant remark—'White headed boy ain't goin' eastward from Eden this trip, I reckon'—sounded like the rippling of water on a drowned rat. Then he saw in his dream, and behold his plain-clothes conductor signalled a cab, whereupon £'s of forfeited passage money surged on his apprehension like the lost legions of Varus on the memory of Augustus. There is no burlesque in the simile, let me tell you, boys, for the question is one of estimation, not of mere magnitude. As with Claudio, the poor fellow had offended, but as in a dream; nevertheless, they were going to make it out a case of attempted wife-desertion within the meaning of the Act. But all this was merely a preparatory exercise, as the machinery of the phantasmagoria fell into working order with a view to grinding out a series of transformation scenes, each more gruesome than its forerunner, and the least intolerable among them throwing his present ignominy into an aspect of idyllic felicity. Edgar is right—'The worst is never come while we can say, "This is the worst."' "Most of us have noticed, or will yet have occasion to notice that when Nemesis gets her second wind."

"Don't, Jeff," protested Thompson sullenly. "I'm anything but a superstitious man myself; still I feel it's not safe to make a joke of affliction, though it may be a person's own doing."

"Your sense of humor must be a subtle one, Steve, if you detect any joke in a tragedy like this," replied the Major with sincerity. "However, Fritz hadn't finished scoring yet. Too much broken up to think of soliciting bail, he passed a night as the guest of Her Britannic Majesty. Next morning, while he was endeavoring to give some account of himself to the Bench various members of the Devil's Brigade put in clients' claims, amounting in the aggregate to something like £600, all of which Fritz paid, in the state of merciful coma which still enveloped his faculties. Then his forgiving wife—cheerfully foregoing the sureties to which she was legally entitled—led him away to listen to explanations which she felt certain would set his mind at rest. It appeared that in addition to the difficulty of the mortgage she had been, perhaps, a little extravagant—a not unusual feature, I notice, in the character of the Irish-Australian. Business men, who knew her as a customer, believed her to be well off and forced credit on her—she being nothing loth. By the time these people had begun to feel uneasy, Fritz was proudly appearing everywhere with her as her accepted suitor; and a word in private between the business man aforesaid and the manager of the bank which honored Fritz's cheques, had paved the way to further credit for the lady. Fritz's personal liability for her prior debts would, of course, date from the completion of his polysyllabic signature to the marriage register. You will perceive that he was still scoring.

"To conclude, Fritz, whose capital was now reduced by nearly one-half, took a five years' lease of the hotel which he had fondly regarded as his own in life interest, and resolutely settled down to redeem his mis-spent moments past. According to the custom in such cases, he interviewed the outgoing tenant as to the quantity of beer sold; and this gentleman's information he privately verified by a conference with the brewer who supplied the house. The result of his investigations indicated a fine turnover, and on this the rental and goodwill was based. It may be worth your while to know that the doctrine of averages—so insisted on by Buckle—maintains a reliable ratio between the demand for beer and for other wets, so that from one factor you may work out the total.

"But Fritz afterwards found that the new owner of his wife's former property—a wealthy and influential M.L.C.—had made it worth the out—going tenant's while, and had also given a hint to the brewer. In addition to this, it was largely a jug business. In addition to this again, Fritz's inexperience soon betrayed him into the indiscretion of reporting a roguish member of the force, whose manner toward the landlady seemed to indicate that policemen are but mortal. After this blunder, the Mistletoe Bough became the best-watched house in Melbourne. The stipendiary happened to be a man who shared Dixon's healthy hostility to people with a foreign accent; and though Fritz did the smallest Sunday business in town, the police and the Bench managed to keep up a good reputation on him. He stood this for six or eight months; but the gradient becoming steeper and steeper, and the Englishman's hell in full blast coming more and more clearly into view, he put down the brake, and went through for three half—crowns in the pound. To return to our old metaphor, he was still scoring. He opened the business at Spring Creek, with a capital reduced to about £200. On leaving Spring Creek, he went through again—this time for one—and-six—and opened somewhere in the Wimmera, with a capital still further diminished. He was in that quarter till Jimmy came of age; then the family removed to the Travellers' Rest, where Mrs. Wetterliebenschaff died. Fritz, having by this time finished his superb break, laid up his cue, and took the back seat he has since occupied. I'm very glad to notice that Jimmy is kind to the poor old fellow. It is only his due, for no man could have excelled him as a gentle, affectionate husband, and a considerate stepfather. May he rest in peace."

The Deacon paused, and lit his pipe, whilst an indescribable something in his manner seemed to denote that he still held the floor, and intended to keep it. The cessation of the story merely conveyed a tacit challenge of comment, and this we all felt; but the silence was broken only by Dixon's muttered rendition of the last pious sentence into Latin, with an Australian intercalation by way of artless adornment.

XXIV

The Moral Bully, though he never swears,
Nor kicks intruders down his entry stairs,
Feels the same comfort, while his acrid words
Turn the sweet milk of kindness into curds,
As the scarred ruffian of the pirate's deck,
When his long swivel rakes the staggering wreck.

—Oliver Wendell Holmes

N ow boys," continued the Senator, "I'm well aware that the sediment of meaning left in your minds by my story crystallises into an emotion of gratitude to heaven that you are not as other men are, or even as this publican. This is utterly and cruelly wrong. To judge Fritz justly, you must imagine him still alive, and with a stake in the country; a man whose obvious interest lies in strict respectability. His sole aim during life was to attain such a position of repute; and, in common fairness, you must judge him as you would wish to be judged; that is, by aspiration and effort, rather than by attainment. Of all the vanquished men I have known—and Legion is an inadequate name for them—not one has died harder than Fritz. He was congenially a man of indomitable purpose, though of flabby principle; therefore, a mean and sordid environment made him a mean and sordid skunk. A criminal environment would have made him a thief, though never a highwayman. A generous environment would have made him a Florence Nightingale, though never an Old John Brown."

"And a religious environment, Mr. Rigby?" ventured Lushington, with a professional solicitude reminiscent of the man who thought there was nothing like leather.

"The word 'religious' has unfortunately so many shades of meaning that I scarcely know how to formulate an answer," replied the Colonel. "But I submit that our hero was, in the first place, mentally limited, and morally neutral, or nearly neutral; therefore I should say, an evangelical environment would have made him a son of consolation, though never a son of thunder—other mundane conditions of tutelage being, of course, duly taken into account, along with the altogether subordinate factor of heredity; and, finally, an almost imperceptible margin allowed for human cussedness. Speaking broadly, the poor fellow's environment is responsible for his failure."

The Major paused a moment in guileful deference to his questioner, then resumed.

"But individual misadventure, rightly used, contributes to general safety. If we locate, identify, and characterise the rocks on which Fritz unhappily bumped his hooker—above all, if we chart the ocean currents and magnetic variations which conducted him to perdition— we shall, in a sense, raise him from the moral status of a stone-broke bummer to that of a universal benefactor. In other words, seeing that he has drawn fire and located the enemy, we ought to honor his memory by acknowledging the service. To my mind his exploit clamors for recognition. Like King John, he does not ask you much; he begs cold comfort, and you are so strait and so ungrateful you deny him that."

Here the Sheriff paused for a full minute, evidently yearning for some assailant with a self-imbedded conviction that the world's crime, brutality, sordidness, ignorance, squalor and general degradation were directly or indirectly attributable to liquor. But our congress happened to lack this species of zealot, so all hands sat silent as effigies, and for a space no man came forth to win the narrow way.

"We all admit that polite environment makes the gentleman and vulgar environment the vulgarian," he continued, metaphorically trailing the tail of his coat slowly along before the meeting, "and this is perfectly correct."

"With certain reservations," essayed Lushington, figuratively touching the coat with his toe.

"With certain reservations," repeated the Judge gratefully. "As, for instance, that the son of the gentleman brought up from earliest infancy in a city slum may, by virtue of his pedigree, unfold gentlemanly instincts, just as an eagle's egg hatched by a goose may disclose an eagle."

"Something of that kind," replied Lushington.

"Good. What Dixon would call the argumentum ad hominem seems justifiable here. Would you like to try that experiment on your own son? Wouldn't you a thousand times rather see him decently buried? And what entitles your son, or my son, or any man's son, to higher privileges than the son of the slum-denizen. I may mention that I am searching these provinces for some educated and intelligent man audacious enough to assert, without phrases, that the Eternal (I should prefer to use a name implying closer relationship, but experience has taught me

JOSEPH FURPHY

that the New Testament conception of Deity is apt to irritate)—some man hardy enough, I say, to maintain that this first cause can possibly sanction the prospective abasement of children unable to distinguish between their right hand and their left. Still keeping to the question of environment—why do we—but—I beg your pardon—may I ask if you are connected with the business?"

"Which business?"

"The business. Licensed victualling."

"No, Mr. Rigby," replied the clergyman, enjoying the joke. "In spite of my unfortunate name I'm a life-abstainer."

"I'm practically an abstainer myself, though not a pledged one," rejoined the Deacon, "and I'm happy to have so much in fellowship with you. Excuse my question. It was prompted by the recollection of what happened to me the night before last at a hotel in Corowa. I had marked an old gentleman of amiable demeanour, though of rather ascetic appearance, who drank nothing but water. We got into conversation and I spent three solid hours in endeavouring to point out to him that one effect of a perfect social system would be to bring alcohol to its true place as a valuable, though somewhat hazardous medicine. I afterwards ascertained that he was the owner of a thriving distillery. But, Mr. Lushington, to what end do we impose restraint on the sale of intoxicants? Why do you agitate for the still closer restriction of Local Option, Prohibition or what not, and why do I argue for State monopoly? Is it not because we wish to alter our environment for the better by making the line of sobriety the line of least resistance? Don't we, in this instance, admit that is allowing a very little for heredity?"

"Come, Mr. Rigby," interposed Lushington, overflowing with academic counsel, "you must acknowledge with all our foremost authorities that dipsomania is a transmitted weakness, or, at least, that heredity is a very powerful factor here."

"A far-reaching one, certainly," conceded the General, "seeing that Noah's unfortunate propensity, latent for—let's see—take Usher's chronology—latent for, say, 130 generations, reappears in the Australian aborigines, a race as susceptible to the temptation of drink as any on earth. Remembering the aborigines, then, along with all other races of immemorial sobriety and allowing as much as you please for heredity, don't we admit that, so far as temperance is concerned, the environment is a matrix wherein the individual is moulded? And does it not become us, for the sake of consistency, to extend the rule indefinitely, first inquiring, of course, whether our social-economic environment is conducive to production of the highest personal excellence all round? If you reply that it is so conducive, the argument is ended. If you acknowledge that here, in an aspiring community, our environment is bad, and we ourselves, from infancy upward, debased by slavery or corrupt by power, then you tacitly concede the advisableness of a radical change in the worldly conditions under which we live."

"Rings the bell every time he's let," whispered Sam to me. "Why don't you fellers give him his head?"

"Your protest is premature, Sonny," I replied in the same tone. "Time and the Colonel against any two, or any two dozen."

But though Rigby was now fairly started, he still failed to connect, and this time the hindrance came from an unexpected quarter.

XXV

Of all the gentle tenants of the place.
There was a man of special grave remark.
A certain tender gloom o'erspread his face.
Pensive, not sad; in thought involved, not dark.

—Thomson's "Castle of Indolence."

I t seems to me that all secular remedies must fail to cure even secular evils," observed Furlong with mild doggedness in his tone, rising from his seat as he spoke, and laying his rod against the steep bank. "The fashion of this world passeth away, and the time is coming to us all when to him that hath—that is, to him that hath chosen the good part which shall not be taken away—to him that hath shall be given, and he shall have more abundantly; but from him that hath not, shall be taken away even that which he seemeth to have—by which we understand, the treasure laid up on earth. 'Seemeth to have' is a fine expression. I'm afraid, Mr. Rigby, the tendency of your moral is to limit, or even to explain away, human responsibility."

I expected to hear a sigh of mental fatigue from the Judge, and my forecast was fulfilled.

"Talkin' about morals," rejoined Dixon, as the trapper climbed the bank, "it's a moral we ain't goin' to ketch no (adj.) fish, no matter how we keep off o'swearin', an' I bin ridin' myself with a martingale all the (adj.) evenin'. My idears is mostly runnin' on that thirty-pound fish you caught here, Thompson."

"Strange how the very same thing has been running in my own mind," replied Thompson pensively. "How little I thought then that I would be sitting here tonight, older and sadder, and not much wiser, thinking of all the changes that have taken place since then. How well I remember it. I had my feet on that root above Tom's head, for the river was—"

"Specify your river, Steve," I interrupted airily, for it seemed evident that either Thompson's reason or mine was reeling on her throne.

"O, shut up. It was ten or twelve feet higher than it is now. Malky Cameron was sitting just above where Mr. Binney is and Billy was away after frogs. Of course, Agnes wasn't allowed to be out after nightfall.

The thought just occurred to me now that perhaps in future years some one of us may sit here again, watching his float and thinking of tonight."

"There is an element of poetry in the suggestion," I remarked thoughtfully. "By the way, when was it you caught that thirty-pounder, Steve?"

"Ten years ago, last May—coming eleven years, now," replied Thompson dreamily. "About three weeks before my unfortunate trip in the canoe."

For the next two minutes, you could have cut the silence into slices with a hay-knife.

"Where's Furlong?" asked the Colonel at length. "Did he take his rod with him?"

"He's only gone to roast a fresh bit of possum for a bait," I replied. "He missed the ghastly disclosure."

"No, he was listening all along," said the unconscious Thompson. "But the vanity of things in general is no ghastly disclosure to him, I fancy. He's had his share of trouble; and he's made the right use of it. Not like me."

"You know him, Steve?" I inquired.

"No, I can't say that I do. I met him once, some years ago. But he's a man I'd take to be as straight as a rule."

"He might have a romance in his life, too," I suggested.

"I wouldn't hint anything to him about it, Tom; he seems very reserved."

"Both you an' him's the clean spud, anyhow, bullocky," interposed the sharp voice of the kangaroo hunter. "If everybody was like me an' him an' you, the world would be fit for a man to live in, which it ain't, not by a long chalk."

During the uncomfortable pause that ensued, the trapper returned, baited his hook, threw his line into the river, and resumed his seat. Then, unconsciously forestalling the Major, he deferentially put in his word, discoursing with the slow precision of a systematic thinker, whose verb had been trained to agree with its nominative. He seemed to speak almost by rote, like a man giving utterance to thoughts perpetually present and garbed in the same verbal attire. (For we always think in words.) His tone bespoke the turtle-dove severity of one reluctantly constrained to draw on behalf of a principle in which his own individuality had become merged and lost. As a mere detail, his sermon was marred by that lamentable mismanagement of the "h," and that disregard for the "r," which distinguishes participants in the glorious charter, deny it who can.

"Whilst listening to your conversation, Mr. Rigby," he said, "the uppermost thought in my mind was the opportunity of usefulness which you allow to pass unheeded, forgetful of the reward which might be yours. Why do you not turn your fine abilities in the right direction? See how closely Daniel xii., 3, might apply to you: 'And they that be wise shall shine as the brightness of the firmament; and they that turn many to righteousness as the stars for ever and ever.' I feel very deeply on this subject, for I myself lived in bondage to Satan for twenty-nine years; and though it has pleased God to call me out of darkness into His marvellous light, I can never recall the wasted time."

"I never flog over them (adj.) idears," remarked Dixon, uneasily. "I'll jist slip across an' shove the (adj.) fire together," he continued. "May's well treat ourselves to a drink o' tea when school's out."

"The lesson my experience has taught me," resumed Furlong, as Dixon escaped up the bank, "is that, so far as secular things are concerned, the one great fact is the watchful providence of God, and the one great duty is unquestioning submission to that providence. But we scheme and strive for easier conditions of life—some for their fellowmen, others for themselves alone—forgetting that 'except the Lord build the house, they labour in vain that build it; except the Lord keep the city, the watchman waketh but in vain.'—Psalm cxxvii, 2. We 'forsake the fountain of living waters and hew ourselves out cisterns, broken cisterns, that can hold no water.'—Jeremiah ii, 13. The real troubles of life are beyond our control; they are specially sent for our good; and instead of endeavouring to evade them, we should accept them as Divine trials of our individual faith. We rightly call them 'tribulations'—the tribulum being the implement used in Palestine for separating the corn from the chaff. Poverty is a severe trial, as I know from experience. Wealth, rightly regarded, is no less a trial—"

"Gosh! I know which specie I'd ratherest tackle," whispered Sam to me, with fictitious jocularity.

"The compilers of the Church of England service," pursued Furlong, "understood this when they wrote: 'In all time of our tribulation, in all time of our wealth, in the hour of death, and in the day of judgment—Good Lord deliver us.' Soon or late, we have to learn that 'all things work together for good to them that love God.'—Romans viii, 28. And the sooner we learn this, the sooner shall our minds be at rest."

"I'll be off, Harold," said Binney aside to his brother-in-law. "Are you coming?"

"Not just yet, George. Stay a minute. We have a discovery here."

"A few years ago," continued the unvalued homilist, wading deeper in his sin, "my mind was full of error and discontent, but, like Paul, I met the Lord in the way, and, like Paul, again, I now count all things but loss for the excellency of the knowledge then vouchsafed to me. I may say that the original word here translated 'loss' has the secondary signification of jetsam—that is, cargo thrown overboard to save a ship. The idea is that life is a troubled sea, and each of us a ship seeking the haven of rest. But our own perverseness leads us to the sinking-point with worldly theories and compromises, with human predilections and antipathies, and unless these go overboard, the ship itself cannot be saved. Paul's dangerous burthen consisted of his Judaic formula. At the present day, one man's lading may be ritualism; another's may be hollow enthusiasm; another's pure worldliness; another's Socialism and Anarchism; but these must go overboard, or their weight will founder the ship. 'What shall it profit a man if he shall gain the whole world and lose his own soul; or what shall a man give in exchange for his soul?'—Mark viii, 37."

"'Bout time for me to travel, Collins," said Sam, in a creepful whisper. "I'll see you in the mornin', as you go past." And he evaporated, like Old Nick at the touch of holy water.

"Anyone who fully realises that 'the Most High ruleth in the kingdom of men and giveth it to whomsoever He will.'—Daniel iv, 25—can never waste his energies in scheming to overthrow or build up social systems," continued Furlong, gathering force as he went. "He will rather be a worker in the field where the harvest is plenteous, and the labourers few. And anyone who, in the right spirit, looks back along his own past cannot but confess that an unseen hand has guided him to the present moment of time; not only sustaining his life, day by day, but interposing hindrances here, compulsions there, benefactors everywhere—all of which were designed to tend toward spiritual growth. And He who is the same yesterday, today and for ever, will continue to sit as a refiner and purifier of silver—Malachi iii, 31—watching and tending the molten metal, and removing its dross, till its surface reflects the face of the Refiner; then it will be taken from the furnace, as worthy of the treasury. But for those who harden their hearts, sinning wilfully, after they have received knowledge of the truth, there remaineth no more sacrifice for sin, but a certain fearful looking for of judgment and fiery indignation, which shall devour the adversaries.'—Hebrews x, 26 and 27."

The trapper paused, but an eerie constraint was upon everyone except Rigby and Lushington. The latter had from time to time been murmuring cordial acquiescence in the speaker's views, tacitly encouraging him to continue; and as for the Colonel, I judged by his attitude that he was metaphorically sharpening his sword on Furlong's door-step.

XXVI

I t has been said that man's extremity is God's opportunity," continued the trapper fervidly. "I can give an illustration of this, and it appears to me expedient that I should do so before we part. I don't wish to force my own petty history on you, but I think you'll forgive me by the time I have done.

"I came out from London just after finishing my apprenticeship as a watchmaker. I'm a poor workman, partly because I have an unsteady hand, and partly because of a natural deficiency in mechanical talent. But, until four years ago, I had never done any work except watchmaking and enginedriving, and since coming to Australia I had never spent three successive days outside of Melbourne. I was married nearly six years ago, and I've been a widower for four years. My wife was a Melbourne native, and her only surviving relations were two brothers, both gone up the country. I found one of them two years ago, and we kept up a desultory correspondence, but I have never heard any news of the other."

"Was that the (person) you was after las' year on the Island?" demanded Dixon, who had ventured back, and finding the conversation apparently purged from spirituality, had seated himself just behind me. "Long-legged, yeller-bairded galoot of a bullocky, you said, with a bay horse. Country's st-nkin' with fellers of that (adj.) description."

"No, Dixon, I've found the man you speak of," replied the trapper, in a voice now hoarse with suppressed emotion. "Let me go on with my story."

"There is always a good deal of distress somewhere in the unseen life of a city like Melbourne, and not long after our marriage the lot fell upon us. I needn't weary you with the details of our struggle against conditions that were too strong for us—the conditions of scanty employment, and decreasing wages, along with the imperative need of money for rent and subsistence. City-bred people, as a rule, can make shift in a city, but exceptions occur. Laura had a weak chest through overwork in her younger days, and now her health began to fail. By this time we reached the limit of our credit. I had nothing to sell but a collection of books, and I parted from these with a regret that seems strange to me now. Laura grew weaker and weaker, and as she needed more indulgence the pressure of our poverty became more severe. No use saying I should have done this or that; I did everything I could; yet I had to watch her fading slowly before my eyes, all the while knowing, or at least believing, that there was health for her, but beyond my reach. I was an unconverted man at that time, and I often felt tempted to do something desperate; in fact, nothing withheld me but the fear of making matters worse. A dark shadow seemed to hang over us; we could read in each other's faces the thought that never left either of us. What was most heart-breaking to me was to see her so resigned. Young as she was, her life had been one long working-day, and she was tired out. But she had the Christian's hope. And you must remember that the awful desolation of the thought that haunted me was made more bitter by such poverty as it is very unlikely that any of you has ever experienced. It wasn't like ruin brought on by some sudden calamity, such as appeals to the sympathy of the world; it was a chronic insufficiency of everything needful to life, and nothing for it but to suffer silently. Yet every moment was so precious to me in those days that the time seemed to fly."

He paused a moment. I felt tempted to throw something at him for playing into the Major's hands after such a fashion. Then he resumed:

"Still there was one hope. A doctor told me that a change of climate might restore her. He suggested Echuca, or the Riverina, and to take her there at once, as the winter was coming on. Just then the little furniture we had was seized for rent, leaving us entirely destitute, and considering Laura's weak state, I hardly know what we'd have done but for two friends, a widow and her sister, working together as laundresses. These good women found room for Laura in their home. May God bless them for their kindness; here and hereafter.

"In the meantime I managed to borrow sufficient money to pay my way, and took the train for Echuca, with a clinging hope that all these fears and troubles might soon be past. But I could get no work at my trade there, though I tried hard. Now, what I should have done was to have refused, in my own mind, to leave the place till something presented itself. No doubt I could in some way have found a home for Laura there, and, ah, well, God's will be done.

"I went on to Deniliquin. I could get no work there, and then, confused and desperate as I was, I took the advice of a very friendly fellow I had fallen in with, and went out to Moogoojinna station, where there was a chance of getting charge of a portable engine. I had a second-class certificate, and I had it with me; yet the opening was so different from anything I had expected that time after time I stopped, half-resolved to turn back. It took me nearly two days to reach the station, and I felt a kind of relief to learn that the place was already filled. You wouldn't believe what a sense of loneliness and desolation comes over a city man when he sees, under such circumstances as I did, what sort of place the Riverina is. I resolved to try Echuca once more, hoping for some kind of success. I didn't dare to think of failure.

"But going back to Deniliquin from Moogoojinna I lost the track in the dark, and next day, between inexperience and anxiety of mind, I got completely bewildered on the plains. I remember that toward evening I found a tank, and slept beside it all night. At daylight I started in what I thought was the right direction. I walked all day without meeting anyone or seeing a habitation, and as evening came on I reached a tank. Next morning I found it was the tank I had been at before. I started off again, and at night I got back to the same tank. How often this was repeated I cannot say, and how I subsisted during that time I shall never know. At last a boundary rider found me, barefoot and bare-headed, half-naked and half-delirious, but still performing this terrible circuit. He treated me with great kindness—I have found opportunity to thank him for it since—and as I insisted upon pushing on, after staying a day and two nights in his hut, he replaced my clothes and boots, and put me on a beaten track. During the day I had often to lie down from sheer weakness, but I persevered until, some time in the night, I found myself close to Deniliquin; then I turned off the track and slept till morning. By this time it was more than a fortnight since I had left Laura. I had written from Echuca, and also from Deniliquin, and I knew there would be a reply awaiting me for some time. When the post-office opened I was handed a letter and two telegrams. One of the telegrams was four days old—'Return immediately. Laura seriously ill.' The other, dated sixteen hours before the time of delivery—'Come home. Laura sinking fast.' I must have dropped the letter; I remember nothing of it except receiving it.

"I walked to the railway station, penniless as I was, and in desperation told my story to the first porter I met. He could do nothing for me. I went to some men loading waggons at the goods shed, but they were too busy to listen to me. I saw a buggy and pair standing at the gate, and an old gentleman approaching it from the goods sheds office. I stopped him, with the most humble apologies. He read my telegrams, and listened attentively to what I had to say; then when I finished by begging the railway fare to Melbourne, he told me that if there were a policeman in sight he would give me in charge. No doubt I looked disreputable, and of course an impostor could have told the same story in the same way; but the refusal nearly broke my heart. I made no further appeal to anyone. My last glimpse of hope was gone; my last vestige of courage was gone; and, without any intention or plan, I started southward on foot, weak and knocked-up as I was.

"I walked along the Echuca road, mile after mile, like one in a horrible, indefinite dream, waking now and then to realise that I was two hundred miles from Laura, and that she was dying, or dead. Gradually, I remember, this numbness of mind gave way to one consciousness—the consciousness of utter isolation, of treading the winepress alone. Terrible as my extremity was, I could do nothing—nothing—to help myself; and I began to see the unreasonableness of expecting from anyone else such help as I needed. Then I remembered Laura's simple trust in an infinite Wisdom, an Immeasurable Love, watching over each one of us continually. This, once for all, brought me face to face with the alternative of faith and infidelity. I struggled against asking myself whether this fearful trouble was consistent with Divine love; but I felt that if Christ were on earth I could appeal to Him with confidence that He would help me, and even this thought brought comfort and peace. You may call it a mere mental reaction; no doubt it was something of the kind; but the moment of that reaction was the moment of my conversion.

"Still I felt no abatement of the desperate impulse to hurry on. My limbs were racked with pain and weariness; but my face was turned toward where Laura lay, alive or dead, and it was impossible to rest for one moment. So hour after hour passed, while I walked eighteen or twenty miles, unconscious of anything around. Then comes a definite recollection. I live it over again every night when I am alone with the memories of the past.

"I seemed half-conscious of a dull aching in my limbs, and a burning pain in the soles of my feet as I walked on. Someone called me repeatedly; and I looked round to see, beside the road, a man lying in the shade of a tree, with a newspaper in his hand; two waggons were close by, and behind one of them a bay horse, feeding out of a box. The man called me again; I went across to him, and sank down in the shade, sick and giddy—"

"Oh, never mind that," interrupted Thompson. "How did you find—how—how was it when you got to Melbourne?" As he spoke, an ungainly self-consciousness was plainly struggling with emotion in his tone. Indeed, between shifting restlessly on his seat, and absently feeling his pocket, he had betrayed an increasing uneasiness ever since Furlong got fairly under way with his depressing tale.

"My dear friend," replied the trapper, in a tremulous voice, "you must allow me to tell the story in my own way. After I had taken a drink of tea and some food, Thompson asked me if—well, he asked me if I had been drinking. I began to tell him my trouble, but, in spite of myself, I broke down completely. I could do nothing but hand him the two telegrams. He read them two or three times.

"'Your wife,' says he.

"I tried to speak, but couldn't.

"He jumped to his feet, looked at his watch, and put the saddle and bridle on his horse.

"'Here, quick,' says he; 'follow this track straight, and it'll take you to Mathoura. Here's money for you'—and he sorted out some notes, and put them in my hand. I mounted, and he altered the stirrups to my length, and buckled his spur on my heel. 'Keep at a good smart canter, and you'll catch the train,' says he. 'But if she's up to time, you haven't got a minute to spare. Hitch the horse anywhere about the station, or jump off and let him go. Don't speak to me. Everything is understood between us.'

"To my unspeakable relief I was in time for the train, and, a few minutes afterwards, I was on my way to Melbourne. Then the physical reaction came. I felt a sudden sickness, with a ringing in my ears, and I seemed to be falling, falling, falling hundreds of feet. My last thought was that I might die before reaching Laura, and, even with the help of my fellow—passengers, I only recovered as the train stopped at Moama. From Echuca I sent a telegram, and about midnight I reached the home of our two friends.

"Mrs. Lacy met me at the door, and told me what to expect. During the terribly cold weather a few days before Laura had taken a turn, and from that time on there was no hope. But now she was restored to me for a few hours longer, and this seemed the greatest blessing life could bestow. She was perfectly sensible, breathing slowly and faintly, and such a smile passed over her white, spiritual face as she saw me beside her. I remember, more and more, every syllable she whispered, so soft and low, for her voice was gone.

"'I knew you were coming, Frank,' she said. 'I prayed continually that you might be near me at the last. This is not what we looked forward to; but it is the best. We've suffered together, my poor love, but that's past for me now; it will soon be past for you—and then think of the everlasting rest of us both. I'll be waiting for you in that new home, as I've waited so often for you in times past; and when you come, I'll never feel my heart breaking for your trouble, as I have so often here. And you'll give yourself to Christ—now—now—for my sake; and be faithful to the end, dear love, so as to meet me where there shall be no more pain, or weariness, or sorrow.'

"From time to time, she whispered half-sentences and disconnected words, but at last her calm eyes rested on my face, and she said:

"'My poor lonely love, don't mourn when you see the grave close over me. Our parting is only for a time. Our Redeemer has travelled the path before us, and made the way sure. O Frank, what we call death is the exceeding great reward. It is sweet to feel the world pass away, with all its cares and sorrows, leaving me to rest with Christ.' The trapper caught his breath and paused, then resumed in a low, steady tone:

"And so, holding one of my hands with both of hers, she seemed to sink into a dreamy state, but sometimes I felt her move her fingers, to assure herself that my hand was still there; sometimes she half-opened her eyes, and smiled as she saw me beside her. At last I heard her whisper softly and bent over to catch the words:

"'Our Father which art in heaven, hallowed be Thy name; Thy kingdom come.' That was all. She slowly opened her eyes, and fixed them on my face, and gave one little sigh. I waited for her to breathe again—waited—but her fingers closed on mine, and slowly relaxed; then I saw the light fade from her eyes; a look of perfect repose settled on her face—an appalling tranquility; she was insensible to my affliction."

He paused abruptly.

XXVII

This world is but the rugged road
Which leads us to the blest abode
Of peace above;
Then let us choose that narrow way
Which leads no traveller's foot astray
From realms of love.

—Jorge Manrique ("Longfellow's Trans.")

For a few minutes we listened to the frogs in the river flats, and the monotonous barking of a dog up at the pub, and the occasional jangle of a bell away in the dark shadows of the bend. The gentle spirit of the evening—previously poisoned by Thompson's unconscious disclosure—was by this time almost forgotten. Seats had, one by one, been selected in sociable proximity, and now nothing but a sense of decorum kept our lines in the river. Presently Furlong, crumpling his hat in his hand, dipped up a drink of water with the rim, and went on with his story—

"Now, my friends, if you think this was distressing, just try to conceive what it would have been if I hadn't met Thompson. It was he who brought me to my wife's death-bed, to make her last moments happy; it was he that saved her from a pauper's grave. O, Thompson, you must meet us both in that better land, where troubles and sorrowful memories are unknown, and all is peace and purity and love. My poor wife never knew in life, but she knows now, whose kindness it was that fulfilled her last wish. And for myself—without even knowing your name—I have prayed for you daily all these years past." Here the trapper's emotion overcame him again, while the sullen hang-dog demeanor of the bullock driver became more pronounced. But, after a minute's pause, Furlong continued, speaking now in a perfectly composed tone—

"When I looked my last at Laura as she lay in her coffin with that angel—look on her face, I calmly asked myself whether I would recall her if I had the power. No, I would not. I was desolate as any castaway on a rock in mid-ocean, but desolation mattered little to me from that time forward, and there was a neverfailing solace in the knowledge that

JOSEPH FURPHY

her gentle spirit had found eternal rest, and that those poor worn hands, crossed on her breast, had done their last earthly work. I knew the time was coming when the assurance of her everlasting safety would outweigh my own sense of loneliness, and that time came long ago. Now that I've met you, Thompson, I haven't one personal anxiety in the world. I am a happy man tonight."

"We all sympathise with you, I'm sure," remarked the kindly clergyman, with a huskiness in his voice. "But you are doubly happy in having found the pearl of great price, and it must crown your happiness to have the assurance that your loved one is safe. You are doing well enough now, I trust, from a worldly point of view?"

"Right enough," replied the trapper, indifferently. "In former times I never imagined that there could be such an opening for me, or any occupation that suited me so well. I'll finish my story in a few words. I turned away from Melbourne with a small kit of tools in my hand, and a few shillings in my pocket, leaving debts behind me to the amount of about twenty-six pounds. My intention was to go round the farms in the Northern District, cleaning and repairing, but after a few weeks I took to trapping, and in course of time paid off my debts, besides buying a suitable turnout. Then I went into other things, feeling my way carefully. I travel over a good deal of country, always doing something. I'm averaging about a hundred and forty pounds a year now, and it costs very little to keep me. Puny as I am, I should have been a bushman."

"I'll say this for you," interposed Dixon, "you're the only feller o' your size I ever see that ain't et up with conceit, an' I dunno one (adj.) man— not if he was fifteen stone—that gits over his work with such credit as you do. You're like the bloke in the disturbance—'I'm little,' says he, 'but, O God.'"

"Mis-ter Dix-on," exclaimed Lushington, naturally shocked.

"Beg parding," replied the vessel of wrath, adroitly veiling his non— apprehension under the mask of urbanity. "Slipt out unbeknownst. Sort o' lapsus (adj.) linguae. I'm a careless (fellow), but I don't mean nothin' wrong."

"And you ought to be on your guard. But, Mr. Furlong, I'm glad to hear of your release from the pressure of poverty. A blessing always attends perseverance in the end. You'll be able to lay by a nice little sum as a provision for the future."

"Well," replied Furlong, with some constraint, "I'm owing Thompson twelve pounds, and—"

"No, no," interrupted Thompson, sourly.

"And I can only pay him about half, and ask him to wait till I earn the rest. You may think it strange that I've been inquiring for him all these years, and never reserved his money, though I've had hundreds through my hands. The fact is, that—that—But what use is money to me now?"

"So it was Thompson you was inquirin' about when I seen you on the Island?" interposed Dixon. "Well, I be (lost). Why the (sheol) didn't you say a (person) with a ches'nut horse? Not a bay. Thompson's remarked for ches'nut ever since I knowed him."

"Any other color's unlucky with me," observed Thompson sadly. "And to prove it—I only had that bay horse for three weeks. Got his hind foot over the hobble-chain drinking at a steep place. Fact, it's as much as I can do to keep even a ches'nut horse."

"I must have a talk with you on that subject," replied Lushington. "We shall meet again, and, I hope, learn something from each other. I should feel sorry to lose sight of a man like you. But, Furlong, I feel really concerned for you. Do you think—if I may be so personal—that you are morally justified in shutting your eyes to the future now that you have opportunity to provide for the old age which, I trust, you will be spared to see? Pardon me for saying that I think you should accept your past experience as an evidence of what may happen again when you will be less able to battle with the world than in your younger days. Believe me, I appreciate unselfishness as a principle, but you should be just before you are generous. You ought to reserve something. You owe it to yourself."

"Well," replied Furlong, hesitating, "I have a kind of provision. It may appear foolish to you, and I won't attempt to justify it. The grave where my wife lies is secured and registered, and I have made arrangements for being buried there with her. It rests with God alone to determine the period of my life and the conditions and place of my death, but when that time comes, those who undertake my burial will find instructions as to my wishes, and a sum of thirty pounds to repay their trouble and expense. The money is safe in the Mercantile Bank, deposited there for that express purpose, and it cannot be drawn until certain incontestable proofs are forthcoming to show that the trust has been fulfilled. I needn't go into the details of the arrangements now, but they are as complete as I could make them. So you see, Mr. Lushington," continued the trapper, deprecatingly, "I'm a little more selfish that I had led you to believe."

"Now, Mr. Furlong, you place me in a painful position. It was with the best intention, and in view of your loneliness in the world, that I threw out the suggestion. I meant it kindly. And all that you have since said makes me only the more solicitous to see you provide for coming years. Now, a series of periodical payments into the Endowment Fund of an Assurance Society, in which I have some interest, would in due time give you a good return, and would much increase your power of usefulness in more advanced life. Shall we talk the matter over quietly tomorrow? I have no commercial motive in proposing it, but I should like to see you safe."

The trapper maintained an uneasy silence. Obstinate in some ways, he was manifestly a man averse to argument. But there was another member of our congregation who, though still more obstinate, had no such antipathy to the intellectual duello.

XXVIII

> . . .Diotrephes, who loveth to have the pre-eminence. . . prating against us with malicious words; and not content therewith, neither doth he himself receive the brethren, and forbiddeth them that would and casteth them out of the church.
>
> —III John, 1, 9, 10

F urlong is safe—if his Bible is worth the paper it is printed on," said the deep resonant voice of the American. "All your financial societies, based on usury as they are, will go to the Father of usury sooner or later—most of them sooner—unless my judgment is strangely at fault. But the postulated president of Furlong's society has given a guarantee which, if not passed over as the wildest extravagance, must be accepted as a pledge that will out-last the solar system. 'And even to your old age, I am he; and even to hoar hair I will carry you; I have made, and will bear; even I will carry you, and will deliver you.' This warranty is repeated in a hundred forms throughout the so-called later revelation, and, most emphatically of all, by Christ himself. Let Furlong be consistent in his working out of the economic problem on Biblical lines. His experiment is being carried out in the spirit of confiding assent; not as a challenge, not even as a test; and such enterprises are of supreme interest in a mercenary age."

"But, Mr. Rigby, I think you take me unfairly," protested the clergyman. "I am entirely with Furlong in full and implicit reliance on divine goodness; still, we must provide things needful in the sight of all men—another way of saying that thrift is an essential of the Christian character. You will surely agree with me in the duty of providing for the future?"

"No," replied the Deacon emphatically. "The only duty that I personally recognise is the very momentous one of forwarding the New Order. Don't wilfully misconstrue me here or confuse the issue by a shifting signification of the word 'thrift.' Remember, I hold that a man's best work, cheerfully rendered in compensation for his livelihood, is a primary component of the comprehensive duty I speak of. I hold the idler as being already in the nethermost pit of infamy—not so much the idler under the bridge, as the idler in the drawing-room at Toorak or

JOSEPH FURPHY

Potts Point—and I hold the prodigal, of high or low degree, as almost equally infamous.

"So I trust we shall agree on the naked question of 'Thrift.' Honest cheerful work, for the sustenance and enrichment and enlightenment of the world we both admit to be a duty—but why tack on to this obligation the altogether alien idea of accumulation? What a despicable subterfuge it is to attempt to carry avarice on the back of industry and economy along the narrow way. Why strive so hard to combine the sense of property with the sense of duty, as if neither could justify itself without the other? Why not allow each to find, or fail to find, its own separate vindication? We are all Goethes—not in respect of literary ability, perhaps, but in respect that we never heard of a crime that we might not have committed. Say, if you will, with Gloster, in 'Lear': 'As flies to wanton boys are we to the gods; they kill us for their sport.' Granted. But that is the limit of their province; they cannot disturb your Individualistic principles, nor my Socialistic fads. Jehovah, through Moses, may enlist and exercise the most formidable—"

"He's fairly started," whispered Thompson to me.

"Not yet," I replied, in the same tone. "This is only a preliminary canter, but he'll start by-and-by."

"Agencies of Nature; but he cannot soften Pharoah's heart when that copper-coloured probationer chooses to harden it. Canute, by his own moral volition, could damn himself—and probably did so—though he couldn't dam the tide; his soul was his own; the tide was God's. Any man may develop his own moral nature, upward or downward—each unit of society being personally responsible for the conditions under which the development of each takes place—but no man can add eighteen inches to his own height; and this last metaphor is the one used by Christ himself to illustrate the utter irreverency of anxiety for the morrow!"

"You take me in a too violent sense, Mr. Rigby," replied the clergyman gently. "Let me put the issue before you with a frankness for which I solicit pardon beforehand, pleading only that the argumentum ad hominem between—"

"Stick to that, young feller," broke in Dixon. "Foller him up on them (adj.) lines."

"Between you and me, at least, does not originate on my side. I presume from your tone that your habit has not been to provide for the future, and I should imagine you to possess independence of spirit which is a very admirable quality. Now suppose that, from the present day, your health and strength fail rapidly—and, pardon me, Mr. Rigby, you are no longer a young man. The decline of life is inevitable, if we are spared to experience it:—

"'From Marlborough's eyes the streams of dotage flow, And Swift expires a driveller and a show.'"

"Which proves in a more literal sense than Solomon intended," said I, "that the race is not to the swift nor the battle to the strategist!"

"Neatly put, Collins," rejoined Lushington. "But, Mr. Rigby, you see that your extreme views place you in a difficult position?"

"A man's life's no more than to say one," replied the Senator gravely. "Notice how my extreme views release me from the position they place me in? When my right hand forgets the exceedingly little cunning it ever possessed, it will still retain dexterity enough to load and fire a pistol. I object to suicide, but only as I object to any other evasion of duty, and I condemn the act exactly as I condemn any other infliction of distress or loss upon those with whom I come in touch. But, in the first place, we presuppose my last task completed, and, in the second place, my unsettled and solitary life has naturally cancelled any claim to the tributary tear. I take no higher ground. Didn't I acknowledge that my religious faith was invisible to the naked eye?"

"What a penalty," murmured Lushington, in real commiseration.

"There is no procedure, right or wrong, but has its accordant penalty," replied the Major. "I daresay that, in the normal sequence of effort and result, it has been within my power to have become a comparatively warm man. But such a condition was opposed to my interests. Let me explain this, even at the risk of appearing egotistic—a weakness which, Heaven knows, is no besetment of mine. An apostle of the New Order, Mr. Lushington, must meet all prospective and actual adherents on a common plane, and the only plane available is that of simple manhood. Think it over. Who teaches poor men must himself be poor. Not only that, but he must refuse all private advantage; he must persist in poverty. 'Axe to grind' is the most deadly charge ever brought against an avowed champion of truth and progress. And the agitator's only safeguard against this aspersion is non-possession of any axe, except the implement which he sedulously applies to the root of this or that social upas. See how this elementary necessity has been recognised by the makers of real history—that is, the history of moral advance. If Gautama, for instance, would put his impress on a race he must voluntarily exchange the degree of a prince for that of the poorest peasant. If Christ would transform the world, He must have not whereon to lay His head.

"If Mahomet would promulgate a creed and found a civilisation he must be seen at the zenith of his power mending his own shoes; he must habitually saddle his own camel with his own hands; and if his successor, Abu Bekr, would complete the work the Prophet began he must not only vie with his poorest followers in plainness of living, but must once in every week leave himself absolutely moneyless. If Wesley would inaugurate the greatest religious departure of modern time he must be as poor as Elijah or St. Paul; he must be able to say: 'If I die worth ten pounds, let posterity pronounce John Wesley a hypocrite and an impostor.' As in religion proper, so in moral science. If Zeno would found the noblest of all schools of ethic philosophy he must teach all day, and by starlight earn his morrow's bread. If Plato would enlighten the world he must die possessed of no gold except his ear-rings. If Epictetus would point succeeding ages to a manlier life he must leave no property beyond his little earthenware lamp. And so on to infinity, Becket in cloth-of-gold was a mere butterfly; Becket in hair-cloth was formidable. All that ministers to lust of the eyes or the pride of life (and here you have a very large order), is fatal to the kind of personal influence a moral leader must exercise. Aurelius was more distinguished by the simplicity, the hardness, the actual poverty, of his life, than by the exalted office he bore solely for the good of his fellowmen, and the air of falsity which pervades the teachings of Seneca is only too easily accounted for by his private wealth. At least ninety per cent. of would be reformers have stultified themselves by drifting into extraneous personal advantage. Here, for instance, we have the secret of Rienzi's failure. I purposely mix religion, ethics and sociology in this inquiry, because they collectively cover so much ground that nothing worth quarrelling over is left in the separate domain of any. It amounts to this: That the man of substance, however he may otherwise serve society, can never do so as a leader in religion or morals, never as a champion of rights, never as a reformer."

"That would shut out such men as Nicodemus and Joseph of Arimathea," interposed Binney.

"As religious or social-economic reformers it certainly would," assented the Deacon. "Mind, I don't mean to say that—taking the men as they are presented to us—the Lazarus of the parable was better than either of the two you have named. We are dealing with special qualifications for a certain task, not with comparative righteousness. I am not presumptive enough even to assert that Lazarus was morally better than the well-to-do gentleman in the same parable. I merely contend that Joseph of Arimathea must have qualified for his traditional mission to Britain by becoming as poor as Lazarus. Touching Nicomedus we infer, from certain passages in the Talmud, that he lived a member of the Sanhedrim wealthy and respected, till the fall of Jerusalem somewhat disturbed his family succession. Doubtless he was admitted to Abraham's bosom as well as Lazarus—but that is not the point. The point is, that having declined to take degrees as a reformer, he missed the reformer's record."

"As achieved by the individual who now stands before us," I remarked.

"If a farthing in the pound can be called liquidation, Tom," replied the Senator, dejectedly.

XXIX

Wer't not for me, the world would roll
Back in the ruts of uncontrol;
Without a master or a guide.
To stem the fierce barbaric tide.

K eep the ball rollin' anyhow," urged Dixon. "Ain't of'en a lot of blokes like us gits together. We don't kill a pig every (adj.) day."

"Well, speaking for myself," continued the Judge, "I consider that the privilege of poverty is worth about 40,000,000 times as much to me as any personal provision which I might have been able to segregate from the public estate. Understand clearly that I have no personal grievance against society; my only fear is that society may have a grievance against me, and I feel bound to guard against that danger. For instance, I hold that every man should have a home of his own, inviolable and independent, but for that very reason I decline to have one whilst better men are homeless. And now see where my spore of fern-seed comes into operation. Generally speaking, I have no fear of being driven to the extremity I hinted at just now. When I consider the finished career of those who have gone before, and note how gratuitous was all their solicitude, my mind is at rest. Take Burns, the poet and spokesman of human nature, as a representative of his race, and think what agonies of apprehension racked that man's soul, to no purpose whatever. The poverty-stricken octogenarian he talked with on the banks of Ayr was his own morbid presage of his future self. He envied the field—mouse its exemption from his own forbodements. Why should he? He never saw his 37th birthday, and he left the world incalculably his debtor—an obligation which the world acknowledged, 25 years ago, by giving him the greatest centenary in history. No doubt he had hard times—thanks to the criminal blindness of his forefathers—but his mere anxiety didn't mend matters, and his honest protest has made times better for us, just as our protest should make times better for our successors. Thinking over these things, I feel thankful that the work allotted to me as a co-operator with the Power in whom we live and move and have our being, is of a much more tangible kind than the providing against the indefinite by means of the elusive. Hence my habitual process of thought leads me to settle down into conspicuously imperfect performance of what I conceive to be the programme of duty, feeling fairly confident that I shall never be condemned to lag superfluous on the pay-sheet."

"Thou art not far from the Kingdom of Heaven," remarked Furlong gently. "But, dear Mr. Rigby, you strike the rock as Moses did, instead of speaking to it in the name of the Lord. It seems to me," he continued with some hesitation, "that your misfortune is want of humility and teachableness."

"Yes; he's got a bit of vacancy there, right enough," assented Thompson ill-naturedly.

"I don't wish to force my view upon anyone," resumed Furlong, "but here is what seems to me a reasonable way of looking at the position we all occupy on this earth. We know that there was a time in each of our lives when we were utterly helpless; but God had a place and a use, and a provision, for each one of us; therefore, we passed the feebleness of that time, and here we are tonight. Now, can we fear that the Almighty arm which shielded our infancy may become paralysed in our age? That is all. The more we attempt to explain away the providence of God, the weaker will our arguments appear. Church tradition, you know, tells of a blind centenarian, led from time to time into the assembly of the disciples at Ephesus, to deliver the charge, 'Little Children, love one another.' Was St. John superannuated even then? No, according to promise, his age was clearer than the noonday. Can we ever be superannuated in the sight of Him who holds our lives in His hand to be resumed when He sees fit?"

"Certainly we can," replied the Colonel promptly, while Furlong writhed in his seat. "St. John was an exception. He wasn't superannuated, simply because in the days of his vigor he had not courted superannuation. It is an aphorism somewhat hyperbolical, I admit—that any man if he is prepared to pay the price, will attain whatever reasonable end he keeps in view; and to most of us, superannuation is the chief aim and object of life. Naturally, then, the person who anticipates a worthless old age, and provides for it accordingly, ensures the fulfilment of his forecast as far as the worthlessness is concerned, though in so doing he defeats the utility of his enterprise; for the moral discipline entailed by his lifework inevitably produces an old age not worth providing for. And that man is superannuated in the sight of his Maker, as well as in the sight of his fellow-men."

"Memento (adj.) mori," observed Dixon appreciatively. "Course when a man's beltin' his way through the world, he can't expect to be every (adj.) thing the doctor ordered; but when he makes a sort of rise he ought to repent. Got to die some time, right enough. Thank Mister Adam (adj.) for that lot. By (sheol)—"

"Good enough for us," moaned Thompson.

"Death," rejoined the Commodore critically, "is no more a serious occurrence than the word 'finis' at the end of a book; which book, long or short, decent, vile or mediocre, as the case may be—cannot possibly contain anything of permanent importance except a record of trusteeship. By the same token, it usually embodies nothing but a scheme of embezzlement, seldom successfully carried off."

"But trustees must live during the currency of their office," suggested the tenacious clergyman.

"A most reasonable claim," conceded the sheriff. "But pardon me, you seem to insist upon something beyond that legitimate demand. Let us get at the facts. We lived in the last decade, in the last year, in the last week. We are living now. But we are not living in the coming week, in the coming year, in the coming decade. Now Human nature dreads the temporal future. There is no getting away from that fact. And to this anxiety some one of three palliatives is applied. Shall we examine these consecutively? The worlding pulls down his barns, and builds greater—or looks forward to doing so. That is the purely secular provision, which is persistently and unmistakably condemned by the founder of the religion we casually profess. Then the Stoic, esteeming all material things as merely auxiliary to self-centred integrity, holds himself prepared to withdraw from the world, rather than become an encumbrance. That is the purely heroic provision, and I confess it has a certain fascination. Lastly, the Christian, concerning himself only with the obligation of life, whilst enjoying its blameless amenities, calmly reposes on the abundant promises contained in that book which he accepts as Divine revelation. That provision is beyond comment, inasmuch as its seeming precariousness never disturbs the confidence of its true partisans. But Furlong has just now said the last word on this attitude of mind. However, these three courses absolutely exhaust the elective possibilities of life. Socialism, of course, simply aims at realising the Christian's provision, per medium of an endowment policy endorsed by the whole community. Meantime, a man may select any one of the three courses I have quoted, but not a combination. Which two can you combine?"

"Any sensible bloke, if he were restricted to one course would select damper and bacon, as being both wholesome and filling," I observed. "And if you could take statistics of the whole human race I fancy you would find a very large number who never trouble themselves over any other consideration. Others care for nothing beyond looking upon the tanglefoot when it is long."

"Your observation would apply with more force to a bygone age," replied the Colonel gravely, "when the would-be worldling was held in his place by the large, flat foot of Privilege; and the would-be Stoic was kept in working order by the threat of having his soul firmly staked down in the bottomless pit, and his body at the nearest cross-roads; while the would-be Christian was cleverly thrown on the herring-scent of royalty, nobility and gentry. Many corpses walk the earth at the present day, no doubt; but, broadly speaking, every living person, from fifteen years old and upward, belongs to one of the three classes. Leaving the Stoic out, we now judge between the worldling and the Christian—between the man who lays up treasure in the shape of property, by exertions on his own behalf, and the man who lays it up in the shape of life's record, by exertions on behalf of others. I maintain that no man can make the two investments conjointly, and I have the argument of congruity with me, not to speak of the four evangelists. The difficulty of the question arises simply from trying to blend two policies, not merely foreign, but mutually hostile to each other. You will remember, Mr. Lushington, that you have just now congratulated Furlong upon having found the pearl of great price? Why, you hardly touched the metaphor. Follow it out honestly, and see where it lands you. I say, Furlong, can you repeat the passage word for word?"

The trapper cleared his throat. "'Again the kingdom of heaven is like unto a merchantman seeking goodly pearls, who, when he had found one pearl of great price, went and sold all that he had and bought it.'— Matthew xiii 45 and 46."

"Thank you," replied the Judge. "You will perceive, Mr. Lushington, that the point brought out is not the discovery of the pearl, but the price cheerfully paid for it. Undoubtedly, from the Samuel Smiles' point of view, this pearl trading is a fanatical speculation. Samuel's pig-philosophy requires a new exegesis of the gospels—an exegesis explaining that Christ was merely giving a lesson in Social etiquette when, in a parable, He charged His followers, on being bidden to a feast, to sit down in the lowest place, and so forth. Yet the metaphor is an exceedingly happy one, for the effort to rise personally in the world merely amounts to an indecent rush for the front seat. Just analyse the figure of speech for yourselves, and its completeness will grow upon you." The Senator paused to let his noisome teaching soak in.

XXX

And she was lost—and yet I breathed.
But not the breath of human life;
A serpent round my heart was wreathed.
And stung my every thought to strife.

"All very fine for you blokes to go fetching out your arguments about right and wrong, and all the rest of it," broke in the young fellow, with a subjective petulance which seemed to size up his Ego. "But what do you think of a man working for a slant to do a thing that's bound to send him to hell straight? Well, that's me. I'll tell you how I came to be in this perdicament."

"To the point—who is she?" murmured the Colonel impatiently, but in a voice audible only to his immediate neighbours. He regarded the audience as his own private diggings, by right of valid pre-emption, and rigid fulfilment of labor covenant.

"It's all through a girl, and she was worth it, no matter how people might cock up their noses at her, if they knew—I'll tell you the whole yarn."

"And you'll be sorry for it in the morning, if I judge you correctly," continued the superseded Major, in his former tone.

"I'm a well brought up man, though I say it myself," pursued the conversational interloper. "You don't hear no (verb) this, nor (adj.) that, out of my mouth. My ole man, he's got a slashin' farm not eighty miles from where we're sitting—no occasion for saying which road. Well, there was a girl come into our district, three years ago, and me and her struck up together, and we was as right as rain for over twelve months, and nobody would a dreamed anything could come between us. But behold you, there comes a new bobby to the township—a feller that was living separated from his wife—and before you could say 'knife' all the girls in the district was gone on the blasted hound. He was an ole bloke too—forty, if he was a day,—but I notice these ole married divils is always the worst. He was just about the ugliest cur I ever did see, with a baird right up to his eyes, but the girls they used to be always blathering about what a splendid-looking man he was. It didn't trouble me; but I hated him from the first day I seen him, an' that cove was the instigation o' me bein' here tonight. I s'pose it was to be.

"Well, he'd got the place to himself, and a feller by the name o' the 'Old Skipper' cookin' for him, an' today you'd see him grinnin' at a bar-maid; an' tomorrow you'd meet him in the bush with a girl on horseback; an' nex' day you'd see another girl yarning with him across a fence; an' all the girls in the district blazin' with jealousy about the lousy cur—an' him a married man. Well, it so happened that Nora had to come a good deal in his road, an' she was the nicest girl in the district; an' O he was this, an' that, an' the other thing, an' your humble servant, an' a polished scoundrel at the back of it all. But she took no more notice of him at first nor if he was a dog.

"But it come around one night that there was a big meeting about Home Rule; an' she was there along o' the other girl that worked partners with her; an' I was there with some blokes I knew; an' somehow or other a row started between some Orangemen and some Gruffs; an' I happened to be in the thick of it; an' up comes my lord, an' grabs me by the collar; an' me nothin' to do with the row, but dragged into it, you might say, through backin' one of the Gruffs that was a friend of mine. Course, I makes a welt at the copper—for I won't stand to be scruffed by any living man if I can git at him fair—but he gits a twist on me, an' he goes out of his way to run me nearly over the top of Nora; an' he stops a minute to apologise, shakin' me now an' again like a dog with a 'possum, an' me helpless on account of the holt he had; an' then he runs me out an' shoves me in chokey, an' back he goes to the meetin'. Course, I was bailed out that night, an' when Court day comes I got clear with only a caution for makin' the hit at the blasted varmin.

"Well, to my surprise, instead of Nora swearing off at him and spittin' in his face if he spoke to her, she seemed sorter taken with him, and naturally this grew into what you might call a coolness between me and her. Well, upon me word, I tried to buck up to another girl, purpose to vex Nora, but I couldn't stummick it no road. Though, mind you, I'll say this for myself," he continued, with a flash of that unaccountable and reprehensible bravado which appears to be confined to the nobler sex, "I was none of your greenhorns that butter wouldn't melt in their mouths, an' frightened if a girl spoke to them. No innocence about me, I promise you. I was edicated up to the knocker before ever I seen Nora.

"Course, I'd got a set on the copper, but I had to sing small; an' after a while I noticed Nora was clean broke off with him, an' they passed one another without a word; an' the copper he sort o' dodged me; an' presently I got thick with Nora again. But she wasn't the same girl she used to be; all her jolliness was gone. Well, it seems the copper's wife had somebody watchin' him, and suddenly there was a flare up, an' he had to resign, or git the run; so he resigned and went up the country horsebreaking; for I'll say this much to his credit, that he was about as good a hand among rough horses as you'd git. Give the devil his due.

"Well, things dragged on for a couple or three months, an' me an' Nora was as friendly as ever; but there was something about her I couldn't make out, no road. At last, one night I was seeing her home from a bazaar; an' it was as dark as pitch; an' suddenly she says.

"'Come an' sit on this log,' says she, 'I got to tell you somethin'; I can't bear this state of things one minit longer.'

"So she started an' has a bit of a cry, an' then she tells me what was on her mind. Seems she wanted to go one Sunday to see another dressmaker she knew in a township about twelve miles away; an' him, he gammoned he wanted to go the same road on some business, so what does he do but he gets a buggy and away goes the two o' them— her kickin' herself all the time for letting things go so fur—an' comin' back he made out he wanted to go the other track through the bush."

The narrator checked himself, then went on with an infirm attempt at nonchalance.

"Well, now, I seen them driving home that same evenin'; and I don't deny I was narked a bit extry; but I had no more suspicion nor. . ." Again he paused; when he resumed there was a subdued and seething fury in every reluctant syllable. "Well, he was a big strong lump of a man, and she was a weed of a woman, so to speak—an'—an'—never mind." The last two words were shattered by a sardonic laugh; then he continued, "It's all very well to talk, but what could she do without making the thing worse—advertisin' herself, as you might say? An' there was him stalkin' about the township as bold as brass for months after, lookin' over my head whenever we met one another; an' me knowin' no more about what had took place nor the man in the moon. O never mind, it's alright—or, at least, it'll be alright yet."

"The scoundrel," exclaimed Lushington. "Hanging would be too good for him."

"Well, I got his wages in my cartridge belt," replied the other grimly. "I'm on his track this time safe, even if I had to kill time for a fortnit—or else I wouldn't be in this quarter tonight. Course, I mightn't git him for another month, but he's booked to go. The laugh will be on my side then. Puttin' in a spoke for poor ole Nora, too—knocking over two birds with one stone, as the sayin' is. Present time I got the patience of Job. I left a good home three months ago to learn him what a fool he was to think I was safe for him to blow his nose on. I got a fair idea where to lay wait for him this time, he's a gift to me when I get him in range. Now I've said it."

"But my dear friend," said the clergyman gravely, "though I sympathise deeply with you, I must condemn your purpose of taking the law into your own hands. 'Vengeance is mine: I will repay,' thus saith the Lord."

"Didn't you say this bloke wanted hanging?" retorted the other. "Is the Lord going to hang him? Does the Lord hang a feller for makin' an Aunt Sally of another feller, an' laughin' in his sleeve all the time?"

"Apart from the stings of conscience, and the retribution of the world to come, God punishes by the agency of our Criminal law."

"Hold on, then; you stick to that," eagerly replied the young fellow, apparently just waking up to his own imprudence in telling the story, and thereby stung to fresh irascibility. "Sposen there's a man in a place called Sussex, in England, an' this man shakes a bushel o' wheat for his missis to boil for the kids to keep them from starving, does God give that man seven years' laggin', and then set him adrift, with his ankles wore to the bone with the irons, and his shoulders like a soojee bag with flogging? Well, that was my gran'father—an' as decent a man as ever your gran'father knowed how to be. Is that God's style of punishing people with the Criminal Law? Don't talk rubbage."

"I admit that, where offences against property were concerned, the law was exceedingly severe in the days of our forefathers; indeed, it is perhaps, too severe still in some instances, but—"

"But God backs it up. Stick to your argyment. We'll see if it's too severe. Sposen a lawyer gets six hundred notes of a cockie's money into his claws, an' then hums and ha's and can't be made to fork it over—does God on'y jist put a set on that lawyer, so's he's got to go partners with another lawyer for a couple o' years. Well, that was what happened to my ole man, when I was twelve or fourteen, an' it nearly sent us on the wallaby. Don't talk to me about law. If it was middlin' decent a cove might spring a bit to suit it; but it ain't even middlin'; it's the rottennest, disgracefullest, d—dest thing from here to hell."

"I admit that it is an unsafe thing to meddle with; but you must consider—"

"Look here, you'll make me disagreeable an' nasty, the way you're goin' on. How the hell fire can the law be a unsafe thing to meddle with, if God's got any say in it? Ain't the law a (adj.) sight unfairer every way nor the cronkest gamblin'? An' people ain't such mullock-brained, flamin' ijiots as to say God bosses that. Mind you I believe in God; but He's just got as much to do with law as He's got to do with—God eternally damn me for a (adj.) fool."

As this amiable young person barked out the last words, he rose and withdrew fifteen or twenty yards farther along the bank, where he mechanically threw his line into the river, and sat down. Lushington followed, and found a seat beside him. Then ensued the low, earnest tones of the clergyman's voice, and the short, sullen replies of the other, equally unintelligible to the rest of us.

By this time the so-called kangaroo hunter and Furlong were the only ones of our party who continued to keep up the procedure of fishing—the former from restlessness, still under the glamour of the thirty-pounder. The sport had hitherto consisted partly in getting our hooks caught on sub merged roots, and partly in having our bait eaten off by the large, prickly crayfish which are always plentiful, except when you are equipped for catching them. But the slope of the bank was such a comfortable angle to recline against, the night was so pleasant, and the seventy or eighty yards of slow-swirling water, so beautiful in the light of an unobtrusive halfmoon, that we felt right enough as we were. Moreover, neither Binney nor Lushington could read midnight in the position of the stars, and the rest of us were not addicted to regular hours.

"Well, our discussion has, at least, effected the ambiguous service of saving an infamous ex-bobby's life," remarked the irrepressible Colonel, addressing his contracted audience.

"Guesswork and prophecy are two different things," retorted Thompson, sourly pedantic.

"Not altogether, Steve. Prophecy is guesswork, made unerring by accurate foresight, and the foresight here required demands only a scientific knowledge of overgrown waywardness. If this young fellow had, in the first place, confided his grievance to a friend or two, he would never have gone on the war-path, even though he had been advised to do so. A mere narration of the affront would have broken that personal equation which has governed his intentions till tonight. 'Affront,' I say advisedly, for observe how frankly our friend poses as champion of his own damaged dignity, rather than of the poor girl's chastity. A lesson in human nature, Steve. A mirror where each of us may see himself at his worst, free from the mask of cant. Hence I honor the young fellow's lack of magnanimity, inasmuch as it implies an equal lack of self delusion or hypocrisy."

"All's well that ends well," remarked Binney, evidently relieved by the Major's prediction.

"Ah, but there is no end to anything," replied that prophet insidiously. "Eternal mutation is nature's law—compulsory as to movement, though dirigible as to tendency; and it rests with us, as the beings most affected by such."

"Think he'll marry Nora," speculated Thompson, absently.

"Could anything be less desirable for either party?" asked the Dictator. "No, Steve, she has cost him too much. Let me explain. Man, in a not unpraiseworthy diversion of selfishness, instinctively overvalues the woman who brings out his best, and correspondingly under-estimates her who brings out his worst—though each woman's influence may operate unwittingly. In speaking of our friend's worst, I am not referring to this gendarme-stalking enterprise, as such, far from it, but to the spirit in which the task was undertaken and followed up. Hit or miss, he would have been, and is, morally deformed from this time forward. In point of fact, Nora's honor is an eminent consideration, the sun and centre of a little universe, while our friend's dignity is a small affair, an insignificant satellite pertaining solely to his insignificant self. But, cramped by a self-centred standard of honor, he began by allowing this moon eclipse that sun; and now he will stultify himself by ignoring both. A strain of Irish-Catholic in his incorrigible Anglicanism would have helped his Australian sensitiveness to a truer sense of proportion, to a nicer point of honor, and a higher perception of justice. And it is the lack of this nobler incentive—felt, though not formulated, which will paralyse his vindictive purpose, and send him home an apostate from vengefulness, yet not a convert to anything better. However, such a capacity for single-hearted resentment commands respect, even though it be so poorly backed by moral discrimination. Sir, I like a good hater."

"Stolen," rejoined Thompson maliciously.

"I forget at the present moment where the expression is from. Do you know, Tom?"

"No," I replied in a still, small voice.

Pluck—swish.

XXXI

"I have slain the Mishe-Nahma.
Slain the King of Fishes," said he.

—Longfellow

I thought I would get him," remarked Furlong quietly, as his pliant rod bent to a semicircle. He carefully rose to his feet, propping both knees against an arched and denuded root. "This is his haunt, Thompson. Now, Dixon, will you take this wooden hook, and watch your chance."

In a few minutes the fish was safely landed in a recess behind a root, and it was a thirty-pounder, as nearly as our carefully concealed disgust would allow us to guess. Probably there wasn't another such fish within miles.

(This, I ought to notice, was not the first catch of the evening. Lushington, a couple of hours previously, had secured a two-ouncer, without losing his bait. But I allowed the little incident to pass unrecorded in order to avoid breaking into one of the Colonel's discussions, which happened to be in full blast. In recounting the event here, I am merely adjusting, not jumbling, the order of things—transposing and grouping my occurrences, after the manner of some more famous, if less faithful, historians.)

"Better tether him in the river tonight," suggested Furlong. "We'll divide him amongst us in the morning."

"I've got the very thing," said I. "Hold on a minute."

I hurried to where I had left my earthly goods; there I let Pup loose, and returned to the river with his chain, with the faithful animal following me down the bank.

We secured one end of the chain to the fish's gills, by means of the strap, and attached the other end to a root. The fish hadn't much room to play, his snout being close to the surface; but at all events, he couldn't get entangled, and he would keep fresh. Then, in tacit unanimity, we all furled our lines, and began to climb the bank.

"Assuredly, Mr. Binney," resumed the Judge, as the two made their way up the steep slope, "a greater number of private fortunes have been dissolved and redistributed (amongst English-speaking people, at least,) since the middle of this century than in the two centuries preceding; and unless my forecast is unusually distorted, the remaining sixteen years of this century will break all previous records, and do it easy. Doesn't every rich Individualist dread the inevitable re-distribution of his wealth more keenly than he dreads any other kind of perdition? And doesn't every poor Individualist long for the golden shower of other people's money infinitely more than he longs for any other manifestation of his Maker's judicious partiality? The spoils to the victor—but only temporarily."

"I beg your pardon," said Binney, good-naturedly. "What time is it?"

"Early yet," replied the Deacon, advancing into the firelight, and hastily glancing at his watch. "Shove on your billy, Steve."

"Under our present system, Mr. Binney, the strong man, armed, keepeth his house only till a stronger than he cometh, and taketh from him his armour wherein he trusted, and divideth—divideth—his spoil. Every man of substance would do well to think this matter over in his intervals of leisure, bearing in mind that the inexorable fitness of things demands some amendment more comprehensive than any patch of new cloth on the seat of an old garment. And I maintain—"

"Good-night," laughed Binney, extending his hand. "I must break loose, sooner or later. Come on, Harold."

"O, hold on, Mr. Binney; don't insult our camp like that," remonstrated Thompson, who had replenished the big billy, and was now adjusting it on the fire. "Great Socialist, Rigby is," he continued, apologetically to the farmer; "but it's more the power of controversy than the force of argument. An ounce of fact is worth a mile of theory, they say; and while he was piling it on sky-high, I just thought of a bit of logic that would knock all his reasons and proofs into a cocked hat."

"Lay on, Macduff," sighed the Major.

"Gregory, remember thy swashing blow," I added.

"You know Stewart of Kooltopa, Jeff?" interrogated Thompson, with forensic keenness.

"I do, Steve. I also once knew a slave-owner named St. Clair—but my abolitionist principles remained unshaken. A fine Socialistic captain of industry is lost in Stewart. What a pity his only son, Watty, doesn't take after him."

"A mortal pity," assented Thompson innocently. "Well, I found the good of Individualism, and the folly of Socialism, three years ago, when I lost that waggon and load in the Eight-mile-Mallee, and went to Stewart."

"One moment, Steve," interrupted the Colonel. "You pretend to be able to track a single beast, day after day, for a week. Now, how could you lose a waggon and load in any mallee?"

"Oh, I could manage it right enough," replied Thompson, relapsing into the bitterness which had governed him all the evening.

"Perhaps you'll take my word for it when you hear the particulars. Tom and Dixon can ball me out if I exaggerate for the sake of proving my argument."

JOSEPH FURPHY

XXXII

The Hills that shake, although unriven.
As if an eathquake passed—
The thousand shapeless things all driven
In cloud and flame athwart the heaven.
By that tremendous blast.

—Byron's "Siege of Corinth."

"I t was one blazing hot day, January three years," continued Thompson, moodily. "I was loaded for Poolkija, with five-ton-fifteen of all sorts. I was pushing on, for I was tied to thirty days, and the station had sent me a letter by the mailman to say that they had a couple of well-sinkers stopped for want of some things I had on the waggon. I was getting eight notes a ton; so I could expect no mercy, and didn't think I would want any. Laughed at the very idea. I knew every drop of water and every bite of grass within five mile of the track for the whole journey, and my team was in rattling trim, but I overlooked the fact that Providence has other ways of killing a dog besides choking him with butter.

"Well, I was making that stage through the Eight-Mile-Mallee, on Birrawong, and, about one or two o'clock, I saw on ahead of me the smoke rolling up as black as a crow. You know the place, Tom, you too, Dixon, and you know it's about the heaviest porcupine in Riverina, and the track through it only the width of a waggon. Of course, I jumped on my horse and galloped on ahead to see which side of the track the fire was on; but I found it coming along both sides about a mile off, blazing twenty feet high, and the draught of it carrying every leaf off the mallee as fast as the flames touched them. I thought I had seen a couple or three decent fires before, but I found I was mistaken. Must have caught alight just before I saw it, for it was no width, but that didn't make any difference to me, considering that we were both in the Mallee together. However, it happened to be a calm day, bar a breath of wind now and then. So when I got back within a couple of hundred yards of the waggon, I lit the near side of the track and gee'd off into the porcupine, intending to get past the fire and then cross the track into the burnt ground. But I had only made matters a trifle worse, for in five minutes the new fire was on both sides of the track. So I bethought myself of an island of hop-bush half a mile away, on the same side as I was on, and I went for it at the rate of knots, with the fire lathering along behind me roaring like fury, and the sun invisible for smoke. The bullocks faced the porcupine without a flinch, for they knew what was up as well as I did, and I'd have made the Island right enough, only for the infernal thing that's on me.

"The first glimpse I got of some galahs in the hopbush, I saw that I was hanging too much to the right, and at the pace I was going I come-here'd and locked the waggon badly. The pole happened to be none too good, on account of a wrench it got the week before, so off it goes by the fetchels. Of course, if there had been time I could have snaked her along with a spare chain; but there was the fire not thirty yards behind, and the bullocks clearing off with a broken pole, so I just unhitched the horse from the back of the waggon, and grabbed hold of my coat on account of the things in the pockets, and got the team safe in the hop-bush without two minutes to spare.

"Well, you know how clean the porcupine burns off, so the moment the fire struck the hop-bush I got behind it, and went to have a look for the waggon and there she was, safe in the burnt ground, with nothing on fire except a case of kerosene standing on top of a big cask of sundries, right in the middle of the load. Certainly the kerosene case was blazing like a tar barrel, for it had been three weeks roasting in the sun, besides being soaked with the leakage of the oil. I daren't poke it down for fear of setting fire to everything, but I had hopes of saving all the load, bar the kerosene and the cask it was standing on, and if the sundries happened to be anything fireproof I might save them, too. At all events, my first thought was full of real pious thankfulness—hedging a little (if you understand me) till I would see how things turned out.

"Well now, I had noticed, in loading the cask of sundries, that it seemed to be a heavy, soddened, old ale-barrel, with a temporary top-end, made of pine-boards, so roughly fitted that the straw and stuff inside stuck out through the cracks. However, by this time the solder had melted on the kerosene tins, and let all the oil down into the cask; so the blaze was something that can better be imagined."

"Don't, Steve," I groaned.

"How sympathetic you are, all of a sudden," sneered Thompson, as he removed the billy from the fire, threw in two handfuls of tea, and stirred it with the axe handle. "Better be imagined than described. But even after the top of the barrel had caved in, the sides were as sound as a bell. I knew they would stand ten or fifteen minutes roasting, and my idea was to get my tarpaulin over the barrel and stop the draught, so as to let the fire choke itself out. I had dragged the tarpaulin into a safe place fifteen or twenty yards away, first go off. So I jumped down off the waggon and went over to it and gathered it in my arms. I just remember turning round towards the waggon, when suddenly there was a flare that blinded me, and an explosion that shifted the firmament, and something hit the tarpaulin such a welt that I went twenty yards before I landed; and there I lay in a heap among the porcupine ashes, with the tarpaulin on top of me. Seems sort of unmanly, you'd think, to follow a person up in such a punctual, unmerciful style, but, of course, it's not my place to lay down the law.

"Well, by-and-by I woke up, sick as a dog, with my face all scorched and I lay down again. When I recovered a bit, I just took an observation of the place, and gave it best. Reminded me of the abomination of desolation. In spite of Rigby's very complimentary insinuation that I'm a skite and a liar, the waggon was gone, body and bones, and the principal thing that was left was a smell of powder. There was a sort of wombat hole in the ground, where she had stood, and a quarter of an acre of the burnt mallee was badly knocked about; and outside of this you might see such a thing as a spud, or an onion, or half a bar of soap, or a partly empty flour bag, or the matting off a tea chest. The hind part of the waggon was about forty yards away, lying in a heap, with the axle torn off the bed and bent two double, and both wheels knocked into firewood, and a whole swag of brass wire out of a piano tangled round the lot. The only thing that was in decent order was the fore-carriage and front wheels, lying upside down, about twenty yards away. It was like something you would dream about. And to make matters better, I had carefully hung my coat on a Mallee near the waggon when I started fighting the fire, and where it went to I'll never know till the day of Judgment."

"(Adj.) sight better to happen to you nor to a pore man, anyhow," remarked Dixon, spreading an old wool-bale on the ground.

"I'm relating this experience merely to prove an argument, and it's for the benefit of people with brains," replied Thompson severely, as he assisted Dixon to arrange the tea-service. "Well, by the time I had found out that the thing was a reality, it was near sun-down. I made my way back to where I had left the bullocks, but they had wandered off across the burnt ground, with the horses following them. I tracked them for a bit, but night came on, and I lay down, with a fearful headache, and a pain in the inside. Off again at daylight, but before I had well started I found the team, tied up in a knot, with the horse close by. I took them on to the Collaman Tank, and loosed out there, and rode across to Rusty Jack's hut, to ask him not to interfere with the bullocks, considering the way I was situated. From there I dodged on towards Poolkija to give an account of my load. I believe I'd have suicided, only I was too infernal frightened."

"Is that your anti-Socialistic argument, Steve?" asked the Major.

"I'm coming to it if you'll only have patience. To give old Forbes his due, he let me off as easy as could be expected. When I told him what had happened, and advised him to send a horse and dray for anything that could be collected, he told me I ought to be the last man in the world to offer advice. Which was perfectly true. 'And now, Thompson,' said he, 'if I might presume to throw out a suggestion to you, it would be to put your horse in the ration paddock for tonight, and go to the hut yourself; and then, first thing after breakfast, clear off this station before anything happens. Jonah would be a safer man to have about the place,' says he. Of course, I followed his advice. Now squat round here, boys, and help yourselves.

"When I got back to the fatal spot, I found a dozen blackfellows having a good time of it, and a lot of emus, and all the galahs and wee-jugglers in the country; for there was over three tons of good tucker scattered about—everything from jam to pearl barley. But I just picked up a few things, and packed them on the fore-carriage, and shook the dust off my feet against that Eight-Mile-Mallee, as the poet says.

"I bethought me that I had seen a good heavy platform waggon in the shed at Kooltopa, besides the one they used. So I drifted across there, to see if I could make some sort of a deal for it. I told Stewart I was just as I stood, for it had been arranged that both pockets of my pants had holes in them at the time of my misfortune, and my coat was gone to glory, with every copper I had buttoned up in the breast pocket of it—so I would have to ask for some sort of terms. Stewart said—'Well, no, he didn't want to sell the waggon, but I was welcome to the loan of it.' And first of all, he wanted me to start for Hay with four tons of pressed skins, and fetch back six tons of stores. So here was a god-send, and it took the feather-edge off my misfortune; and, if you'll believe it, from that day to this, Stewart would neither take the waggon back or listen to one word about paying for it. 'Damn your soul,' says he, 'can't you keep the (adj.) thing till I ask for it?'"

"Well, strictly speakin', Stewart don't count," observed Dixon. "Divil thank him, he's a (adj.) Christian, he is. Here, wire in, young fellow" (this to Lushington), "what the (adj. sheol) are you thinking about? What's come o' the other gentleman?"

"He has retired to his camp," replied the clergyman, helplessly. "He wishes to be alone."

"At first it made me feel as mean as a lord chamberlain," pursued Thompson, "but a person gets used to anything in course of time. Now, help yourselves, boys; no politeness here. That's the same waggon," he added, by way of clinching the argument, "only I got her thoroughly overhauled before going out last wool season."

There was a pause. "Well?" said the Judge, interrogatively. "Well," replied Thompson, defiantly.

XXXIII

How subject we old men are to this vice of lying.

—Second Part of King Henry IV, Act III, Scene II

As the Social-economic controversy re-commenced, Dixon
deferentially touched me on the back with the edge of his pannikin.

"Say, Collins—onna bright—what does non omnia possumus (adj.)
omnes stan' for?" he murmured aside, unconsciously displaying a
fearsome mnemonic power of an unlettered but brainy man. "Is she
straight? There ain't no 'possums in the ole country. I got that on good
authority."

"I think she's straight, Dixon, though I can't give you the small
change for her. I fancy you'll find her in any good list of Latin phrases."

"Must 'a missed her some (adj.) road. Hunt her up tomorrow. Say,
them ole Latiners knowed how to git the loan of a feller (adj.) quiet.
Right. I'll work the (phrase) for all she's worth."

Then we turned and took part in the conversation, which, by the
united efforts of Thompson, Binney, and Lushington, had been forced
round to Furlong's thirty-pounder. Some very good fish stories were
told during the repast. I remember I narrated how I had once caught
half-a-hundredweight of fish with one large fat maggot, on a small
hook, and still had the maggot to the good. I think I laid the scene of
this miraculous draught on the Murrumbidgee, but no matter. I had
made the haul with a night-line, which I had casually—though, as it
happened, fortunately—attached to the top of a very limber whipstack
sapling, trimmed clean of its leaves and twigs, and growing on the brink
of the river. On visiting this line in the morning, I had found the sapling
bent down to the water, and had easily landed an exhausted codfish of
thirty-two pounds. Inside him I had found another of fifteen pounds;
inside him another of six-and-a-half pounds; inside him again, one of
two pounds; inside him (if the cynical reader can stand it), a bream of
half-a-pound; and, inside the bream, the maggot still serviceable. This
story had grown, by healthy and unconscious accretion, round a small,
central core of fact, retaining so perfectly the form of its nucleus that,
if you were to hear me tell it, you would perceive in a moment that the
relation held no loop or hinge to hang a doubt on; so you would just try

to excel it. This was what the other fellows did; but when Lushington over—reached himself with a haul of eels from a Northward running Victorian river, our synod broke up in grief and mortification, though the unhappy man remained unconscious of his own outrage on decency.

"I'll probably see you in the morning, Collins, before you leave," said he, reaching up to unhook his two-ouncer from the twig where he had hung it for safety. "I've arranged to spend the forenoon with Smith. Good night." So the kangaroo-hunter's name was Smith.

Then all the hands dispersed, and silence settled down on the camp. By this time a sickly half-moon was past the zenith, and the stars indicated half-past one or thereabout.

The Colonel, seeing me fold the aborigine appurtenance of my slumber, with the woolly side in, and spread it on a clear space, near Dixon's waggon, removed his own bedroom suite from the waggonette, and pre—empted an allotment contiguous to my selection.

Contemplating him there, as he enjoyed the best smoke of the day, I couldn't help reviewing his works and labours and his infatuation during the quartercentury he had devoted to meddling in matters beyond the workman's legitimate field of enquiry, and I retrospectively noted the perverse and enthusiastic young Bayard slowly and surely petrifying into the perverse and crotchetty old zealot, though, necessarily, in this casual memoir he passes with barely an introduction.

"Memoir," I repeat, with sadness, for character is no creation of a diseased fancy. Independent of the leaders, and apart from all organisation, there are men—intellectual giants very frequently—behind the nefarious Socialistic movement, poisoning the public mind with aspirations for a state of things which would make life worth living. Our ancestors knew how to silence these fellows. If legal process seemed doubtful, or public execution seemed undesirable, there was a quieter way. You might have approached any one of my own Irish forefathers, furtively pointing out a superfluous individual of the Rigby type whilst jingling a few shillings in your hand.

But, setting aside expediency, there is something well worth study in the spectacle of a man, subject to the needs and restrictions of flimsy mortality, challenging principalities and powers, and fatmen of all descriptions, with the easy assurance of Jack-the-Giant-Killer; and all gratuitously. Penalised by voluntary poverty, future blind as to himself personally, and indifferent as well, yet conscious, like St. Just, that there is no rest for revolutionists but in the grave, such a man, be he right or wrong, certainly attains manhood. But he is a stranger to manhood, who has never suspected an impudent libel in the term "interested agitator!" Ah, heaven. Conservative as I am, no sophistry could blind me to the fact that any man gifted with the special order of brains requisite to agitators can bring his goods to a market where profits are greater and returns quicker. The alternative of apostasy is always open, and there is joy amongst us over one blackleg of maximum ability and minimum integrity. But the agitator is a man who, for reasons satisfactory to himself, though inscrutable to people of self—bounded horizon, chooses the dinner of herbs and hatred, therewith, rather than the stalled ox where love is. Not that he is enamoured of the many uninviting personal traits generated and fostered by poverty; but that he hates these moral blemishes bitterly enough, and wisely enough to attack them at their source. One object only he has in common with the mass of his disciples—the object, namely, of their own economic advantage. Beyond this point, his Satanic isolation begins. To Brown, Jones and Robinson material prosperity is in itself a sufficient end, an end beyond which their sober wishes never learned to stray; to him the same temporal well-being is but a necessary means toward unprecedented expansion of latent moral, mental, and physical faculties. He recognises, as clearly as we do, the chaste beauty of plain living and high thinking; but he also knows that when living is forced down to a certain degree of plainness, the thinking is not likely to be as lofty as could be desired; and herein lies the goading motive of his harsh evangel. To brand him fanatic, is just—the just penalty of being born too soon; to picture him wild-eyed, long-haired, and unwashed, may or may not be just, and indeed makes little difference either way; but interested in the way intended, merely furnishes impertinent people with a standard whereby to gauge the moral stature of the censor.

I am in the habit of relating a pretty stiff lie about Rothschild and a Socialist. One of the Rothschilds, travelling by rail in France, encountered an interested agitator, and the two fell into discussion. Finally, Shylock took out his tablets and made a calculation: "My fortune is so many million francs; this, amongst so many millions of population, comes to so many francs, so many sous, per head. There is your share, mon ami; take it and hold your tongue."

My custom is to assume that this neat little fib sizes up the whole question; but, between ourselves, it does nothing of the kind. It only sizes up the man Rothschild. The points unintentionally illustrated in the parable are—this fatman's sordidness of soul, and his unwarrantable judgment of an ideal altogether beyond his apprehension.

But my under-current of thought was persistently dwelling upon that glimpse into the Never-never of my companion's soul, happily vouchsafed to me when our acquaintance was only a couple of years old.

Again and again I recalled that incoherent outburst of undying love, which showed the effective and confident lord of creation to be commanded like Cleopatra, by such poor passion as the maid that milks and does the meanest chores. These memories were, of course, associated with that mysterious, end-shaping operation of Providence which had brought the sundered Down-Easters together at last.

But to what purpose? There seemed to be some sort of rift in the banjo. Surely I couldn't be mistaken unless there were visions about.

XXXIV

This wreck of realm—this deed of my doing—
For ages I've done, and shall still be renewing.

—Byron's "Manfred."

I t moves, Tom."

"I know it does, Colonel, but we needn't force that fact on an unscientific public. Galileo got into trouble through not being able to keep the same item of information to himself. Let it move. By the way, you struck form tonight; I've seldom seen you more insulting to visitors."

"Was I? Possibly my conventional pliancy was disturbed by some good news I received this afternoon—or rather a hansel of good to come."

"I'm glad to hear it," said I with sincerity. "I couldn't make you out tonight at all. I fancied there must be some hitch in the sequence of things, and I was beginning to despair."

"Hardly as explicit as it might be," observed the Major, complacently critical. "However, as a Conservative, you have reason to despair. The Socialist harvest is plenteous, however few the labourers may be. That Furlong, for instance, is worth looking after."

"Just you let the man alone, Deacon, he never did you any harm."

"Binney's a hard case, by reason of his stake in the country," continued the Judge reflectively. "Lushington is impervious, because of his pernicious training. Steve is hopeless, owing to his constitutional lack of ardour. Dixon, of course, is Dixon, and for yourself, motley's the only wear. But I have Furlong already tempering between my finger and my thumb, and shortly will I seal with him."

"Oh, you're speaking of your commission with the Emperor Nicholas. Don't you see it's a failure, and likely to continue so?"

"And why, pray?"

"In the first place, General, a reformer ought to have a programme, and you have none; in the second—"

"One moment, Tom. Don't mistake me for an organiser. I'm merely an agitator, a voice in the wilderness, preaching preparation for a Palingenesia. The programme is hidden in the order of events, and will be evolved in its own good time. To be fettered by a programme now would be fatal. The 'man of affairs' will not be lacking; let us recognise him when he appears. The formulation of a hard and fast system is the prevalent mistake amongst apostles of our cult. Principles only are vital; and how often have these been obscured and subverted by insistence on details. If we assuaged our zeal by bearing in mind that Socialism is relative, not absolute—that it must come by evolution, not by miracle— we should be much further ahead than we are. As a matter of course, each parable relating to the Kingdom of God gives us one aspect of Socialism. In this instance, you will remember that a morsel of leaven was hidden in three measures of meal, till the whole was leavened."

"Why, then, did you lead Binney to believe that Socialism meant the abrupt confiscation of farms, and the degradation of farmers to the ticket—of-leave level?"

"Do you think he apprehended it so? How far is it to his place?"

"A mile and a half as the crow flies."

"I must give him a call. But, to meet your objection satisfactorily, I'm only a watchman, imperfectly qualified, I admit, though Divinely commissioned. And, as with Jeremiah's sentinel, if I fail to sound the trumpet, I shall render myself responsible for the catastrophe which a timely warning may avert. I pretend to be cognisant only of certain facts, which may be ticked off consecutively. Here they are. Up to the present generation popular intelligence advanced, at best, by arithmetical progression. The outcome is a thing that serves all the useful purposes of oppression. Oppression maketh a wise man mad. A wise man mad is formidable; and wise—at least, relatively wise— men are not as scarce now as formerly. Nothing but large and repeated concessions on the part of the classes can avert a collision. The classes will make no adequate concession, and the new wine will burst the old bottles. There you have the argument of a drama in which the Socialist takes no part beyond that of the Greek Chorus—mouth of the author's principles and sympathies. But at the close of this drama, the Socialist takes the leading part. The blind reaction from an individualism grown unendurable will not take him by surprise. His spirit is acclimatised to the new order; and he is therefore qualified to stand as the prophet of hope in a doomed and perishing system. Now, let's hear your second quibble."

"It's a homely one, Doctor; yet it contains the number one key to your magnificent failure as a mischief-maker; 'altruistic,' and 'deontological,' and 'iconoclastic,' and 'ochlocratical' are the simplest words you use; and the trackfaring bloke, being clothed with his illiteracy as with a garment, errs in his interpretation. In a word, you are too sesquipedalian."

"Meant sarcastic," murmured the Colonel. "Perhaps my rhetoric is rather reminiscent of the sequel to the First Book. So mote it be. I speak to be understanded of the people, not to entertain hearers who must have a gig or a tale of bawdry, or they sleep."

"You were on the religious racket tonight, Deacon," I remarked.

"All things to all men," replied the Judge sententiously. "Talking to an agnostic, I dwell on Proudhon's 'Property is Robbery'—talking to a so—called Christian, I dwell on the Psalmist's 'The earth is the Lord's'—the same solid axiom, varied slightly in expression. But broadly speaking, I'm always on the religious racket; for my game is man, and man is a religious being; moreover, the person whom you would call non-religious I usually find the most apt, inasmuch as he is already free from the incrustation of sanctified selfishness. State Socialism must be built on a foundation of religion rightly so-called. There is no other foundation possible. Note any moral characteristic, or social usage, of any race or nation, and you'll find some religious tenet underlying it. And what appears to be the most inspiriting sign attendant on our movement is the intensely religious, the fearlessly righteous tone of its current literature. The opposing literature is of necessity frankly materialistic, if transparently evasive; and herein lies the most encouraging weakness of the individualistic position. But even that position requires the soothing justification of religion; wherefore the clergy of all denominations, by judicious suppression, perversity and manipulation, of what they call the revealed will of God, make shift to meet the requirement. The resultant is a poor religion, sir, an ill favoured thing, sir, but their own. This leads up to another consideration; to wit—"

"I beg your pardon, Major," I interposed, "You were saying you got a pleasant surprise this afternoon?"

"Ah, yes. I got two letters today, forwarded from Echuca. One from Waghorn, acknowledging my notification that I expected to place the result of my work in his hands very shortly, and informing me that he had collected some statistics which had not been available to me. But my gratification arises out of the other letter. It was from Milligan Brothers. You may remember that about four years ago I parted from them on the very best of terms, after a couple of years fairly successful exporting of the Mohawk wirebinder. They're importing a string machine this year—good enough for a new thing, but as yet requiring a certain amount of brain—worry and objurgation. However, I had the opportunity to watch the two trial machines that were in operation last harvest, down in the late districts, and at the sight of the trouble, my spirit lusted to undertake the old game with the new machine. So a fortnight ago—the end of my present engagement being then in sight—I wrote to Milligan Brothers, offering my services again, and leaving the question of wages with themselves. I had their reply this afternoon, written as a memo. on the corner of my letter. They declined to employ an agitator."

"And you find satisfaction in this?"

"Well, I should say so. While any far-reaching reform is in the air, it excites no opposition worth mentioning, but rather a sentimental sympathy; once it approaches what is conventionally known as the range of practical politics, it will suit any active advocate of that reform to be a single man. At last the hand writing is visible on the wall, Tom. . . Still, I don't know. . . The memo. was written by Leslie Milligan; and he's the most astute man of my acquaintance. He can see ten years further ahead than the average Conservative does—in other words, he can see a decade ahead at the present moment. I mustn't build too much on his hostility." The Deacon sighed, and placed his pipe carefully on the rim of his hat.

"It was so in Wesley's time," he resumed. "The Episcopalian clergy were interested and amused by his discovery of the 'new birth' and so forth; but when the State Church was menaced by defection, the thing seemed to have got beyond a joke. Then those ministers of the gospel thought they were doing God service by hounding the little apostle from parish to parish, with all available ignominy. It was so in the time of Rousseau. While reform seemed an affair of the Greek Kalends, his diatribes, crowned by the 'Social Contract,' entertained and interested the aristocracy. (Strange, by the way, how unwarrantably temperate the tone of that epoch-marking book appears to us now.) He never lacked patrician patronage, resent it as he might. The inveterate misery of his life was owing to unfortunate personal qualities, not in any way to his resolute challenge of the social lie; but if he had lived a few years longer, a handsome reward would certainly have been offered for his head. And there was a time when negro emancipation was sentimentally discussed by slave holders as an interesting moral question. In the guise of an abstract idea, it was highly fashionable; but presently it assumed the form of a concrete policy, and then, then, the righteous anger of the former sentimental theorists found expression in assasination, lynching, tarring and feathering. So it will be with Socialism. But passive waiting is weary work. De Foe, in the pillory for liberty of conscience; earless, but unconquerable; Wesley, dripping from a horsepond, yet intrepidly preaching what he conceived to be the truth; old John Brown, doggedly insisting upon his own execution as a felon by State Law; it seems to me that under such stimulating conditions the squalor of human life is half cancelled, and pride becomes pardonable."

"My word, you're right, Colonel," I replied, controlling my emotion.

The Major paused and lapsed into reverie. But Dixon, reposing close beside us in his waggon, had been following the thread of argument with his usual crude intelligence, and now remarked in a thoughtful tone, "Yes, chaps, I was readin' about them (adj.) things las' winter, on Kooltopar. 'The Army of Martyrs' was the name of the (adj.) book. Swapped 'Harry Stottle' for her. Awful the set them Catholics used to put on pore misfortunate individuals, jist for bein' too (adv.) good. Frightened sheol out of me at the time, on chance of another (adj.) persecution. Wouldn't suit me no (adj.) road. I'd say, 'Slack off, for Goesake; I'll confess anything you (adv.) well like.' Cripes, yes; like a bird. (Adv.) little pigheadedness about this child, if there was any get out. Anyhow, them sort o' things is did away with now; an' we got a right to be thankful, if you ast me anythin' about it." A long sigh of relief; a few half-intelligible expletives of devout gratitude; and presently the slow, regular breathing of the Australian Cuddie Headrig proved that the sectarian discords of former ages had little power to break his rest.

Again my mind reverted to the marvellous tactics of Destiny, as revealed to me during the day; and I wondered at the apparent pettiness of the issue. I would dissemble—

"Thinking of the mad days you have spent, and how many of your old acquaintances are dead?" I conjectured, after a pause.

"No," replied the Judge; "my thoughts took a more cheerful, and no less quotable turn. I was sending my bright, far-seeing soul three centuries in the van."

Again there was a minute's silence.

"I say, Sheriff, did you ever notice that in the 'Shakespeare Plays' there are more women named Kate than anything else? Why is this thus?"

"I never noticed it; but I believe you're right. And those characters are all amiable, or piquant or both. The wherefore of the thusness, I should say, might possibly be found in the hypothesis that the author loved some woman of that name. Now if you ascertain by historical research, or by the shorter cut of nomenology, whether this applies to Bacon or to Shakespeare, you'll be doing work worthy of your ambition."

Another minute's silence.

"Asleep, Colonel? Do you know what was the name of the original Flying Dutchman?"

"Van Straaten, originally; but known to British sea-gulls as Vanderdecken. A profitable and engaging study, I should say, in view of the couple of years you have to live."

"Life itself is a dream," I sighed, "and the world is not even a stage— it's a badly dislocated magic lantern picture; and the men and women are not merely players, they're barely phantasms. But lux ex (adj.) orient, as Dixon would say. Nothing exists but Brahm. Far away back in the genesis of time, Brahm took 40 winks; and what has seemed to happen since then has been a fugitive dream, that is still crossing his mind. He may wake at any moment, and we will pass away, as if we never had existed. In fact, we never did exist, except as immaterial conceptions in that momentary."

XXXV

Nay, lay thee down and roar.
For thou hast kill'd the sweetest innocent
That e'er did lift up eye.

—Othello, Act VII, Scene II

"_____"

It was about the third time, during an intimate off-and-on acquaintance of twenty-three years, that I had heard such an expression from the Major. He sprang to a sitting position, and glared at me in the sickly moonlight.

"Fie for shame, Deacon. A snake?"

"O, damn you, Tom. Why didn't you remind me?"

"Remind you of what?"

"How came you to suggest that name, just now?"

"Simply through wondering to see how little interest you took in an old acquaintance. I've been thinking of her all the evening."

The Sheriff groaned. "It's not your fault, Tom. I beg your pardon. No one is to blame but myself. I'll tell you what I've done. I was engaged to spend the evening with Miss Vanderdecken—and you see how I've managed the thing. O hell."

"Well, to tell you the truth," I replied, "I wondered to see you leave her so soon, and take it so coolly all the evening. You knew her in the old country—didn't you?"

"I believe I did. I'm certain I did. Talking to her, this afternoon, my mind was in a haze; there seemed to be some old memory associated, not only with the people and places the spoke of, but with herself. I couldn't determine just then, whether it was an actual reminiscence or an occurrence of unconscious cerebration—a thing I'm very subject to—and I was afraid of committing myself by pretending to recognise her and remember her, when I might turn out to have been merely a resident of her neighbourhood when she was a child. On the other hand, if I actually did know her, it would never do to have forgotten her. Women are very sensitive to this kind of remissness; they regard it as a slight. So, in order to gain time, and to get a better grasp of the position, I excused myself for an hour, on the plea of attending to something at my camp. I intended asking you to post me up a little, for you have spent an hour or two in her company, and she talks well. I was to have returned at eight o'clock—but then, the ruck of the company and that accursed thirty-pounder. . . What will she think of me now? Heaven above."

"You can apologise to her in the morning," I suggested.

"Of course I shall do so, but that doesn't cancel this hideous default. This is the kind of thing that makes me tired of life, Tom."

There was a short silence broken only by an occasional exclamation or a deep sigh, from the stricken agitator. I was just dropping off to sleep with the thought that there is something not altogether unpleasing to us in—

"I say, Tom."

"Here, your worship."

"Do you know, I fancy I made love to that woman once."

"I don't believe you, Senator."

"I can hardly believe myself. . ."

"Yes. . . Kate Vanderdecken. . . Same grey eyes. . . Same bright hair. . . Same soft, slow voice. . . The old forgotten memories are coming to light."

"'Like Roman swords found in the Tagus' bed,' as the poet says," I suggested sympathetically.

"Kate Vanderdecken. . . Yes, Kate Vanderdecken," pursued my Azim—hero critically. "And she remembered me. . . What on earth. . . I'll never forgive myself. . . Now she particularly impressed me, this evening, as being decidedly the most engaging woman I ever met. Indeed I remember that, as I came down along the fence, I fairly shuddered at the thought of having such a flower of womanhood for a wife."

"On account of the imaginary other fellow?" I conjectured. "The thought was unworthy of you, General."

"Now, for heaven's sake, don't judge anyone else by your own standard. I was thinking of the time I would lose if I lived in such an atmosphere. That is accounted for now. And to slight her after this fashion. O hell. I've put my foot in it this time."

And the Colonel, whose verbal cynicism veiled the most sensitively considerate spirit that ever made man miserable, writhed and fumed in undignified remorse.

"Surely there's some variety of sickness that might come on a person in the evening and go away before morning without leaving any trace?" I hinted.

"O shut up. It's dreadful—damnable—beyond precedent, and beyond forgiveness—" And thus the unfortunate Major continually reviled himself, whilst I dozed off to sleep, tacitly accepting his penitence as sufficient atonement for a default which, after all, would add some twelve or fourteen hours to a twenty-five years' estrangement.

XXXVI

See; thou dog, what thou hast done;
And hide thy shame in hell.

—Macaulay's "Virginia."

About three hours later—just as the middle distance was becoming faintly visible in the cool, fresh dawn, and about 50 cocks were vigorously proclaiming the neighbourhood an agricultural, not a pastoral, one—I was awakened by a weight across my neck, a stertorous breathing close to my uppermost ear, and an overwhelming smell of fresh fish in my nose. Then I became aware of the faithful pup lying at my back, his throat pillowed on my neck, and his fine, Osiris-like muzzle resting against my moustache. The pulmonary systems already noticed, together with the capitalistic contour of the noble animal's stomach, when I turned to look at him, bred a suspicion which was verified when I jumped up and ran to the river just as I was.

I had noticed the water falling rapidly whilst we were fishing, and since that time it had gone down something over a foot. Now, here was Furlong's fish, partly dragged and partly swung to a horizontal root, just above the water level where the skeleton still lay, and all round the wet clay was impressed with tracks very much resembling those of a large kangaroo dog. Thus everything was explained. As a rule, only fishermen's dogs will eat fish; it is an acquired taste, like the appreciation of Walt Whitman amongst ourselves. But the kangaroo dog is independent of all epicurian rules and limitations. Like the Gentiles, he is a law unto himself.

I took a branch of prickly scrub, which had been stranded among the roots, and threshed away all the tracks; then threw the branch into the river. Everything being thus nicely tidied up, I slipped back to my nest and went to sleep again—after noticing, by the way, that Smith was saddling his horse for an early start. Another good hand at keeping appointments, I thought.

"Awake, Æolian lyre, awake."

It was the Judge's voice, as he laced his boots. The sun was showing through the river timber, eastward, and all the fellows were up for the day. Furlong passed by, with a cordial salutation, and went down the bank—the Colonel following him, to assist in the convoy of his fish. By the time I was dressed, the two had returned empty-handed, and were dawdling across where Dixon was putting a fire together. Thompson, with Dixon's pipe in his mouth, and heaven's own felicity in his face, was going straight towards the relics of the fish for a bucket of water. I joined the group at the fire; and presently Thompson returned with his supply of water.

"This'll hold enough for all hands," he remarked, as he filled the big billy and stuck it on the fire.

"Aren't we going to have some of the finny spoil for breakfast?" I asked, with the lust of a gourmand.

"Spoil by name, and spoil by nature," murmured Thompson pleasantly, as he arranged the fire-sticks around the billy.

"I move amendment to snake up the (adj.) fish, an' fry a dollup off o' the (same), if Furlong's agreeable," suggested Dixon.

"First catch your fish," drawled the Major.

"I said, 'If Furlong's agreeable,'" replied Dixon pointedly.

"O, most certainly I'm agreeable," said the trapper, with his melancholy smile.

Amongst well-bred bushmen, lack of information is always carried off by august indifference; otherwise there would be derogation of dignity. Of course, in cases where assistance can be rendered or advice given, a certain chastened interest is even justifiable, but this interest must be purely objective, and entirely foreign to anything like curiosity or solicitude. The bushman must know all that may become a man; anything that he doesn't know (to quote the antediluvian proverb) isn't worth knowing. So, after a seemly interval, Dixon yawned, stretched himself, glanced round the sky in casual observation of the weather; then took down a towel from the branch of a sapling and a piece of soap from the stump, and sauntered towards the river. Each of us equipped himself in a somewhat similar manner, and listlessly drifted in the same direction. We found Dixon, with his back to the fish, ostentatiously washing his face, and we all followed his example, conversing apathetically about one thing or another. "Native cats?" I speculated at last, indicating the organic remains by a backward inclination of my head, after I had done washing.

"Couple of dozen of them," said Thompson, carelessly. "Swear to their tracks. Fish has kicked himself out of the water, and got lodged on that root. I must be off; the billy'll be boiling over.

JOSEPH FURPHY

"'Native cat' is a misnomer," remarked the Senator, as we climbed the bank. "The animal belongs to the Dasyuridae, not to the Felidae. The distinction is an extremely far-reaching one; it is more than specific, it is generic. Worth knowing, that the Dasyuridae are peculiar to Australia, Tasmania, and New Guinea; whilst Australia, Madagascar, and the Antilles are the only parts of the world destitute of the indigenous Felidae. Apparently, however, the native cat is icthyophagous upon occasion like the domestic cat."

"Well, no; he ain't," replied Dixon, politely captious toward a rival pedant. "He's always spotted—white on top o' yallerish grey. Now an' again, he's spotted white on top o' black, but that's on'y a case of exceptio probat (adj.) regulam, as the sayin' is. Curious thing, Rigby, the natey cat, he'll eat any (adj.) thing, and no (adj.) thing'll eat the natey cat."

However, we had no fish for breakfast.

That relatively impoverished meal being over, the Deacon arrayed himself to wait on his country woman. I offered to accompany him, and he gladly consented, waiting with some impatience whilst I recovered pup's chain and secured the faithful animal in a shady place to give his banquet a chance of sacking down wholesomely. Thompson on his way to Binney's rode beside us as far as the Pub. Then the General, silent and perturbed, followed me into the front parlour.

XXXVII

Go for my wandering boy tonight;
Go search for him where you will;
But bring him to me, with all his blight.
And tell him I love him still.

—Sankey's "Collection."

W onderful weather for this time of year," remarked Mrs. Maginnis, who was re-arranging the things on the mantlepiece. "Think we'll get some rain with the change of the moon?"

"Hard to say," I replied critically. "The sun looks very dry this morning. Can we see Miss Vanderdecken, or Miss Flanagan, please?"

"They're gone," replied the landlady. "Went away just after sunrise. I was up early this morning, for we set some bread last night. Miss Vanderdecken heard me, and she came out in the passage, and away goes the two of them and the boy. She made me send the boss to harness up her buggy, and I had to waken the boy whilst Lizzie was hurrying up some sort of a breakfast. She said she had a headache, but it would go away with the fresh air; she wanted to get back to Echuca; and she couldn't touch any breakfast herself; and I begged and prayed of her not to be in a hurry, and so did Miss Flanagan for she looked real bad."

"I should like to have seen her before she went," remarked the General, absently contemplating a porcelain shepherdess on the mantlepiece.

"Well, she was expecting you last night, and quite uneasy," replied the landlady. "She as good as sent the boy down to see what was keeping you."

"The young brat never came," replied the Sheriff with ready malignity.

"O yes, he did, Colonel," I interposed. "He was sitting beside me all the time you were diverting us with the history of old Fitz,"—a shudder ran down my boots as I bethought myself—"Fitz—Fitz?" I continued, racking my memory, "Fitzgerald?—Fitzpatrick?—yes, Fitzpatrick. The boy was fairly fascinated by your inferences and admonitions. You entertained a disciple unawares this time!"

"But he never gave me the message," said the Major, doggedly.

"She didn't send any message, properly speaking," explained the landlady.

"'Sam,' says she, about 9 o'clock, or five minutes past, 'ain't you going to see Mr. Collins?' Says she, 'you was taken with him today,' or words to that effect. And the boy said he'd been thinking of going down, to give Mr. Collins a few wrinkles about one thing or another; and I spoke up and said he had nothing to do but follow the fence to the river. 'Well,' says she, 'when you're there, you might take notice if you see Mr. Rigby; you'll see if he's busy or not. Course, you're going to see Mr. Collins on your own account,' says she, 'but I'd rather you wouldn't speak to Mr. Rigby, nor let him see you if possible.' So, in one sense of the word, she didn't send him. But she was very uneasy till he came back."

"And did he report himself to Miss Vanderdecken?" I asked.

"How? O yes, she had a long talk with him—or, properly she sat and listened to him for a good half-hour—and, in the course of conversation, he said all hands was fishing, and Mr. Rigby was spinning yarns that a person would go through fire and water to hear."

(There was an envious inflection in the woman's voice as she spoke the last words; then she proceeded in her usual tone), "Well, after that, she went to her room, and Miss Flanagan with her, and I've never seen her again till this morning. She came from the same place as you, Mr. Ribgy, didn't she?"

"Yes," replied the Senator absently.

"I thought so. She told me in the course of conversation that she knew a lot of people that you know. I'm sorry you didn't see her again. Well, you must excuse me; this is one of my busy days."

"Tom," muttered the Deacon, as we passed the bar, "can you suggest any form of penance that would meet the merits of this case?"

"I can. Will you follow my advice?"

"I'll follow anybody's advice, now, even yours."

"Then leave your waggonette in charge of these people and borrow Steve's old horse for a day or two. That's all practicable. Follow Miss Vanderdecken to Echuca; you'll be there almost as soon as she. Apologise to her; grovel if necessary, for I'm afraid that, in the face of Sam's evidence, nothing but the truth will serve. Still, you can tell the truth as to leave the impression that your default was in some way owing to a certain greatness of soul inscrutable to the girl mind. Wait on the ladies for a couple of days; show them the lions; exchange reminiscences; compare conclusions; in a word, quit yourself valiantly, and let the Lord do as seemeth Him good."

"Not to be thought of, Tom," murmured the Commodore aside to me, for Maginnis was in the bar, and Fritz was entering. "How could I force myself upon her, after what has happened? I must just let the wretchedness and infamy of the transaction (goodmorning, Fritz) die out by the process of the suns. And a hopeless prospect that is, for if there is a man alive whose whole moral being is one comprehensive register of foregone sensations (What'll you try this morning, Tom?) that man is myself. Constant as the northern star, of whose true, fixed (What's yours, Fritz?) and moveless quality there is no fellow in the firmament. The penalties of this irrational and involuntary fidelity of mine (I'll take a cigar, this time, Jimmy), transcend its advantage by a very long way (pass the jug, please Jimmy, and an empty glass). Here's to the good time coming, boys—in honest water, that never left man in the mire."

"You goot helt, yentlemence," interposed Fritz, raising his tankard. "Peer vor der Yarmance, unt Yarmany vor der peer. Minezelluf, I schall pe ver podiclo mit mine trinks. Ven the Yarmance knog (sheol) der French mit dot last var'—"

"Don't imagine that my solicitude is for yourself, Colonel," said I, when we had left the bar and turned toward the river. "I was thinking of Miss Vanderdecken—

Must she too bend, must she too share

Thy late repentance, long despair.

Thou throneless homicide?

I'd rather than anything you would take my advice. You're pledged to do so, remember. I never was more serious in my life."

The General shook his head. "Is there any use in asking you to stand off and contemplate the position you want to place me in?" he asked wearily. "Don't you see that we must view this thing from Miss Vanderdecken's standpoint, not from ours? Don't you see that she is judge, jury and prosecutor in the case; that the case is closed and cannot be reopened, except for exonerative evidence; and will you tell me where such evidence is to come from? What use is there in my approaching her as a penitent, when she must of necessity view me as an interested hanger-on? Be sure she has taken my measure; and though she has perhaps taken it wrongly, I have lost the right to protest. Why, she would very probably consider herself justified in asking me how much I would take to let our acquaintance drop. Granting that I deserve her contempt, why should I invite a further instalment of it? Not for her sake, surely; and though I leave myself out of the question not for my own sake, either. Your estimate of the whole matter is warped, I am happy to think by friendship; and she is the aggrieved party, not you. For my own part I have lost a friend, possibly a co-operator—and heaven knows that is a loss which taxes my patience. By the way, do you know that boy's name? Sam what?"

"Fernyhurst," I replied, after a moment's consideration. "Sam Fernyhurst. You'll hear of him at the—Hotel, Echuca." (And the boy's name did turn out to be Brackenridge. A nut for your nomenological sceptics to crack.) "That's where you'll find Miss Vanderdecken. I'll never speak to you again if you don't take my advice."

But the Deacon was obdurate. Returning to the camp, we found Dixon platting a whip, and Lushington sitting beside him on one of the oil drums used for carrying water on the roads. The clergyman, finding that Smith had forgotten his appointment, was turning his attention to the somewhat urgent case of Dixon, and, with a meed of success, for the bullockdriver, won from his up-country reticence by Lushington's genuine sympathy, was now giving his own spiritual experience with child-like frankness and vivacity, though in language too manly for reproduction here. Altogether the honest fellow expected to get to Heaven in the end, though he would be content to shave every post on the course; nevertheless he had hopes that the fire and brimstone of the other place were in the nature of a brutum (adj.) fulmen. There was nothing novel or interesting in this, so I caught my horses, and refusing to shake hands with the Major, went my way.

XXXVIII

Spare her, I pray thee if the maid is sleeping.
Peace with her, she has had her share of weeping.
No more. She leaves her memory in thy keeping.

—O. W. Holmes, "Iris, Her Book."

If any reader of romantic temperament should share my own strong personal interests in the further fortunes of Miss Vanderdecken, I shall be pleased to lay before her the only scrap of information I possess. But I warn her (the reader, of course, not Miss V) that I have only style of narrative—take it or leave it.

Towards 3 o'clock on Saturday afternoon, six or eight weeks after the events just recorded, a swagman rode slowly past the Deniliquin football ground, where a crowd, numbering (to speak circumspectly) five or six hundred bodies, indicated a coming event of some local importance—no less, indeed, than the first match of the season. Actual interest in the game was yet abeyant, and the organisms were collected in idle groups pending the inaugural bouncing of the ball.

The swagman jogged along, his mental upper-current noting the assemblage, the weather, with other accessories of the scene, and meanwhile construing the pace of his horse into the different distances of three several paddocks, each available for duffing. But your swaggie, as well as yourself, has two separate personalities; and this man's second self, as represented by his mental under-current, was lapt in higher thoughts—though, to be sure, these were not rigorously devotional for he had 16/—in his pocket. In fact, he was composing a sonnet to the evening star. The bay mare, with her equipment, had cost 45/—at a saleyard in Hay, and was not likely to fetch a higher price in Echuca. She was a broken-down racer, blind in one eye, and the saddle and bridle kept her countenance. A partially obliterated map of dried blue clay, covering her near ribs and shoulder, also extended over the rider's left side from boot to ear, indicated that she had been down somewhere in the salt-bush country; whilst a corresponding patch of wet mud on the near side, and somewhat sandy in quality, betokened a spill of more recent date. But her philosophic master was one who accepted the Spanish proverb that 'it is better to ride a goat than to walk.'

Close at the heels of the mare came a large, slate-colored, kangaroo dog, perfect in every point, yet not too fine. And it is worthy of remark—though by no means remarkable—that the football crowd scrutinised the dog with hungry interest, and viewed the mare with sympathetic regard, whilst overlooking the traveller himself, as a bloke of no account.

With one exception. As the swagman came abreast, a well-grown boy advanced from the crowd. He was clad in an ulster made for some man of 7 ft. height, which garment, thrown open in front, disclosed the scanty uniform of Echuca Juniors. The mare stopped spontaneously. The lad laid one hand on her mane, and, with grave cordiality, extended the other to her rider.

"How you poppin' up, Collins? I s'pose you was a bit cut up at bein' disappointed o' seeing me that mornin'?"

"Well, I did feel it," I replied, as I scanned the self-possessed but ingenuous face, and mentally reviewed the past few years, trying vainly to establish a connection.

"Same here. But I reckoned you'd hear the rights of it from the Maginnises. Say, I had an idea you was goin' up for a mob o' cattle. Contract tumbled through some road, seemin'ly?"

"Well, yes. In a certain sense the thing was a failure. Where's Miss Vanderdecken now?"

"Went back to Melbn'e. What's come o' them two black horses o' yours?"

"Gone."

"Sold?"

"Shook."

"You was tellin' Em you had two mates in a speculation, how about them?"

"Same box. Similarly cleaned out. Right with me in sour misfortune's book."

The boy uttered a low, soft, self-respecting whistle, and I continued:

"When did Miss Vanderdecken leave Echuca?"

"Let's see, a fortnit after that time. I seen her off. Got any idea who worked the oracle on you?"

"Two fine, smart, up-to-date chaps; men that knew every inch of the country from here to Diamantina; Pete Davis and Dan Scott—stage names probably. Spooner picked them up on his way from Wagga, and secured them for our trip. Was Miss Vanderdecken in good spirits when you took her back to Echuca?"

"Miserable as a bandicoot. How'd you manage to let them fellers git the loan o' you so cheap?"

"I'll explain. According to appointment, I reached Hay on a certain Sunday, with my own two horses, and two more from Yarrawonga. Spooner met me on the bridge, and went with me to where our mate, Rory O'Halloran, was camped on that Common, a couple of miles from the town, with these two chaps, and five more horses. We were to pick up another man with a horse of his own at Booligal. Our plan was to start from Hay first thing in the morning. Couple of hours before sundown I walked back to the town to leave Pup in charge of a friend of mine—a man that I knew to be trustworthy and careful. I ought to have left him with Mrs. Ferguson in Echuca, but I couldn't bring myself to part with him at the last moment—"

"Better if you'd 'a give him to me when I run across you that time."

"Economically, yes. As you shall hear. I stayed yarning with this friend till the middle of the night, and then cleared for our camp, with a strong dust-storm in my face. Not a star to be seen for dust, an' no moon that night. Not a spark of fire where I expected to find the camp, but I came to the conclusion that Spooner and Rory had been dainty enough to shift somewhere else on account of the wind. So I lay down, and went asleep with an easy mind. At the first break of day I woke up, half-buried in sand, and the first thing I distinguished 40 yards away was a man shaking the sand out of his ears. It turned out to be Spooner. He had slipped over to the town just before sunset to have three more words with a drapery-girl that he had been engaged to for the last couple of years. She wanted him to attend Evening Service with her, but he excused himself on account of his clothes, and so missed the chance of balancing for a busy day spent in worldly affairs. A lame pretext, too, for the clothes were brand new; and he wasn't in a position to be independent—if he had only known it."

"Right. I bin there myself," interposed Sam, approvingly.

"At all events, he left the town about 9 o'clock; and from that time his experience had been something like mine. I don't think either of us had any uncharitable feeling toward Rory; we knew him to be an average bushman, and we judged he had some sufficient reason for shifting the camp. So we were about setting out to explore the river timber, when up comes Rory himself, battling against the wind. He had been groping around after the camp for some hours as well as ourselves.

"The fact was, the poor fellow had a little girl buried in the Hay cemetery, and the thought of the child had grown upon him as night came on, till he could stand it no longer—he had to do something. So, just after dark, he had gone across to the cemetery, and had sat by the grave for some hours. Then he spent the rest of the night wondering why the camp had been shifted.

"What had taken place at the camp in the meantime is no business of ours, unless we want to be impertinent. It is a matter that rests solely with Pete and Dan, on the one hand, and the Recording Angel on the other. Our only concern lies in the fact that our whole plant was gone, and gone in a sand-storm that hadn't left five yards of identifiable horse-tracks in the county of Waradgery. But if there's any sense in the balderdash about foeman worthy of your steel, we had at least the satisfaction of knowing that our fugitive antagonists were past masters in geography. An experience of this kind helps a person to realise the magnificent extent of Australia. That's all. Did you see much of Miss Vanderdecken during the time that she stayed in Echuca?"

"A lot. Where do you think them blokes has got to?"

"Where are the leaves of Autumn, Sam? Where is the lost Pleiad? Where is the boy that stood on the burning deck? Where is your own lost youth? Did the Colonel get back to Echuca before Miss Vanderdecken left?"

"No. Just missed her by the skin o' your teeth, as the sayin' is. Why ain't you follerin' them coves up?"

"That's what I was foolish enough to do for some weeks. Finally, eight or ten days ago, I met a man riding one of Spooner's horses, faked to perfection; and this man had bought the horse from a tank-sinker away back on Poolkija; and I knew the tank-sinker to be straight. Saw the receipt and recognised the signature. That was the only trace I got; and it satisfied me. But I understand you to say that Miss Vanderdecken stayed in Echuca for a fortnight?"

"So she did. Is your mates follerin' them blokes yet?"

"Also, I understood from the Major that he would fall back upon Echuca in a week or so to do some writing up. Did he not call on Miss Vanderdecken?"

"He was some days longer'n he expected to be. But I was askin' you if your mates is follerin' them gallus-birds up?"

"Well, Rory has gone back to Goolumbulla, in hope of getting into his old billet again. He has two horses there, to go on with. The poor fellow came out like a man when we fell in. The whole speculation had left him nothing less than a hundred notes out of pocket; and he offered Spooner and me fifty notes each, to repay our loss and disappointment. Of course, we weren't on; but eventually we accepted a fiver each to help us on the war path. Spooner's in chase still, last thing I heard from him. So Miss Vanderdecken was gone before the Deacon came?"

"She went away in the morning, and he come in the afternoon. Think Spooner's got any possible o' collerin' them coves?"

"Not merely a possible, but a moral. Let him once see their tracks and he'll overhaul them hand over fist. He may have them by this time, with whatever plunder they've got left. Did Miss Vanderdecken know that the General was coming to Echuca shortly?"

"Dunno. Arty did. I say, Spooner'll give them chaps a matter o' five years without the option."

"What for?"

"Horse-stealin'."

"They didn't steal the horses. You're sure Miss Flanagan knew—"

"Illegally in possession, then."

"They're not illegally in possession. Let Spooner alone. He's as shrewd as he's straight, and that's saying something. He has receipts, witnessed by a police magistrate, for my two horses and Rory's one; and the rest were bought by himself. If he finds any of them in the possession of our absent friends he'll just watch his chance, and quietly re-shake them. Then he'll call round in a business-like way to claim the saddles and things. I think he'll recover them without difficulty; and if the other fellows are impudent enough to demand so many week's wages, they'll find him a bit of a lawyer as well as a bit of a bushman. But that's his business, not ours. You're sure that Miss Flanagan knew that the Senator was coming?"

"Yes, I told her. She used to call at our place of an evenin', to see me; an 'about the fust time she was there she says, 'Wonder when Mr. Rigby's comin' to Echucar, or if he's comin' this road at all?' An' it happened to be that when the Colonel was goin' fishin' that night, after he'd been yarnin' with Miss Vanderdecken, I heard him tellin' Maginnis he'd be goin' to Echucar in a week for good. Course, he didn't get there for another week. Great ole preachin' we had that night down at the river. Mind you, there's a lot in it. Things is drawin' towards a change, an' us Socialists is no more responsible for the comin' revolution than the petrel is for the storm it prognosticates. Mere matter of evolution.

A hundred years ago we thought all we wanted was a fair field an' no favor, on a gospel accordin' to poor Richard; but now we find that sort o' thing means the survival o' the greediest. Restraint's the thing we want now, considering that the old order gets shunted, makin' room for the new, for fear of one good system blue—mouldin' the world; an' God fulfils himself in lots o' ways. Mind you, Individualism would suit me all to pieces. I'd strip for the spin from Log Cabin to White House, figuratively speakin', without givin' a beggar how good the company was; but I'm thinkin' about the fellers that can't run for sour muck, no odds what dons they are other ways. It's so in social—economics. An' it's no use sayin' the dominant classes ought to do this an' ought to do that. Ought, be dashed, they won't do it. But it'll be did all the same. They tell you inventions an' science an' all manner o' labor savin' things ain't goin' to stan' still for the sake o' the workin' class. 'Right,' says we, 'Excelsior's the watchword of science at large,' says we. Social— economic is quite as much as physical, an' social-economics ain't goin' to stan' still for the sake o' the sharkin' class. Same time, we ain't ready yet. . . We ain't schooled. As Gronlund says—or I wouldn't be sure but what it's the prophet Hosear—'My people are destroyed for lack of knowledge.' But how long'll it take to break the galoots in? Couple or three generations, says you? Well, it'll take about ten years, at the outside. You'll edicate a man up to it in two years—if he ain't a fat- head altogether—an' it don't take any longer to edicate a million head o' fellers nor one straggler. See, I'm allowin' eight years to come and go on. Fust the poet and the sage has got to enlighten the people; then the statesman's got to organise the national policy; then, you see, we got the man with the rifle—an' that's the beggar we want. We want to sling the onus of rebellion on the monopolist. Course, he says, 'Hold on, I stand out,' 'No, I'm dashed if you do,' says we; 'fall into line quick, or by gosh we'll straighten you.' As Pompey said to the Memertines, 'Why will you prate of privileges to men with swords in their hands?' Makes me laugh."

It didn't make me laugh. Insanity is rampant in our family, and I was feebly wondering what the premonitory hallucinations were generally like, when a wholesomer idea struck me.

"Have you been talking to the Colonel the last few weeks, Sam?" I asked.

"Stacks o' times. Me an' him's like brothers. Gosh, ain't he a man of a thousand. He didn't come down with the las' rain. Pity that sort o' bloke ever dies. I'd give a trifle to be like him—though I ain't half-rotten when I throw my ears back. No loss o' time now, I promise you. When I ain't readin' or argyin', my thinkin' tackle's goin' like fury. I'm doin' my level. Course, I belong to the club, for the sake o' gettin' in touch with fellers that's got their brains lower down. Anyhow, athletics is no objection to study, s'posen you don't gamble. Poor heart that never rejoices. Greatest athletics in the world was the classic Greeks, an' in Plato's 'Republic' you'll fine—"

"How did Miss Vanderdecken pass the time away while she stayed in Echuca?" I asked uneasily, feeling as the simple-minded reader would feel if she heard, or fancied she heard, some baby of a fortnight old asking for his pipe and tobacco.

"On'y seen her a couple or three times for the fust week, though I often seen Arty. After that—me bein' out o' work waitin' for a new feller to start in the shop—Arty used to git me to hire a horse an' buggy every afternoon, an' take the two o' them out for a bit of a drive up the river road, where you an' us begun to overtake one another, if you remember. I say, why didn't you snap Miss Vanderdecken? She was fair collared on you that afternoon. I could see it stikin' out a mile, simple as I gammoned to be."

"She knew the Major in the old country, didn't she?" I conjectured.

"Noddin' acquaintance, likely. Gosh, ain't he a disy? Knows everything, dash near. Sort o' bloke I'll be when I git fairly goin'. I say, we must go into the social-economic subject properly when we get a slant, an' you'll find I can give you a couple or three wrinkles. I'll introduce you to a swag o' fellers o' my way o' thinkin', an' you'll see I'm the daddy o' the ridgment. Strikes me, my little star ain't a bit too st—kin—' is she? Used to wish I was an ole bloke, but now I'm glad I got so much in front of me. I'll just be in the thick of it—won' I? Great! As Paine says, 'If there be war, let it be in my time that my children may have peace.' That's my idear, too, I'm thinkin' about my kids. Different from Hezekiar—that ole cock-tail says: 'Good is the word that the Lord hath spoken, for there shall be peace in my time'—knowin', mind you, that his kids was going to drop in for it hot. Well, them times is past now: swallered up in the evolution of humanity. Thanks first to Gutenburg, an' then to the long line o' prophets, from Rousseau to Bellamy, there is at last a Daniel for every Writin' on the Wall; a Curtius for every yawning chasm; a What-you-may-call-'im for every—"

"Did the Deacon seem to take much interest in hearing about

Miss Vanderdecken?" I interposed hastily, for I wanted to hear my own voice.

"Well, yes; even if it did seem to make him sort o' melancholy. But I say—onna bright—you look's as if you was gone on her? Can't blame you—fact, I give you credit. She's a ding-donger. Bin along that track myself. Same time, Arty's more my style. Natural enough, considerin' she's the dead spit o' my missus, though, of course, my missus is a lot younger."

"Who did you say was a lot younger?" I asked, with renewed disquietude of mind.

"My missus—my wife."

"What is this for?" I murmured reproachfully, with an upward glance.

"Eh?"

"Nothing, Sam."

"Want o' sleep, an' general worry; that's what's shakin' you up, Collins. Ain't surprisin' considerin'. Take a couple o' days spell at our place when you git to Echucar. We got a spare room. Goin' fur down into Vic?"

"Uncertain. I'll know better when I get to Echuca."

"Anythin' up your sleeve, so to speak?"

"Well, yes; just when I met you at Maginnis's the Colonel had been refused a billet on account of his jossless irreverence toward our institutions, and I've made application for a cut-in at the same sphere of usefulness. I stand a good show, if there's a vacancy."

"Yes, the General was tellin' me about the sort o' jar he got, that time. S'pose you've took degrees in string binders, before today?"

"Haven't been privileged to see one of them yet, though I spent some of my earlier years among machinery, and not without a share of reputation. But I have higher qualifications than mere skill. I belong to a powerful clan, strong in two electorates, and we're all known to be constitutionally sound on the one thing needful."

"Handy thing to have in the fam'ly s'posin' it don't blind a feller to the social-economic question," replied Sam gravely. "Anyhow, you jist go straight to our place when you git to Echucar. Expect the Major'll be in tomorrow, if it ain't rainin'. He's takin' levels for the irrigation racket these times. An' what d'you think—we got Furlong swore in. The Colonel rounded him up. Grand little chap, but he's got notions. Don't do to be a feller o' one book, no matter if that book's the Bible. Course, the Major goes in strong for Scripture, too; but he ain't spiritually-minded. No more ain't I. Mind, all of us gives Furlong credit for his religion, considerin' his heart's in the right place—"

Here, a long, shrill whistle sounded from the crowd. Sam, too dignified to look round, stuck two fingers in his mouth, and replied in kind.

"Central Umpire," he remarked indifferently. "S'pose I must go and have a welt at this bag o' wind. I'm goal-sneak. Wish you could stop and barrack for us, but considerin' the track's a bit greasy, I think you better be shovin' along. Now mind you don't forget to head straight for our place. Missus'll be glad to see you, for I told her you was a cove worth takin' by the hand. Mrs. Ferguson'll tell you where we live. So long."

And the petrel of State Socialism towed the tail of his ulster towards the arena, whilst I resumed my way, reflecting on the unsatisfactory issue of a romance which at one time had seemed to contain all the elements of happiness.

XXXIX

The gentle Knight, who saw their rueful case.
Let fall a down his silver beard some tears.
"Certes," quothe he, "it is not even in grace
T'undo the Past, and eke your broken years."

—Thomson's "Castle of Indolence."

B ut after all what is happiness? "Felicity" is its closest synonym, and you will observe that both words have the alternative import of Compatibility, or Accordance—as when we speak of "a happy combination," "a felicitous phrase," and so forth. Such a coincidence in double meaning is not without significance, since it betokens an instructive sub-consciousness that Happiness must not be incongruous, or out of place, in respect of Universal Harmony. Doubtless, our field of thought is invaded by a prophetic forecast, a twilight revelation of completer life, not directly formulated, though finding cryptic register in every-day speech. Then—taking Happiness in the double intent of the word—who shall presume to interpret its manifestation, or limit its scope? Passing over the vanishing happiness of the moment, the ephemeral happiness of the day, and the scarcely less transitory happiness of the lifetime, may not the Ultimate Happiness of the Moral Universe be in some way consistent with the cross—purposes of human life? Further, may not this Final Felicity (whatever the term may imply) be directly subserved by what appears to our myopic scrutiny as untrammelled thought wedded to marionette action; as painful heart—thrift mocked by prodigal waste; as poetic augury refuted by prosaic anti-climax? And if there be a Universal Purpose, beyond individual welfare, and apart from the wayside interests of existence—if each lifetime be but one pace of Humanity in a decreed journey towards some Ultimate Good—then, measuring the consummation by its incalculable cost, that Good may be taken as the Inconceivable Best.

Ay, but—mortal men, Hal, mortal men. And women still more inveterately mortal. Mortality is here emphasised, not in trite confession of its precarious nature, but because of its abject servility to terrestrial conditions. The brain which explores the arcana of Science, or seeks new horizons in Thought, is apt to ache consumedly. We are not such stuff as dreams are made of, but precisely the reverse. In fact, the avoirdupois will assert itself, carrying not only its physical vulgarities, but also those attributes interwoven with its texture. The gravitation which anchors human feet to the earth has its analogue in the super-physical province of life, where (to speak frankly) the Interminate is just one step beyond the Empirical. Setting aside the "illative sense" as unscientific, we have within easy reach, here and now, the line where verification ends and Conjecture begins. For in no terms of experiment, in no formula known to research can the authentic story of an extra-mundane Scheme of Life be told. There was a door to which Omar Khayyam found no Key; there was a veil past which he could not see. To sane minds, the Universal Plan is the enigma of ages; detached, objective, and wholly intangible— any attempt at solution thus being a capricious speculation, shaped by the proclivities or by the experience of its projector, and varying even with his mood.

But current Emotion—of the earth, though by no means earthy— is a matter of certainty, not of supposition. Here, at least, we have, comprehended within the secularised Ego, a radical incentive which governs its own containing individuality, as magnetism governs the compass-needle. Hence, for instance, the maid called Barbara was left with nothing but her song of "Willow," and she died singing it. What availed the Scheme of Life to her?—though she held debentures therein, equal in face value to yours, or mine, or Kate Vanderdecken's. . . Invite her to "eliminate the hedonistic calculus." Why the words would die on your lips, in pure shame of their cruel falsity.

Romeo also found that Philosophy could not make a Juliet. And so it fared, to a considerable extent, even with the self-sufficient Colonel. That incident marked an epoch in his thought-life. The old record, sweet, tender, elusive; the Eden-song, written in rose and gold, now reappeared on the palimpsest of Memory, never again to be obliterated; and from that time forth an accession of sadness was observable in his bearing, with an abatement of the cynicism which had lent a kind of fascination to his homilies. Despite his habitual reticence, all this was evident to me.

But each nature is tripartite in super-physical faculty, and the influence of that echo from the past, however potent emotionally, had no curative effect on the Major's mental and moral elements. What can arrest the momentum, or disturb the bias of half a lifetime? When the Ego has ceased to be a hobby-ridden man, and has culminated into